MAKE ME NO GRAVE

HAYLEY STONE

MAKE ME NO GRAVE

©2018 HAYLEY STONE

Published by Aethon Books LLC.

Print and eBook formatting, and cover design by Steve Beaulieu.

DEDICATION

For Becky, who always inspires me to be better

ACKNOWLEDGMENTS

I wish to express my sincerest gratitude to Rhett Bruno and Steve Beaulieu of Aethon, both of whom were willing to take a chance on this book, and whose support and insight were invaluable throughout the revision process. To my parents who have always supported my dreams, and to my friends and first readers who offered either feedback or encouragement—Rebecca, Adriane, Jace, and Missy—thank you. I would also like to thank Joshua McKinney for the writing prompt that began this whole endeavor. As always, to my partner, Jasper: you keep me sane in a profession that breeds madness. Thank you for laughing at my jokes. I love you.

ASHER

Kansas, 1873

CHAPTER ONE

Almena Guillory corkscrewed in the middle of the room, turning round and around and around, drawing out some stubborn thought. I asked her to sit down, please, weren't no sense in her wearing herself out like this before we'd even reached the courthouse. She told me to go to hell.

"Already been, ma'am. Spent a summer once in Texas."

I hoped the joke would cheer her. To tell the truth, I was troubled by the indignity of the scene. Guillory was the Grizzly—*or was it gristly?*—Queen of the West. That was what people took to calling her, anyway, but she didn't look like any bear I ever saw. She wore the sun in her skin, arms just starting to freckle. Her brown hair was falling out of her high-crowned hat in stocky strands, and her lips were cracked hardpan. Every now and again, I noticed blood weeping from the crevices. Sort of wished I could do something for the lady. Criminal or no, I felt sorry for her.

"He'll come for me, Marshal," she said. It was the same tired refrain she'd been at for the past few hours. Since being holed up in this here little hotel room, she hadn't said much. Cursed some. And continued insisting *he* was coming. Some lover, by my guess.

3

"I'm not sure who you mean," I replied. "Ain't nobody coming to free you, Miss Guillory."

"When are we leaving?"

Thought about lying to her, but there was something in her glare—a flat awareness, you might say—made me reconsider. "First light tomorrow."

I wasn't blind to the way her gaze ricocheted off my leather.

"That's a fair idea," I said pleasantly, "but I surely wouldn't recommend it."

Both of my guns were holstered, the polished butts half-concealed by the flap of my coat. Seemed a mite unfriendly to have them out, and I didn't see a need. However high she esteemed herself, we both knew I'd pull faster than anything she tried.

The Grizzly Queen sneered at me, lips pulling back in a feral smile. Pretty sure hers were the whitest teeth I'd ever seen on a wanted man. But then, Almena Guillory wasn't no man, and try as I might, I couldn't help noticing that, too.

She was still wearing the saloon dress I'd caught her in. Except now, she'd torn open the frilly collar, clawed off the buttons at her neckline, and stripped away her black gloves, exposing the flesh of her forearms and a long, jagged scar, possibly from a cattle fence. Supposing she was hot, I offered to open a window, but she only took it as permission to do it herself. She walked over, threw back the shutters, and stuck her head out, baptizing herself in the spinning coolness of the evening. I heard her gasp or maybe sigh. Her hands clutched the windowsill, and in the new stillness, she trembled. Shaking like a leaf.

And then came the words again—hushed, prayerful words. *"He'll come for me."*

This time when she said them, I tried to imagine the man she meant to hear them. Some shadowy loner blown in from the Territories, most like, or maybe an ex-Confederate displaced from the war—tall, broad-shouldered, an able-bodied sort. Probably had a fine horse. But, and I'll grant you this may've been a reflection on my poor imagination, I couldn't invent a face to go with all my idle wondering. She wouldn't give him up, and for some reason, not one person had yet to name the Grizzly Queen of the West's consort. Man was a spook.

I leaned forward. "Mind if I ask you something?"

"What?"

"Why red?" It was the color of her lips and her dress. "I know you had a whole closetful of costumes you could've chosen from —I had a peek backstage. Yonder ladies were very… solicitous. What I mean is, and don't get me wrong here, Miss Guillory, it's not a bad color on you, but it ain't exactly what you'd call subtle now."

Almena had been slouching against the windowsill, but now she straightened. She shook her head with a short, cruel laugh. "Don't you know your religion? Isn't your name disciple or something?"

"Apostle," I corrected. Even that wasn't my real name, not the name I was born with, but when you go barreling through life, names have an odd way of attaching to you like stickers from a bramble bush. I wasn't about to split hairs with her on the matter. "And depends on whose religion."

"Red is the color of Catholic martyrdom. When Mary, Queen of Scots went to her death, she wore red to protest the execution."

"You're a Catholic then?"

"Do I look like a Catholic to you?"

"You look like a woman entitled to her beliefs, same as anyone else."

"I just like red," she said. "That's all."

Maybe that was the God's honest truth, but I couldn't help thinking it was more symbolic than that. That wearing red was somehow proof of her faith to this man she was waiting for.

"Fancy the color blue myself," I said to break the silence. "Mind if I ask you something else?"

She lapped at the fresh blood on her lips. "You're awfully chatty for a marshal."

"Yes, ma'am. I've been told that. Just this thing's been niggling around my head since I started searching for you…"

"Hunting me."

"—but if you *do* mind, I can stuff my curiosity. It's nothing what won't keep."

She rolled her eyes, but I guessed she was grateful for the distraction because she replied, "I can't stop you from asking."

I displayed the palms of my hands, as though I were holding both options up for her. "Just to clarify: is it grizzly, like the bear —or gristly, like a tough piece of meat?"

I'd heard a lot of wild stories since moving out West, of men turning into beasts under moonlight and the dead lurching back to life, hungry for the living. Folks out here were tough, but they were also paranoid as all get-out. Sometimes for good reason. I'd experienced my fair share of strange happenings on the plains, including the time I'd heard the infamous call of the Indian death bird right before a shootout. This other time, I swear I saw the ghost of one of the Bloody Espinosas—Felipe, I think—walk up to a bar in Canon City, Colorado and order himself a drink.

But nothing, not even these small instances of weirdness, approached the level of myth surrounding the Grizzly Queen of the West. They called her a witch. Said she couldn't be killed. Said the last men who'd tried had ended up dead themselves, wearing the same wounds they had given her. The rational part of me wanted to explain away these tall tales as being nothing more than local superstition, but maybe there was something to them. For the first time, I didn't have to rely on secondhand accounts. I had the woman herself right here to answer my questions.

Something softened in Almena's face. Her hands stilled, nails hovering over the grain of the windowsill, their tips blunted from digging shallow graves out of the wood.

"Grizzly. Like the bear. Why's it matter?"

"Don't." I leaned back and stretched out, crossing my ankles in a show of casualness. "Unless you're planning on turning into one."

Almena looked partly amused. "You're worried I'm going to turn into a bear?"

The way she said it, I knew that story at least was untrue. Probably the rest were, too.

Feeling foolish, I quickly changed the subject. "Are you sure I can't convince you to sit down, Miss Guillory? Rest a little? You're starting to look a bit piqued."

"No," she said.

I sighed. "Only trying to make you more comfortable."

I followed the path her gaze took around the hotel room, eying the tired carpet, worn to the floorboards at places, and the wallpaper bowing away from the walls.

"In a manner of speaking," I amended with a small smile. Heck. Even the furniture looked to have seen better days. The bed was missing a post and had notches of wood taken out of the remaining three. Saying nothing of my chair's bad leg.

For a split second, forgetting herself, Almena smiled back.

I decided to keep trying. "Can I get you something to eat? Something to drink?"

"Whiskey."

"Not whiskey. Something else. Something not liquor."

She gestured vaguely, and when she thought I wasn't looking, began sawing her teeth across her nails. Back and forth, back and forth, like a prisoner trying to file her way through an iron bar. I thought it best not to comment on.

I got up. "You know, why don't I just have Dorothy bring up whatever she's got leftover from dinner."

"Yes," Guillory said, but she wasn't looking at me. "You do that."

Instead of heading to the door, I went to the window first, checking for trouble. A few folks were out, taking advantage of the long evening. Some portly rider had stopped near the saloon, watering himself and his horse. A little farther on, a man with a shock of orange hair and his lady friend strolled down the boardwalk, passing through slits of rusty light between the store overhangs, talking low and glancing discreetly at one another. Two businessmen wearing ditto suits stood outside Robert's General Supplies across the street, chewing the fat. I recalled seeing all of them when I rode in, except the rider, but he appeared halfway to Sunday with drink, all red in the face and sweating, so I judged him no great threat. It was clear he wasn't here for Guillory. If he were, he was going about a jailbreak all wrong.

I turned from the window—and straight into Almena who had moved in, stealthy as a cat. In one slick movement, she thrust her hand inside my coat, groping for my Colt.

At the same time, I drew my other piece, rolled the hammer back, and shoved it between her ribs. Her hand remained inside the flap of my coat, the hard line of her body edged against mine, her shoulder pressing into my collarbone. I was also well aware of the location of her leg wedged between mine, her knee dangerously close to my most precious bits. Worse still, I couldn't be sure she didn't have the gun cocked, her finger tight on the trigger, ready to put a hole in me.

I frowned, more at myself than her. "Probably shouldn't have gotten so close."

"Probably not," she said. Her breath grazed my lips. "Back up."

I took a step back but kept my gun kissing her side.

In a quiet, yet sturdy voice, I said, "You don't really think he's coming, do you?"

Her eyes shot to the window and back to me. I half expected to feel her gaze, given how many times I'd heard those eyes described as *piercing* over the past few months. But as I stood there, watching her watching me, they were just gray eyes. Could've belonged to anyone.

I tried to hold her gaze, but she kept pushing it to different areas of the room. Looking for a way out, or maybe another weapon. Judging her odds.

"I'm betting that's why you're so anxious," I continued. My mouth tasted sandy, a familiar backwash of fear on my tongue. Anyone who's had a gun on them and says they didn't experience the same is either a liar or a fool. "You're worried on account of him not being here already. On account of him not being here when you needed him in the first place."

She shook my gun, rattling the barrel against my thigh. "What do you know about it?"

"I know what it's like to be let down by someone you love. Someone you trusted." I wished this was only theater. Some pretty offering of sympathy to settle her. But I suspected she'd see right through me if I tried anything of the sort. "Believe me, Miss Guillory, when I say, 'I know,' I'm being neither kind nor cunning."

To my surprise, she smiled. Pressed in closer. Wasn't grizzly bears came to mind then. I was thinking what any man wading through tall grass thinks. *Snake.* "You imagine just because we have something in common, that means I'm not going to shoot you?"

"I was hoping it might give you pause."

She snorted. "Don't try appealing to my better nature, Marshal. I don't have one."

I looked down. The sight of her slender hand disappearing into my coat remained an unsettling one. "Might be you're right about that."

"Move towards the door."

"Can't do that."

"Then I believe this is what one refers to as an impasse." She wasn't looking at the window anymore.

"Let go of my gun, Almena." It was more request than demand. "Please."

By now, some marshals would've shot her dead. I knew half a dozen men—good solid lawmen—who would've put her down the moment her fingers brushed the fabric of their coats. But that wasn't my way.

Sweat collected on her forehead, and she worried her bottom lip between her teeth. "I'd like to, Marshal, seeing as how you asked so nicely, but we both know if I let go of your gun, I'm a dead woman."

"I won't shoot you. You've got my word on that."

"Even if I thought you were telling the truth, and I'll grant, you seem like an honorable man…"

"Thank you."

"That still leaves me at the mercy of the court as soon as we get to Abilene." Her eyes were flat and tired. "They're going to hang me, Marshal."

"You'll get a trial. A decent shake."

"A decent shake," she murmured. "How comforting."

"You've committed a crime, Miss Guillory," I reminded her.

"I've committed multiple crimes. That's why they're going to hang me."

I sighed. "If you don't release my gun, ma'am, I am gonna have to shoot you."

She stiffened. "You do that, and you can be sure I'll take you with me."

"I didn't say it'd be a pleasant experience." My arm threatened to sag, fatigued from holding so damn still. "But this can't go on for much longer, and I can't just let you go. It's my job to sit on you until we get to Abilene. Now, I could've done that anywhere—an outhouse, back of the grocer's. I could've tied you to the post out there with the horses."

She glared at me from underneath the cliff of her bangs. "Why didn't you, then?"

"Because, despite your colorful moniker, I don't think you're an animal, Miss Guillory. I don't think you should be treated like one neither."

Her lips parted, but she didn't speak. Small grooves appeared between her eyes, a sign of indecision, doubt.

"Just slide your hand back now, nice and slow..."

For a moment, I thought she might come to reason. Might trust me... but, no, there was someone out there she trusted more. The specter of rescue clung to her like a shadow.

"No. Regardless of what you believe, he *is* coming for me. But that doesn't mean I can't make it easier for him when he gets here. Now *move.*"

I took another step back, but this time I turned, yanking her arm with me. Throwing my weight at her, I pushed her back into the wall. I heard the terrible sound of a skull meeting wood, a gun going off, and then Almena cursing up a storm, swearing like a man who's just lost his shirt at the poker table.

When it was over, my hand still gripped my piece, but hers were empty. She swung several times at my face, which surprised me a little. From her, I expected claws.

Leaning away, I managed to keep her pinned by one of her shoulders with my free hand. She was stronger than she looked, but I still had the advantage of height and better footing. I trained my gun on her but rested my finger outside the trigger guard. I glanced down briefly, wondering where the bullet landed. Whether either of us had been shot.

"Are you hurt?" I asked her. When she refused to speak, I

pressed her shoulder and said more firmly, "I asked if you were hurt."

Her chin jutted out, and I thought she was gonna spit at me. But she just shook her head and released fistfuls of my coat. I knew the following day would bring bruises where her fingers had briefly dug into my arms, but at least there'd still be a tomorrow, for both of us. That was something.

"I'm gonna have to tie you up now. You understand why."

"I could've killed you just now," she said. I had her tearing strips of linen off the bed at gunpoint. Dorothy wasn't gonna be happy about it, but it wasn't like I carried rope around with me. I was fully prepared to add it to my bill.

"You wouldn't have been the first to try," I said.

She tore another long strip, looking down at her hands. "That wasn't me trying."

Could've fooled me.

CHAPTER TWO

The hunt and capture of Guillory had robbed me of nearly two nights of sleep, and I was feeling tipsy moving into the bright morning. Dorothy brought me a plate of eggs over toast, and stayed with me while I ate, distracting me with some light talk about a problem she'd been having with the young couple I saw walking yesterday.

"I don't mean to be a gossip," Dorothy said, which is what she always said right before sharing some local bit of hearsay. "And I don't mean to be crude, but they're just so... *loud*."

"Newlyweds, I'm guessing?" I asked absently, regarding my breakfast like a rattlesnake. My stomach was in knots. Not since my first time catching a wanted fella near St. Louis had I felt this uneasy. Unlike Almena, he hadn't been willing to come peaceably. I'd had to put him down outside a tailor's shop; the storefront had blue shutters and a sign missing its vowels. Funny I still remembered that.

"Naturally," Dorothy said, rolling her eyes. They were a pretty shade of blue that contrasted nicely with her brown skin. Shame most folk didn't spare her a second glance, often more interested in her younger sister, Sara, who enjoyed singing for customers at the saloon down the street. It was their loss, far as I was concerned. Dorothy kept a fine house, and she took care of me every time I came through.

"Something wrong with my cooking?" Dorothy asked after another minute of watching me shuffle food around my plate. At her offended look, I stuffed some yolk into my mouth, but chewed slowly and swallowed with difficulty.

"This business with the lady fugitive's got you all twisted up, ain't it?"

"Something like that."

I watched sunlight paint the sky through a window at the end of the hall. It filled in the space around some harmless gray clouds. By all accounts, it was gonna be a beautiful day.

Dorothy touched my elbow, encouraging me to keep eating. I gave up on the eggs and attempted the toast. "You think she's innocent?" Dorothy asked.

"No, don't imagine she is."

"Then what's the problem?"

I set my slice of toast down in a bed of crumbs, still only partially-eaten. The egg yolks stared up at me like a pair of rheumy eyes, one bleeding into the other. I was fighting a losing battle. Nothing was gonna stay down 'til Guillory was safely delivered to the courthouse in Abilene. Maybe not even then. She was the closest thing to a celebrity in these parts, after all. The marshal's office in St. Louis could end up asking me to ferry her there instead if they felt the district court wasn't gonna do its job. They loved their hangings in Missouri.

"Probably nothing," I said, offering a smile. "Just too much time in my head's all. Anyway, think you could bring Miss Guillory something to eat?"

She pinched her lips together. "What's a criminal like to eat for breakfast?"

"Eggs'd be fine, some more toast—and juice, if you have it."

Dorothy shuffled off, but the cold stone of nausea in my belly persisted.

A short time after that, Sheriff Jedediah Strickland and his boys rode in.

————

Marshals are encouraged to work with local law enforcement, but my neck crawled seeing the sheriff and his men arrive, and so early in the morning. Boded ill. Among the men Jed brought with him, one or two proved good with his hands. Soon after arriving, the men purchased wood and nails from the general store. I saw the writing on the walls even before the men got to work digging a small trench and putting up the post. They were building a poor man's version of the hangman's scaffold. There were too few trees in the area, and of those, none with branches strong enough to support a man—or, in this case, a woman. Sheriff wasn't about to let that stop him. He was determined to see Almena Guillory swing.

I stood outside the hotel, barring the entrance, my coat tucked behind my leather in a subtle threat. Jed wanted to move Almena from the hotel room into a small windowless shed behind the grocer's that smelled like rotting wood and salted meat, but I put a stop to that.

"Don't be such a soft touch, son," Jed said with a mouth full of apple. Sun provided plenty to see by, but it also drove deep shadows into the caverns of his old face. As long as I'd known him, coming up on a few years now, Jed had always been a fair, reasonable sort. I couldn't say what it was, but something about Guillory turned him mean. "It's just for a few hours. I'm sure she's stayed in worse accommodations."

I removed my hat, tousling my dark blond hair. "My issue

ain't just with the shed, Jed, but while we're on the subject, I don't see why you wanna put her in there."

Jed pried off another chunk of apple with his two front teeth. Little pieces of meat sprayed from his mouth when he spoke, others fell into his black, thistly beard. "She's a notorious outlaw. Where else would we put her?"

"What's wrong with the room in the hotel?"

"The windows, for one."

"She's not gonna *jump*."

Jed shrugged. "Seen it happen before. Best we not take any chances." He grabbed my shoulder and shook it gently. The action reminded me of my father. I clenched my jaw, averting my gaze. "Relax, son. You did good tracking her down. Your job's over now. Time to let justice run its course."

"Wasn't aware you'd summoned a judge and pulled together a jury," I said, meeting his eyes again. My face felt hard and stiff. "You hiding state's witnesses in that thatch?"

Jed tossed the apple to the ground, kicking it away. He wiped his hands off on the front of his vest, spat out the side of his mouth. "You're a good man, Apostle. Decent. But that's your problem. Decent men don't know when to be hard—too busy being *decent*, you see? But a righteous man…. A righteous man knows there's a time and place to get biblical if you take my meaning."

"I take it fine. Don't mean I agree with it."

Jed smiled tightly, and stared up at the cloudless sky, letting out a breath. I noticed more lines in his face I'd never seen before. "Maybe not, but you'll respect my decision. Won't you, Apostle?"

He looked straight at me. Again, I flashed back to my father jostling me by the shoulders, the whiskey on his breath beating me over, his eyes bright and wild, him repeating, *you'll respect me, so help me God, you will respect me* while my mother cried somewhere in the next room.

"No," I said, concentrating on a spot near the porch overtaken by yellow weeds, and then at the teardrop stain of tobacco on Jed's boot. For some reason, it was hard for me to look at him directly. My fingers flexed at my sides, releasing a fist. "I can't in good conscience say I will respect it, Jed. Or you, if you try hanging that woman. I said it before, this ain't how we do things."

Jed frowned. "You know why they call her the Grizzly Queen, don't you?"

"Jed…"

"No, you're gonna hear this. You think she deserves a *trial*. You think she's *owed* it. You think I'm just after—what? Frontier justice?" His voice closed on my ear, low, controlled, but angrier than I'd ever heard him. "If you knew half of what she's done, you wouldn't be here judging me. You'd be out there holding a hammer, too. She's not some innocent girl accused of shoplifting from a goddamn lady's boutique. Almena Guillory is a murderer. Her and her ilk rob trains and mail coaches; they've held up saloons, rustled cattle, stolen horses. Hell, I wouldn't be surprised if she's responsible for shooting the *goddamn President hisself*!"

Jed had gotten himself all worked up. Only thing for it was to let him rant, burn himself out.

"Before she moved out here, you know what they called her? Back in the South? *Killin' Al Guillory*. They say she dressed like a man during the war just so she could see some action. Make no mistake, son. Killing's in her blood. Given half the chance, she'd cut you down and wouldn't bat an eye."

In the moment he stopped to take a breath, I thought back to a different conversation.

I could've killed you just now.

You wouldn't have been the first to try.

That wasn't me trying.

"I don't know about that." I rubbed my jaw where Almena

had managed to land one good hit earlier. "Sometimes people surprise you if you let 'em."

"And sometimes they don't. Sometimes they shoot you in the back and stand there watching as you bleed out in the dust."

His words inspired a sudden epiphany. I looked at him critically. "Is this personal, Jed? Did she do something to you? Guillory?"

"After tomorrow, it won't matter what she's done," the sheriff answered stiffly. "*She'll* be done. And then we'll go after her man, and the rest of her gang."

"Sounds like you're looking to rack up quite the body count."

"If you were interested in the business of saving souls, Marshal, you should have become a preacher."

———

There was no more hammering, sawing. No one at work. The sheriff's boys were done fiddling with the structure, or near to it. Already people stood around on the boardwalk, and in the street, passing curious glances at one another.

Dorothy caught me on the landing of the stairs, going up while she was coming down.

"What's a matter?" she asked.

"Trouble. You mind I check out a bit early?"

She shook her head, short hair bobbing around her cheeks. "Course not. Do what you gotta."

I thanked her and continued to Almena's room. Once there, I knocked on the door with the toe of my boot. "Miss Guillory?"

"What do you want now, Marshal?"

"I'm coming in. Back away from the door, please. Try anything, I won't be responsible for what happens. Clear?"

I listened a moment, heard her steps retreat, and went in.

"Look, Marshal," Almena said. She was sitting on the edge of the bed, wagging her foot. When she stretched, I noticed stains decorating the spots beneath her arms. She'd popped more buttons near her chest, no doubt her answer to the hot, sweaty darkness of the room, and her hat lay discarded in the corner by the piss pot. "Unless you fancy letting me go, better you leave me be. I've nothing more to say—"

"Some men downstairs. They're planning on hanging you." I grabbed up my pack, same one had all my basics—stale biscuits, bag of coffee beans, tinder, couple pieces of string because you never knew when you'd need some good string—then adjusted my belt. I hoped I wouldn't have to use my guns today, but I always had to prepare for that chance.

She blanched, then tried to cover it. "You sound surprised."

"Disappointed, more like."

A cough or maybe a laugh. "It'd save you some time and effort, though, wouldn't it?"

Her words pricked me. She thought that little of my integrity?

"No, ma'am. Didn't go through all the trouble tracking you down and capturing you alive just to let a bunch of locals string you up. Now come on, we're leaving." I headed for the door, then stopped and turned back when I didn't hear her move. "I bear you no ill will, Miss Guillory."

"You *bear* me no ill will? Is that supposed to be humorous?"

"No time for this." I retraced my steps and snatched her off the bed, half-dragging her toward the door. I'd never handled a woman so roughly in my life—minus my first meeting with Guillory when again, she'd forced my hand—and I lamented having to do so now, but she gave me no choice.

"You're worrying for nothing," she said as we booked it down the hall. Noticed she had no trouble keeping up for someone claiming to be unconvinced of the danger. "I'm not going to swing. Not today, anyway."

"Almena. Your lover ain't coming. You've got to make peace with that."

"You keep your fictions, Marshal, and I'll keep mine."

Dorothy was downstairs, and she wasn't alone. Sheriff and his boys were with her. I pulled Almena behind me, leaving her a few steps back, and met Jed on the ground floor. My stomach lurched, what little breakfast I'd had threatening to come back up on me. This wasn't gonna be any kind of pleasant.

"Jed."

"Apostle." His eyes shot to Almena, full of loathing. He snorted. "Not so tough now, are we, sweetheart?"

"How's your son, Sheriff?" She appeared to suddenly remember something. "Oh, wait."

The sheriff jerked forward with a snarl, ramming my shoulder. I barely managed to keep him from climbing the stairs.

"*Bitch*!" he snarled.

Almena just stood there wearing an eerie smile that didn't reach her eyes.

"You see? What did I tell you? She's a godless piece of northern trash." His beard glistened with spit.

"Come off it, Jed. You're provoking her." Though I did wonder what Almena meant by her words. In all the time I'd known him, Jed never mentioned having a son, though judging by what had just passed between Almena and him, I gathered there was good reason for that.

"Enough of this." Jed motioned to his boys. "Take her."

"Now wait just a minute—"

Two of the sheriff's men bull-rushed me. My head smashed into the wall, loosening my thoughts like dust. I considered drawing down on the men, but Dorothy was standing right there, along with that couple from before. The young missus looked right terrified, especially when her gaze caught on Almena. I wasn't about to risk anyone innocent getting shot, and I didn't like my odds against such a large coalition of vigilantes either. My guns stayed put.

Ignoring my protests, the remaining two deputies barreled past, clomping up the stairs in their noisy clodhoppers, tracking grime all over Dorothy's nice carpet. Guillory resisted, but they got hold of her linen binds, dragged her down, and thrust her outside. She blinked rapidly in the sudden light like an old hermit, recoiling from open sky. Before her eyes had a chance to adjust, the sheriff's deputies started pushing her toward the road.

She smelled like urine passing by, which I hadn't noticed before in my haste. My frown deepened. What had she been thinking? If the lady needed privacy to relieve herself during the night, all she had to do was ask. But, no. Instead, she'd pissed herself. I swear, the woman was stubborn as sin.

Still, that remained for a judge to decide.

"Easy, boys," Jed said, heading out after Almena. "That there's a federal. Don't want to leave any permanent damage."

A moment later the men released me, running to catch the spectacle. All save for one sorry bastard who decided to teach me a lesson. His bony knuckle slammed into my gut, folding me over. Air fled my lungs, causing me to wheeze for a few seconds. I didn't see the fiend leave, but when I stood back up, he was gone.

No one stopping me from pursuing, I lit out the door after them.

CHAPTER THREE

A lmena's red gown looked gaudy in the sunlight, glittering and cheap. Matching tears reached up both thighs that I didn't remember being there before.

Despite Dorothy's kind and unexpected offer to lend Almena something more appropriate to wear—*"no lady, saint or sinner, should swing with her undercarriage flapping in the breeze!"*— Jed made Almena keep the dress on. He said it suited her, and his men laughed, describing her in words not worth repeating. I was embarrassed, both by their language and the intention behind it; these weren't true deputies of the United States government. They were boys giggling at the sight of bare skin. But they were also angry, maybe a little afraid, too, and that made them dangerous.

"Sheriff!" I quickly caught up with the group. Guillory glanced back at me, but I couldn't read her expression. One of the deputies shoved her forward, and she turned back toward the sun. "Sheriff, I'm asking you to reconsider."

Despite my effort to intercept him, Jed didn't slow. "I'm not having this conversation with you again, Apostle."

Where most of the sheriff's deputies appeared giddy, bumping into one another as they trailed behind Guillory, Jed's face was drawn, his brown eyes empty. Having forgone his duster in the heat, the sheriff held the front of his suspenders with tense knuckles, as if he were pulling himself forward. I hoped he was having second thoughts.

"I don't think you're thinking clearly." I spoke quietly so Jed's boys wouldn't hear. I didn't wanna humiliate the man, though I wasn't above it either if that's what it took.

Jed turned to me suddenly, placing a hand on my chest. The deputies halted to stare at us. With a sharp, impatient gesture, Jed motioned for them to keep walking.

"What's gotten into you? You sweet on this woman, son? That it? Think she might show you a little friendly gratitude if you keep her from swinging?"

"Hell, Jed. You should know me better than that."

He got into my face, cheek twitching beneath one eye. "And you should know better than to question my judgment. Stay out of my way, Apostle. I mean it. Don't push against this."

He turned his back on me, walked away.

"*Jedediah*!" I called to him.

When he turned back, his shoulders slumped. I knew how I must look: coat pushed back, guns exposed to the glare of day.

Ahead of us, the deputies fought Almena to get her into position. Judging by the way one of them was lying on the ground holding himself, seemed she'd managed to get a leg up. A few of the others were laughing at him, and jeering her. Town folk continued to hang back near the stores, pretending occupation with something else.

I watched the sheriff, steady. "I'm not asking now. I'm telling you how it's gonna be. Call off your boys."

"And if I refuse? What then? You planning on shooting me?"

"This has gone plenty far, Jed. You put the fear of God into her. What more do you want?"

"I want her dead. Thought I'd made that pretty clear."

I started towards him, real slow, the soles of my boots crunching grit. "It doesn't have to be like this."

Although I tried to keep my focus on Jed, the activities of his deputies forced me to extend my attention to the area around me. My eyes kept veering to Almena, her red dress standing out against the white sky like a battlefield pennon. They'd secured her arms behind her, rebinding her wrists, but with actual rope this time. Same kind of rope the sheriff's men were now tossing over the horizontal crossbeam.

And just like that, the scaffold became a proper gallows.

Someone I didn't recognize as a deputy—probably an employee of the general store—rolled a barrel up to the foot of the structure. So that was how they were gonna do it. Crude, but it'd get the job done.

"That's close enough." Jed held out one hand, his other settling around the grip of his revolver.

"Hey, sheriff!" one of his boys shouted, oblivious to the growing quarrel. "You want that we should string her up now?"

"There's some things a man can't come back from, Jed," I warned.

"I thought *people could change*," he mocked.

"Sheriff!" The deputy again.

"Goes both ways," I said.

"I don't expect you to understand, Apostle," Jed said, "but you're right. I do know you. I know you won't pull on me, not so long as you value your badge. A judge'll understand letting Guillory die a whole lot more than he'll understand you shooting a fellow lawman."

Incredibly, he let his hand fall away from his piece and turned to face the gallows. Almena watched us, leaning away from the man who had his hands on her, the rope creeping into her neck. Faith drained from her eyes. *She knows he's not coming.*

"Sheriff!" I jogged forward. Tried to stop him.

Tried.

Jed cupped his mouth with his now-free hands, hollering back to his man:

"*String her up*!"

Guillory refused to be hefted onto the barrel and headbutted the luckless deputy who tried to force the issue. Another man came up behind her, wrapping his arms around her belly. His hand brushed her bare thigh. The man reeled away suddenly, as though he'd been smacked in the head. He windmilled before falling backwards, landing hard in the dirt. Almena spat on him.

The remaining men pulled their firearms. Sheriff included.

"Marshal's service!" I shouted, finally drawing in the same fluid motion I'd used dozens of times before. I gained some looks, a few curious, others disgusted and impatient. Jed's mouth went slack inside the cave of his beard. Almena glanced over at me with a feeling I'd never seen before in her scornful eyes: relief. She must've guessed I was all she was gonna get as far as allies went.

"Let's everybody be calm about this. Lower your weapons and step away from Guillory. She's under the protection of the United States government. You touch her, and you're in breach of federal law."

"You don't want to do this, son." Jed stepped toward me. I pointed my piece at him, and it was like an invisible string between us pulled tight, stopping him cold.

"You're right about that," I agreed sadly. "But you're not giving me a choice."

Jed's frown was so deep, I worried the rest of his face might fall into it. "You'd choose this *criminal*, this *whore*, over your own brothers-in-arms?"

"It ain't like that, and you know it. You're breaking the law, Jed."

"*She* broke the law!" he spat, pointing at Almena. "Her! I'm the one trying to set things right!"

"By lynching an unarmed woman?"

Jed raked his beard with an agitated hand. "You still can't see it, can you? A woman—she ain't no woman. She's a devil, Apostle. And you're playing right into her hands. What's to say she won't escape before you get her to Abilene? What's to stop her from killing again?"

"I won't let that happen."

"You'd stop her?"

"Already have."

Movement continued in my periphery; one of the men tied a cloth around Almena's mouth to prevent her from spitting on them again. Another adjusted the noose around her neck, tightening it. She made a vain effort to kick one of them and missed. Her shoe went flying to the dirt.

"Are you boys stubborn or just plain stupid?" I asked the deputies, pulling my second gun in the time it took them to blink. The white ivory handles glinted in the sun. "I said step away. Go on now."

Only two, the youngest members of the posse by the looks of it, obeyed. The rest held their positions, heads cranking back and forth between us, waiting for confirmation from the sheriff.

The crowd stirred behind me with growing restlessness. Some of the men disappeared, which worried me. I suspected they were going to fetch their guns.

"You told me yourself. She was caught resisting arrest," the sheriff said.

"To be fair, I wasn't being too gentle neither," I replied, continuing to split my attention between Jed and his boys. I didn't know how, but they'd gotten her up on that damn barrel. I guess I had the answer to my earlier question. *Just stupid then.*

"Be a shame if she tried anything else."

"Last warning. Tell your boys to stand down."

"*Men!*" Jed barked without looking behind him, without seeing the baleful outline of the L-shaped hangman's scaffold against the empty Kansas countryside. He hesitated, the man I'd never known to be anything but decisive. The man I expected to be better than whatever personal vendetta curdled in his heart. I considered myself a fair judge of character, but in that moment, I knew I'd judged Jedediah Strickland wrong.

"*You know what needs doing!*" he roared.

My first bullet punched through the foot of the man who attempted to kick over the barrel, penetrating flesh and wood with a meaty sound. My second caught his compatriot in the neck as he started to pull Almena off the barrel by her legs. His dark blood sprayed across the front of her dress. She stood on her tiptoes, half-dancing, eyes wide with panic, desperately trying to keep her balancing act.

A more enterprising deputy returned fire, taking out a few hapless weeds at my feet. Rather than stepping back, I moved forward, advancing slowly but surely, firing several more shots. The remaining men dove for cover behind the wooden scaffolding. Unfortunately, one of the youngsters made the unfortunate decision to crouch behind Almena's barrel. Kid was starting to tip it over, intentionally or otherwise.

"Hold your fire!" Jed was shouting. Least, I think that's what he was saying. I kept losing his voice amidst the loud percussion of gunfire, but he had his hands out, gesturing wildly to his men. "*Hold your fire, goddammit!*"

I watched the boy behind the barrel—and I watched Almena, leaning at a sharp angle, her situation growing more precarious. With the rope choking her, I worried she'd black out before I could cut her down. I needed to make a quick end of this, but I couldn't see a way to do that that didn't result in more bloodshed.

Making matters worse, the crowd of onlookers was growing

in number behind me, men drawn by the sound of gunfire. They held Sharps rifles across their chest, and one woman even whipped out what looked like a Derringer—but no one seemed to know who to aim at. The rest of the ladies had wisely scattered, most ducking inside whatever storefront they'd been standing outside of, alleviating some of my concern for civilian casualties.

About that time—while I was yelling for the bystanders to get back inside, and Jed was screaming for his men to stop shooting —Almena slipped. Or the boy upset the barrel. Either way, she was swinging, the noose pulled up to her chin. Her body rotated like a fish on the end of a line as she panicked, fighting to get air.

Well, shit.

The drop had been gradual enough, hadn't broken her neck, but that was a small mercy while she continued to dangle there, suffocating. The surviving deputies fumbled bullets into empty chambers, and I took the opportunity to move closer, firing an occasional warning shot whenever one of them peeked out from cover. I had only two more rounds before I'd have to reload, so I tried to fire sparingly.

Almena's lips were moving, but I was still too far away to hear what she was saying. I brought my gun up, intending to shoot through the rope.

Pulled the trigger.

And was promptly laid flat by someone else's bullet.

The world pounded and receded away from me in witless agony from a point close to my stomach. I couldn't *breathe*, never mind move, though my hands still twitched uselessly for my gun somewhere nearby, fingers clawing at the hot dirt. The taste of copper burned my mouth.

Jed hovered over me, a dark silhouette bleeding into the pale sky. All I could make out was his bushy black beard which shook when he spoke. "I'm sorry, son." A prolonged sigh as he removed his hat, knelt down next to me. "Dammit. You just couldn't let it lie, could you?"

When I opened my mouth, tried to speak, blood drooled from the corner of my lips.

"Guillory," I choked. I needed to know if she was all right. Seemed a waste to die for nothing.

Jed went real quiet and looked away from me, standing back up with a grunt of effort.

"You missed," he said.

CHAPTER FOUR

Hell looked an awful lot like a room in Dorothy's hotel: same furniture and everything. The musty curtains were drawn, heat settling on me like a blanket, and the devil himself bore a striking resemblance to Almena Guillory.

She sat across from me with her back to the wall, a pistol in her lap. *My pistol.* Instead of the saloon dress, she had on a plain white blouse too big for her judging by the deflated folds of fabric in the front, and a tanned-leather skirt covered her legs all the way down to her ankles. I wondered where she'd gotten the change of clothes.

"—my dead?" My lips stuck together when I tried to speak, dryness rolling back into my throat like a tumbleweed.

"You've got strange notions of heaven if you're asking me that," she said, but her voice lacked the same vitriol as before. Her entire expression was kinder, and to look at her now was like peeking around a mountain to the eroded side you never saw. I didn't know what to make of the change.

"Could've been the other place." I rested my eyes a moment. "Seems rude to presume upon the Lord's judgment."

"Well, you're not dead. But the Lord's got nothing to do with it."

"That so?" I found that if I put my mind to it, I could sort of struggle into a sitting position. "Do you know who shot me?" My heart broke to think it might've been Jed, but I needed to know, one way or another.

"It was that young one, with brown hair. I don't know how else to describe him."

"One hiding behind your barrel?"

She nodded. This surprised me at first. When I gave it some more thought, however, the picture came together.

I relaxed back against my pillow. "He must've thought I was aiming at him when I went to shoot you down."

Almena shrugged. Apparently, it didn't matter to her.

"How bad was it?" I asked, meaning the gunshot.

She absently rubbed her side and took a moment to peek outside the window before answering. "Bad."

I nodded. "Most times is."

I'd yet to investigate my wound, but did so now, tentatively moving my hands beneath the covers. I'd been caught by friendly fire in the backwoods of Kentucky once, and I recalled the misery of walking back to civilization, listening to the wet brown dirt sucking my boots, taking one step after the other after the other. Couldn't focus on much else but moving forward. When I finally got back to town, the bandana I'd borrowed and used to hold in my juices was drenched through. You could've twisted it and it would've rinsed like a laundered shirt.

I knew something wasn't right as soon as I began to probe my side. Instead of that instance of revolting pain, there was nothing. Throwing back the covers, I stared down at myself, stupidly wondering where my bullet hole had run off to. Some blood remained—dark, crusty. It'd dried in a crooked streak down my stomach, originating from a spot of solid, naked flesh.

"A genuine miracle," I breathed.

"Not quite."

My head shot up, and my eyes immediately met Guillory's. She shifted in her chair. My pistol slumped into the hammock made by her skirt when she spread her legs. She picked it up and set it on the nightstand beside her. Maybe it was a gesture of trust, or perhaps she was tired of having a loaded weapon in her lap. Her other hand still cradled her side. Had she been injured during the shoot-out?

"What would you call it then?"

"Probably a mistake," she said quietly.

"How's that?"

She stood, turning away. "You saved my life. I saved yours. We're even now, Marshal."

"Wait—"

Almena didn't get far on her own power. Something inside her seemed to crack, like a tree limb overburdened by snow. Her legs buckled. I instinctively reached out to catch her, but of course, being that I was trapped in my bed, I was too far away to do any good. She lingered on her hands and knees long enough for me to break the sluggishness the blood loss had caused me. Not saying I was graceful any. I moved with all the elegance of a drunkard stumbling home after midnight, but I managed to get up and stagger over to her.

Almena swatted my hands, but the action caused her to grimace, and she doubled over again, clutching her side.

"Here, let me help you up."

She spat blood, gooey as a wad of chewing tobacco, and used her knuckles to wipe her mouth. "It's fine," she told me when I made another overture of helping her to her feet. "Don't touch me."

"You're hurt."

"You'll be hurting in a second if you don't get the hell away from me."

I gave her the space she wanted and went to look for my shirt instead. I'm not normally self-conscious, but I didn't relish the thought of being found in such a compromising position with a known criminal. A known *female* criminal. Someone was bound to arrive at the wrong conclusions.

"The woman took it," Almena said. "Your shirt. That's what you're looking for, right? She said she was going to try and get the blood out before it set."

"Woman?"

"The one who runs this place. Dorothy?"

My brows bounced up. "We're still in Asher?"

"Where else? I certainly wasn't going to drag you halfway across the country on my back."

I rubbed my forehead, trying to defeat my rising headache. I went and collapsed into the chair Almena had previously occupied, sort of hoping she'd take the bed. She looked like she could use it more than me.

"Maybe you ought to start from the beginning. What happened after I passed out? And where's the sheriff now?"

Almena felt her way to the bed, shaking. She curled up on top of the covers like a cat, tucking her arms in protectively around her abdomen. Rather than look at me, Almena focused on the curtains past my head, breathing as evenly as she could manage. Every exhalation sounded strained.

"You sure there's nothing I can do?"

"You've done plenty." Her tone was waspish.

I pushed my fingers through sweaty hair. I was getting frustrated, but at the same time, felt I needed to keep calm. "Please, Almena," I said gently, leaning forward, trying to capture her gaze. "I'm just trying to understand, and I could use your help making sense of all this."

"Don't you get tired, Marshal?" she asked me.

"Of what?"

"Of being so damned polite all the time."

Her lips threatened a smile—a *real* one, not the arsenic-laced expression she'd tried on me before. It was a lucky man got to see a real smile from Almena Guillory. With that thought, my mind banked hard toward the Grizzly Queen's consort, the nameless bandit who hid in the shade of her infamy. He hadn't come after all. Wondered what Guillory made of that, but I was smart enough not to bring it up just then.

"You want to know what happened," Almena said after another moment.

I exhaled. "If it's not too much trouble."

She barked out a laugh and shook her head. "You've been nothing *but* trouble for me since you showed up."

Almena sat up, brown hair tumbling onto her shoulders. Her fingers arched over the edge of the bed, digging into the mattress. The smile faded, replaced by—I don't know what. Sadness, maybe? She wasn't frowning, exactly, but something about her haunted look hit me hard. I knew the number of ghosts living inside me, knew them all by name. How many ghosts did Almena Guillory carry? What were *their* names?

"You want a neat summary?" she said. "I chased off the sheriff and his men, healed you, and dragged you back here…"

"You chased off a posse of armed men?"

"Yes."

"By yourself?"

She ignored my disbelief and continued. "They'd have left you for dead. *I* should've left you for dead."

"Why didn't you?"

"Before you go getting any ideas, it's not because I like you. You did defend me, though, and I honor my debts."

"Thought there wasn't supposed to be any honor among thieves."

"You'd be surprised."

Already was. "So how'd you get free?"

She arched a dark eyebrow. "What do you mean, how'd I get free? You fixed the rope with a bullet. You shot me down. Don't you remember? It was a hell of a shot."

A sour taste filled my mouth. *Jed.* "I was informed I'd missed."

"Well, you were misinformed. If you'd missed, neither of us would be here now."

"You said you...*healed* me." One of my hands drifted to my side, visiting the empty site of the injury. "How'd you manage that?"

Almena picked at the roots of her nails, idle-like, but I wasn't fooled. Especially when she did it enough to make them bleed. Insanely, I thought about reaching out, taking her hands inside mine, stopping her from harming herself further. I repressed the instinct, knowing she wouldn't take kindly to the contact, and I'd no right to initiate it. Finally, she threw her hands down into her lap. "Oh, what the hell. It's not like half the town didn't see me do it. Bruising. What I do, I call it bruising."

I frowned, not following. "That a scientific term?"

"No, it's not *a scientific term.* Here, it'll be better if I just show you."

She moved on me, grabbing my wrist. With my free hand, I reached for my piece on the nightstand. I only realized I'd done it when I heard the hammer roll back, chilling in the silence. She froze in front of me, the muzzle inches from her belly. Her lips curled back from her teeth like an animal's grin, more sneer than smile. "What? Still don't trust me, Marshal?"

"I'd like to, but your reputation ain't exactly pearly. Trust's not something I hand out freely these days." *Not anymore.* "You want me to trust you, you've got to show me you're worth trust-ing. Simple as that."

Guillory gave me a long-suffering look when I didn't immedi-ately back down. That look puzzled me with its familiarity. I remembered it belonging to a different face. "Look, Apostle, if I'd wanted you dead, you'd be dead. Simple as that."

She had a point. If nothing else, she'd at least earned the benefit of the doubt. Hadn't she?

Fighting the tight lump of nausea in my gut, I set the gun aside.

Her grip on my forearm eased, claws retracting into fingers again, not quite a lady's touch but nearer to it.

"How's it work then?" I asked. "Bruising?"

"Like this."

She snatched the pistol from the table and fired a shot into the ceiling that left my ears ringing. While the mouth of the gun was still hot, she pressed it to my chest. It burned like a son of a bitch, reminding me of the time I'd accidentally grabbed hold of the wrong end of a cattle prod. I yelped, half from the surprise, half from the pain.

My body was still trying to respond when Almena casually discarded the pistol and pressed her hand to my naked shoulder. She winced, but otherwise never so much as blinked. I watched in wordless amazement as the red, blistering scorch mark that had only just bubbled to the surface of my skin started to disappear. Seconds later, the mark had vanished, along with any sensation of the wound.

While I fumbled for something intelligent to say, Almena grabbed the collar of her blouse and tugged it down, revealing the same mark in the same place on her chest. After a moment, the mark disappeared. Like it was never there at all.

I jerked to my feet, toppling my chair. *Maybe Jed was right. Maybe she is a devil.*

I'd heard rumors during the war about men and women shrugging off bullets, tearing apart enemy soldiers with their bare hands, but I'd always taken them for hyperbole. Legends grown out of the senseless carnage of wartime. No one had ever proven the presence of witches at Gettysburg, nor that wizards—artificers, by a fancier name—had destroyed the Wrightsville Bridge. All that was just talk, soldiers letting off steam.

But maybe it wasn't. And if it were true, even in part...

God help me, I've rescued a flesh witch from the noose.

Except devils didn't use their powers to save lives. And Almena Guillory had surely saved mine. Regardless of my beliefs, seemed mighty uncharitable to think badly of her.

"You're wondering if it's witchcraft, right?" Almena guessed. She stood and approached me, and it took every ounce of willpower to react as she got closer. Her lips broke into a smile at my discomfort. "Oh, don't look so concerned. It doesn't involve pagan rituals or anything that might upset your dainty sensibilities."

My hands were shaking. I planted them on my hips to try and stow my nervous energy. "How's it work?"

"How do you remember the words to a hymn or know to close your eyes against a glare? How do you catch yourself when falling? It comes naturally, like living. It's almost a reflex more than anything else."

"So it ain't magic."

"I didn't say that. I sure as hell don't have a better word for it."

I considered that. "Can you start and stop it?"

"It's not a beer tap, Marshal. But if you're asking if I can control it, then yes. To an extent. I don't take any injury I don't want, and my body heals most injuries I can't survive, unless I interfere. Is that enough to satisfy your curiosity?"

Before I could respond, the door slammed open, nearly flying off its hinges. Twin barrels preceded Dorothy as she pushed inside, shotgun in hand.

"What the blazes is going on up here?" she demanded.

"Everything's fine," I assured her.

Dorothy frowned, looking top-heavy with that shotgun. "I heard a gunshot."

"Just an accidental discharge," I said, lapsing into my Marshal's Voice; that careful mix of coolness and professional calm. My wife had given it the name, though it was usually in the context of *don't you do that, don't you dare use your Marshal's Voice on* me. "As you can see, nothing to worry about. No need for the gun."

Dorothy lowered the shotgun so now if she fired it would only blow away Almena's feet, instead of her head. "I'll be having no funny business from you," she warned the other woman. "If you start giving him any trouble—"

"Thank you, Dorothy," I interrupted, "but I think I have things covered here."

With a little more encouragement, and my repeated reassurance that the hole in the ceiling would be compensated for, Dorothy retreated. She gave Almena the evil eye the whole time as she backed out of the room.

"I like her," Almena said, soon as Dorothy was gone.

I gave her an odd look.

"I mean it," she said. "I admire a woman who's willing to risk life and limb for the ones she cares about. That's a woman unafraid to defend her own. Good for her." She looked away sharply, as if embarrassed by her own sentimentality, then waved her hand impatiently. "Go ahead and ask the rest of your questions, Marshal. You look ready to burst."

She was right about my interest. Like a man discovering the stars, I wanted to know more. "Does it work on every sort of injury?"

"Most. There are exceptions."

"Like what?" Only by her incredulous look did I realize I'd asked something personal and inappropriate. I'd crossed a line. "All right then. Does it hurt you to do it?"

She crossed her arms low, shielding her abdomen. "Of course, it hurts."

What kind of ability could look and act like magic without having any of the perks? I wondered. After all, wouldn't true magic prevent any harm to its user? The anatomy of her gift confused me, but in the pleasant manner of a puzzle. I was probably risking eternal damnation prying into Almena's dark art, but I swear the devil himself would've been curious.

"Providing you can—wait, is it healing or bruising? What's the term for when you're healing yourself?"

"They're two sides of the same coin. Call it whichever you like."

"All right. Providing you can heal yourself like you do, why didn't you get rid of those cuts and bruises on your face after we first tangled? Couldn't you have healed yourself right quick back in the hotel?"

She shrugged and swung herself down onto the bed, fiddling with the chamber gate on my pistol. Each time it closed with a hefty snap. "I could have. But wouldn't you have found it strange if I didn't have a mark on me?"

"Fair point."

"Besides, it's far easier to simply pass the injury on to someone else. I guess you might say I was saving them for a rainy day."

"And that scar?" I glanced down at her arm.

Almena snapped the cylinder closed again. "We all need reminders."

I grabbed my chair and righted it, leaning on the back. "Almena, mind my asking why you're still here? I'm grateful for your help and all, but you know I'm still duty-bound to turn you in."

She snorted. "I'd like to see you try. And since when are we on a first-name basis?"

"You're carrying my bullet wound; I'd argue that makes us fairly close."

"Don't flatter yourself. You're not my first."

I started to say something, but cut off at the sound of someone racing up the stairs.

The next instant Dorothy appeared in the doorway, breathless and huffing. She wasn't holding the large-barreled shotgun this time, though my relief at that was short-lived.

"Sheriff's back," Dorothy announced.

Almena rushed to the window, opening the curtain with a single crooked finger. "Brought some more men with him, too," she observed.

Dorothy looked at me, and I swore it was the same way my wife used to look at a meal just starting to burn—sadly, but with some hope of rescuing it still. "Maybe now is a good time for you to acquaint yourself with my attic, Marshal."

"And why's that?"

"Because he's telling everyone you conspired to free Miss Guillory there because she's your woman"—Almena made an unladylike noise—"and that's why his boy shot you. In short, he's calling you a Judas. And if he finds you're still alive, I think he's going to try and kill you."

CHAPTER FIVE

Dorothy herded us into a storage room on the second floor, quietly shutting the door behind her once we'd all filed in. It was dark and windowless, but once my eyes adjusted, I could make out crates and barrels. Like much of the hotel, the room held the reassuring smell of aged wood.

It would've been a tight fit for two people, let alone three, and while I did my ample best to give Almena some personal space, as Dorothy jostled her way to the back of the room, there was no helping us bumping up against one another like cattle in a pen.

I lifted my head, casting my gaze toward the ceiling to avoid noticing how close mine and Almena's faces were to one another. Her freshly laundered clothes couldn't hide the smell of the day on her—a hard mixture of dirt, blood, gunpowder, and sweat— merely covered it some like a thin doily laid atop a set stain. I knew I couldn't have smelled rosy myself and was grateful for her lack of comment on it. Maybe she appreciated the dire situation we were in, or maybe we were finally starting to get on, but whatever the reason, she kept quiet while we waited for Dorothy's instruction.

"Given what I'm risking to help you both, I trust you two'll be discreet about what you're about to see," Dorothy said, and I wasn't sure what she meant until she drew a small match from her pocket and struck it.

She held the tiny flame up, and it quickly ate through a false image of the ceiling like a spark shooting through a spigot of gas, revealing a scuttle hole and string. Dorothy tugged on the string, the panel opened, and a ladder followed.

It wasn't the strangest thing I'd seen today, but it wasn't nothing neither. Between Almena's fleshcraft and Dorothy's illusion, I had to wonder if everyone in Kansas wasn't hiding a little magic.

"Well," I said, "ain't that something."

Almena stared at Dorothy, almost as if she were seeing her for the first time, and when she spoke, her voice held newfound appreciation. "I haven't seen that trick since before the war. Were you part of the coalition?"

"No," Dorothy said as she ushered us up the ladder. I went first, letting Almena finish her conversation, but only because I also wanted to hear Dorothy's explanation. "My momma was a Blesser, though, worked as a conductor back before the war. Never lost a ticket."

I was barely following now. I guessed the conductor and ticket had something to do with the Underground Railroad, but the rest shot straight over my head. "Blesser?"

"A witches' coven mostly consisting of abolitionists committed to helping slaves escape the South before the war," Almena explained. How she knew that was beyond me. I'd only just learned a year ago about the spirituals used to signal slaves to escape.

Dorothy nodded. "She was no Moses, only made a few trips, but she did what she could to help any fugitive slave come her way. Even once the war was won, she was afraid the peace wouldn't last, and our people would be put back in chains, so she taught me a few tricks like this one. Useful for hiding, if hiding's what's needed. Now get yourselves settled up there and stay quiet. I'll come fetch you when it's safe."

Almena finally joined me, but not before turning back to Dorothy. "Your mother was a brave woman."

"You think I don't know that?" Dorothy said, but there was a note of pride in her voice.

"Fleshcrafters and abolitionist witches," I said, soon as Dorothy left. I shook my head with an incredulous smile. "Next you're going to tell me all them sewing circles up North are made of ladies practicing the dark arts."

Almena smiled. "Not *all* of them."

She looked like she might say more, but just then I heard Jed's gravelly voice, muffled but distinct, barking orders to his new posse. I held a finger to my lips. We both listened as men shuffled around on the second floor below, and I found myself holding my breath whenever it seemed they were right beneath our feet.

Almena, on the other hand, looked perfectly relaxed. She had chosen to sit across from me, back against the wall, legs extended and crossed at the ankles. While we waited, she licked her thumb and attempted to rub out a small dirt smudge on the waist of her borrowed shirt. Every now and again, the sound of furniture screeching against the floor made her flinch, but otherwise, she minded herself well, just biding her time.

I sat on my haunches, holding on to a low crossbeam for balance, anxious to move around but knowing I needed to stay quiet. Almena glanced up at me once and shook her head. Guessing she had a lot more experience with this sort of thing than I did; normally, I was the one stomping around downstairs, not hiding in a crawlspace.

Eventually, the sounds died off. That was when Almena tensed.

After another few minutes, we heard steps.

The small scuttle hole opened with another puff of brown dust, joined by the sharp smell of a burnt match. I held a hand out to Almena. She bent beneath the low ceiling, looking ready to—I don't know what. *Pounce* was the word that came to mind. Whatever she planned to do, I can't imagine it've been gentle none.

Dorothy peeked her head inside. "All right, y'all come down now. They've gone."

"What did you tell them?" Almena asked, hanging back.

"Told them I was hiding an outlaw and a disgraced marshal in my attic. What do you think I told them?"

Almena grinned. I couldn't help thinking these two women could've been friends under different circumstances.

"I said you'd split," Dorothy continued, "and he'd gone after you. Again. And if anyone else comes around asking, that's what I'll tell them, too." She looked at me, a promise in her eyes.

"Thank you, Dorothy." I grasped her hand. "I owe you."

She nodded, looking half embarrassed by the gratitude. "Owe me for the ceiling and the sheets, too," she said.

"I'll make good on it. You have my word."

"Where are they heading next?" Almena asked as we climbed down from the attic. "Which direction did you point them in?"

"They asked me which way y'all went, and I said I didn't know, what with it being night and my eyesight what it is, but that I *might've* heard you talking about trying for Ellis. It was the first town I could think of."

"Ellis," Almena repeated with a nod as if this conformed nicely to her plans.

Made me nervous thinking she had a plan at all.

We headed down the creaking stairs, gathering in the back kitchen. Without being asked, Dorothy started the hearth, blowing the embers into living flame, not for warmth but a little light. She also lit a few wax candles. Our shadows made hard, starved

46

figures on the walls, their edges shivering whenever we passed too close to a flame.

At my request, Dorothy went to fetch my coat and badge. I had a sense I'd be needing them both sooner rather than later.

"I hope you're not getting any ideas," I warned Almena, who stood a little too close to a butcher's cleaver. I sat perched on a stool nearby, checking my revolver with some intention of cleaning it. That was when I discovered I was plum out of bullets. Whether Almena knew it at the time, she had used the last of my ammunition with her little presentation back in the room. On the off chance she didn't realize I was at her mercy, well…I wasn't going to be the one to tell her.

"I'm curious to hear what you think is going to happen now, Marshal."

She sauntered past a cutting board that still had half a loaf of brown bread on it. She picked up the abandoned knife, glancing at me while she did so, and proceeded to hack into the loaf, cutting off a thick slice. I let my hand fall from the grip of my empty revolver and moved my finger off the trigger out of habit.

"I'm going to take you somewhere Jed's got no jurisdiction and won't be tempted to try something like this again. I'm going to rent a courtroom and some jail space, hire a bailiff, find a judge willing to preside—which I don't think will be too hard, given your reputation—and call in the jurors and witnesses."

Almena chewed with her mouth open. "Sounds like a lot of work."

"Why they call it a job."

She smiled, still holding the knife, bare wrist resting against the side of the cutting board. "You know what I think is going to happen?"

"What's that?"

"I'm going to get away."

"You sound sure of yourself," I said. "Just like you were sure your man would come."

Her shoulders stiffened. I'd struck a nerve.

I stood and walked toward her, feeling brave, or maybe stupid from the blood loss. "Let's say you did manage to get loose again—what would you do? Go after him?"

She faced me. Shadows settled in the exhausted lines of her face, but her eyes were bright and wild like the lights over a swamp. Couldn't help thinking how easily those eyes might lead a man astray. "What's it to you?"

"There's a reason he didn't come, Almena."

"You're right. Something must've stopped him. It's likely he's found trouble himself."

"Could be," I agreed. "Or could be he chose himself over you."

The flesh of her knuckles tightened, showing an outline of bone as she squeezed the handle of the knife. "Are you looking to get stabbed?"

"Not particularly."

"Then stop talking."

If I was quick, I could maybe disarm her, but I needed her more distracted. "Before, you said you weren't trying to kill me. I've been wondering about that. I know you've killed men, so it can't be the killing you've an aversion to." I scratched the back of my neck. "So what was it stopping you?"

"Maybe you just caught me in a good mood."

"I don't think that's it."

"What then? You think I fancy you?" She laughed, but to my ears, it sounded forced. "Think I've gone all soft for your *yes ma'am, no ma'am* gentleman marshal bullshit?"

"No, ma'am."

The suspicious way she looked at me—like she couldn't tell

whether the joke was at her expense or not—killed my pleasure. Poor woman didn't seem accustomed to humor.

Dorothy returned, and Almena set the knife down. I couldn't say what inspired me to be so reckless with her. I'd thrust my hand into the burning bush, and had come away miraculously unhurt. Probably best I not try for seconds, though.

"I couldn't save your shirt," Dorothy said, already chatting away as she entered. "Too much blood. But you're welcome to keep Jasper's." Jasper Hansel, Dorothy's late husband, had died in a bad accident some years back. Only thing I knew about him was that he'd been a fairly large man in life. His shirt made me look small, like a boy who'd gotten into his father's wardrobe.

Dorothy had more luck with my coat. It looked cleaner than it'd been when I first arrived, with my five-pointed marshal star pinned to the front. A tremendous amount of relief rushed into me at my badge's return, like I'd been missing a part of myself without it. I thanked her kindly.

"You want some butter with that?" Dorothy asked Almena who'd abandoned all pretense of table manners and was devouring the rest of the loaf, tearing it apart with hands and teeth.

She paused just long enough to answer, "If you have it."

Dorothy was obviously being facetious, but now that Almena had asked, she behaved as though honor-bound, obligated to see that her guest was properly cared for under her roof. Even if she was a criminal.

"I offered you something to eat earlier," I said. "As I recall, you declined."

Almena wiped some crumbs from her mouth. "That was before you got me shot."

"Technically, I got myself shot."

"Keep talking, Marshal. See where it gets you."

Instead of hogtying her like I knew I ought to, I went back to my stool, feeling tired and achy, wanting a hot meal and a warm bed and to sleep for days. I knew I'd have to secure her again, but in my condition, and her with her flesh magic, I didn't see how that was going to be possible. I wanted to put off tangling for as long as possible, least until I recovered some of my strength.

But then the new missus—one I'd seen earlier walking along-side her beau, same one Dorothy had complained about being… vocal—appeared in the doorway, initially beheaded by the shadow of the doorframe, so I didn't recognize her until she stepped forward into the light.

I did, however, recognize the gun that pushed out from the dark ahead of her.

It was my missing piece—a Colt .45. The Peacemaker, it was sometimes called, though it wasn't making me feel peaceful none to see it in the hands of a stranger.

The woman kept me on the business end and moved into the kitchen.

"Marshal," she said, making tremendous effort not to get too close or make eye contact with me. Her lip quivered, but she kept the gun steady. "I'm very sorry about this."

I said nothing, mostly seeing as I had nothing nice to say.

Missus kept on until she stood in front of Guillory, and hesitated when the outlaw opened her hand to receive the weapon. "You won't shoot him, will you?" Missus asked, holding the gun against her chest, away from Almena.

"That'll be up to him." Almena wriggled her fingers in an impatient gesture before going ahead and snatching it from the other woman's loose grip. Seeing her holding it made me a little sick, my brain conjuring thoughts of bread, butter, and blood as Almena wiped her fingers off on her skirt and dragged her mouth across her shoulder.

"You two know each other?" I finally asked.

"Apostle Richardson," Almena said, with the relish of one

who's pulled off a very neat trick, "Meet my cousin, Nelle Guillory."

"It's Shaw now," she corrected meekly.

Then I was made to go outside, my own six-shooter pressed firmly against my lower back.

———

People were always jawing about family resemblance, cooing over babies having *his eyes* or *her smile*, and talking like it was the most important thing in the world—looking like someone else. Most of the time I didn't see it. Maybe it was owing to my lack of imagination, but in the case of Nelle Guillory (or Shaw, as it were), I especially wouldn't have guessed any relation.

If you stripped away the cuts and bruises, maybe held her head underneath a faucet for a while, I suspected Almena would emerge looking aristocratic with her pointed nose and high jawline. Nelle, on the other hand, could only be described as soft —one might even have called her delicate-looking, though it had nothing to do with her size. It was the way she carried herself, keeping her hands close to her stomach like she would tuck into a ball and roll away at the first sign of danger, sort of like an armadillo. She had a round face and pillowy arms, pinched off by the lacy sleeves of her nightgown, and curves in place of Almena's bony angles.

But the most striking difference between the two women was Nelle's dark, sloe-eyed gaze, which together with her warmer color made me think she had a little Indian blood in her. Cherokee or Chickasaw, maybe. She and her cousin shared the same brown hair, but that was the only similarity, far as I could make out.

"You said this wouldn't happen again." Nelle spoke to her cousin in a harsh whisper. "You *said*…"

I watched them out of the corner of my eye while I saddled a horse—Guillory's ticket to freedom. It was possible she'd tied off some poor creature somewhere else along her route, that way she could change to a fresh mount and outride any would-be pursuers, but it'd been nearly two days since I'd caught her. That poor animal couldn't be doing any sort of well.

"I know," Almena replied in a voice I'd never heard her use before. Tender-like. "I'm sorry. But it wasn't as if I'd planned on getting caught."

She glanced my way, and I dropped my eyes to the iron stirrups, pretending I wasn't hearing every word. I doubt she was fooled, but my eavesdropping didn't seem to disturb her. Maybe she wasn't worried because she didn't plan on leaving me as a witness to her having a heart.

"You know, you're aiding and abetting a fugitive of the US government," I said without glancing up. "That's a federal crime. Punishable by hanging."

"He's right," Nelle said. "You shouldn't have come. You should've left it well enough alone."

"You knew when you wrote me what I'd do. Don't pretend otherwise. And don't worry about the marshal. I'll take care of him."

"Where's Bratt? That's his name, isn't it? Your lover."

Silence followed, the tense kind that filled a confessional when the sinner wasn't ready to admit guilt.

"That's his name," Almena answered at last.

"Well, why wasn't he here to take care of this?" Nelle demanded. "Why's it been left up to me?"

"He got held up."

"They were going to *hang you*, Almena! What could've possibly been more important than being here?" Even upset, Nelle's voice never grew beyond a loud whisper. I glanced over, and she was slouching, chewing on her nails in the same way

Almena had back in the hotel. She kept looking over at me with sad, worried eyes.

"I don't know," Almena admitted, "but you can trust I'm going to find out. Marshal, you about done with that horse?"

"Nearly," I answered. My warm breath cooled in the night air.

"Well, hurry up."

"He saved you," I heard Nelle remind her cousin after another moment.

"Only after he arrested me in the first place."

"Is it true then?" Nelle asked, and now there was something solid in her voice. I imagined her standing straighter, and glanced over to confirm it. She'd lifted her chin, just like I'd seen Almena do when she wanted to look tough. Her gaze was steady. "All the horrible things they say you've done. Tell me straight."

I stopped fiddling with the saddle, wanting to hear Almena's answer.

"Not everything," she said.

"The robberies. The killings…"

"Yes."

"Why?" Nelle asked quietly.

"Why doesn't matter. I have my reasons, but they're *my* reasons, Nelle. They're none of your business. Go back inside. Climb back into bed. Enjoy your new husband. Tomorrow, this'll be nothing but a little column in the paper. A few days after that, it'll be feeding someone's fire. That's the way it goes. Good, bad… in time it's all forgotten. I'm only the monster until someone else does something worse."

Nelle's footsteps crunched in the dirt as she walked away. I finished securing the saddle, double-checking the girthing, more out of habit than any real concern about Guillory sliding off.

As I turned, Nelle also turned back, saying, "The war did something to you, didn't it."

Wasn't a question.

Almena said nothing. She readjusted her grip on my pistol.

Nelle finally met my gaze, the first time she'd made direct eye contact for longer than a few seconds. "She wasn't always like this. She used to have a conscience. Used to care about things. People."

"Nelle." Almena made her cousin's name into a warning.

"Best listen to your cousin, Mrs. Shaw," I said, not wanting the woman to get caught in any crossfire that might take place.

"Again, I'm very sorry about this, Marshal. I didn't have a choice…"

"She's blood," I said, understanding.

Nelle looked over at Almena with a queer expression. I wondered what it was like to see two people standing in place of one.

"Yes. Blood's all she is now." Nelle headed back inside.

———

Even with the night black and cool, the heat of the day still radiated up from the ground, warming my feet through the soles of my boots. Out here, most men didn't want to die with their boots on, but I couldn't imagine going any other way. Seeing as I spent more time in my boots than out of them, just made sense to finish the same.

I stood facing Almena Guillory for what I felt was sure to be the last time. Calm. Ready to face my maker, if that's what it came to.

She took the reins from my hands and ordered me to stand back. I half-expected her to shoot me outright, put one into the back of my head and leave me to bleed out beneath a messy canvas of stars. Just like Jed said she would.

Instead, she stood there a moment, holding back the horse who seemed eager to walk on. Each time the horse pulled, she winced, and I knew it had to be my wound acting up again. Though she hadn't said so, I suspected severe injuries took longer to heal. And mine had damn near killed me. It also explained why she hadn't blown out of town before I'd woken up. Riding at full gallop required skill enough without adding the pain of a gunshot wound.

"You ever tire of wearing the white hat," Almena said, "you come find me, Marshal."

Her words led me to believe I'd live to see another day, and I dared to hope, even as I replied, "Sorry, Miss Guillory. I'm flattered by the offer, but I've already got a job."

She lifted the pistol's sights from me, barrel pointed harmlessly at the sky. "I'm not offering you a job. I'm offering you a brand new life. A chance to reinvent yourself. An escape."

"Escape from what?"

"Everyone's got something they want to get away from."

In my mind, I saw a man, a woman, and a train. I smelled warm, seedy smoke as it rolled out of the stack in coughing spells. That odor had lasted on my clothes for days, partially because I didn't change them for days.

My face must have given away the memory.

Almena nodded. "Like I thought. This could be your one and only opportunity to break free. Leave it all behind. Become someone else entirely."

As Almena went on, she drew teasingly close to me, like she had when I first caught her in the back of Asher's saloon, when she'd leaned her hip against mine and with bright gray eyes said, *I don't suppose I could change your mind about arresting me?* Of course, right after, before I'd even given her a reply, she tried shattering my kneecap with a bottle.

Almena caressed the side of my jaw with the front sight of my pistol, ever so lightly. The iron kiss sent an ugly shiver down my spine, and I leaned my head away.

Frowning, I asked her, "And who exactly would you have me become?"

"Up to you, of course. But if you need a starting idea, how about going by Devil Richardson? Has a nice ring to it, don't you think?" Her teeth showed white, even in the dark.

"I think changing your name don't settle the past. You can't run from the law forever."

Almena pressed the end of the barrel into my chest, pushing me away from her. Clearly, she was disappointed with my answer.

"If that's the way you feel, then I recommend you keep your distance. Don't come looking for me again."

Knowing the truth would likely earn me a bullet and a dusty grave, I kept silent, letting her believe what she would. The Grizzly Queen mounted the horse in a single motion, pulling herself up by the saddle horn and only grimacing once from the discomfort.

I stood back from her wheeling horse, knowing I was beat. "If you find Bratt, you be sure to let him know I think it mighty ungentlemanly of him to leave his lady in the lurch. Even if she is a cold-blooded outlaw."

Almena lifted her chin, threatening another smile. "You'd do well to forget that name, Marshal. It's not yours to know."

She turned south, and as she rode off, she didn't look back once. I couldn't help thinking, *There's a woman who's used to riding away from a trail of bodies.*

And I hadn't stopped her.

THE DEVIL YOU KNOW

CHAPTER SIX

W eeks after Guillory's trail went cold inside Saline County, the new district judge gave me a fresh appointment: hunt down a ruthless gang of bank robbers along the state border, mighty close to Indian territory. I shipped as far south as I could on the train, and saddled the rest of the way. By the time me and my deputies rode into Baxter Springs late that evening, my poor horse was worked into a shiny lather along its tack, and the action was already over.

Some local photographers had their equipment all set up, ready to document the dead as proof positive for a reward, but the bodies of the outlaws were still too wet to stand. As I hitched my horse to the rack in front of Collier's Hardware, I saw them struggling to operate the dead men whose heads kept slumping down into their chest and whose legs refused to hold them. One of the lawbreakers barely had any head left to speak of, having been on the receiving end of a Winchester carbine. Another had taken a bullet to the throat, and the flesh was still dribbling blood. The other's injuries were discreet enough that I couldn't tell by a cursory glance what'd done them in. It was only as I got closer that the blossoming spots of red on the fronts of their shirts came into view.

I showed my badge and introduced myself and my assistant deputies as we approached, noticing the anxious looks from some of the men nearby. There were four of them standing out in front of the Springs Hotel. One smoked a fat cigar. They all had their weapons sat against the wall or railing, well within reach. Still expecting trouble, I wagered.

"Hey, Marshal," someone called to me. A kid, couldn't have been more than twelve. Probably the son of one of the photographers. "Want to see something neat?"

"I surely do," I answered, being friendly, certainly not anticipating what the boy would do next.

"Watch this," he said, smiling.

The boy took the arm of the outlaw who'd been shot in the neck and began to work it up and down like he was priming a pump—only instead of water, blood came pouring out of the wound, gushing down the dead man's sternum. The boy did it a couple of times, glancing up at me with excited blue eyes, wanting to make sure I saw and approved of his discovery.

"My god," one of my companions, Dempsey du Pont, murmured. "Is this what passes for fun out here?"

The Du Pont boy came from good stock, which was a fancy way of saying he had a lot of important relatives. Yankee entrepreneurs and the like—the kind of men other men called *richer than god* with a dirty look, thumbing out their own empty pockets. Of course, all of the Du Ponts were back in Delaware, prospering off the thousands they'd made during the war selling death in the form of reasonably priced American gunpowder.

For reasons he didn't like to talk about involving a falling-out with his family over his close friendship with an old schoolmate, Dempsey had exchanged cushioned seats for leather saddles, going west without more than a penny to his name. I'd met him a short while ago in Independence. He was working for the local sheriff as a part-time lawman, part-time grocer. Asked him if he was interested in retiring from grocery service to pursue more dangerous work, and he said, "Yes, sir." Asked him if knew how to shoot, and he'd answered, "With a gun, sir." I did the only reasonable thing I could do at that point: I deputized him on the spot.

My other deputy, Wade Prough, just smiled at the boy's trick. Where Dempsey's looks were fair but frequently brooding, Wade showed just the opposite. He had an old, weathered look despite being only a few years older than me, his skin ripened from long hours in the sun. Short, wrinkled hair curled around the tips of his ears, and his dark moustache grew into a pair of the most impressive burnsides I'd ever seen on a man. But he was always quick to smile—and quick on the draw, too. I'd known Prough for years; he'd been the one to accidentally shoot me back in Kentucky, but as he liked to say, what was a little buckshot between friends?

Wade normally prowled near the railroad, imposing order on the dozens of cow towns along its tracks, keeping men honest with his presence, and throwing down with the ones who decided to try their luck on the owlhoot trail. After my bad run with Guillory, I'd telegraphed him, asking for his help with this new gang, and was lucky enough to get it. We met up near Kinsley, and I made no comment about how gray he'd gone.

"What are you smiling about?" Dempsey asked Wade peevishly. "You're just going to encourage him."

Wade tilted his head, inspecting the boy and the dead outlaw. "I don't know. Seems like an improvement to me, career-wise. Rather ingenious little trick, too. What do you think, Richardson?"

"Grat!" snapped one of the photographers, an older fellow with greying black hair who shared the boy's blue eyes and large ears. I expected he'd admonish the youngster for playing with the dead, but he just said, "Now you leave the good marshal and his friends alone."

"Come over here and help me get this one up," the other photographer said, only one side of his mouth moving with his words..

"Excuse me," I said to Grat's relation, ignoring Wade as he leaned down to try his hand at working the corpse pump. "You know where we might find the local sheriff?"

He frowned, exchanging a look with the men on the wooden porch. "Should be down at the parlor, with the rest of them."

"Saloon parlor?"

"Undertaker's parlor," the man with the cigar corrected, letting out a small smoke ring. "Sheriff's dead."

"You said with the rest of them." Wade stood back up. His face was dark and serious.

"Yep. Killed some of us." The man's eyes were moist, and I didn't think it came from the smoke. I realized my mistake in thinking him casual about what had happened here. The cigar was a disguise, the same way a lady hid her grief behind a veil. Once I figured that out, the rest of the signs were obvious: the men all stood too straight, too still, and they kept drawing their mouths into their cheeks, fighting back hard emotion. *No wonder they still have their guns with them. They're angling for blood.*

There was a bright flash as the photographers took the first of their shots. Dempsey startled, automatically reaching for his sidearm, but Wade placed a hand on the younger man's arm, steadying him. Dempsey let his hand fall, cheeks warming.

"What can y'all tell me about the outlaws who came through here?" I asked.

"What do you want to know?"

"How many of them there were, for starters."

No one could agree on a number. Some said six riders, others seven. One swore there was an eighth man—someone from the town who'd gone ahead to reconnoiter Baxter Springs. None of the others corroborated the story, and seeing as the man looked a bit wobbly, I couldn't be sure the eighth man wasn't just a figment he'd conjured from a bottle. They also argued about who shot who, not on account of the reward, but as a matter of honor. Seemed the only thing the Springs men *could* agree on was where the outlaws had hitched their horses—back behind the hotel, just down the street and across from the First National Bank they later robbed. Prime location to get in and out, slick and easy.

I shared a look with Wade, who nodded at me and then looked at the ground, still nodding. I knew what he was thinking. There should've been no need for killing.

I set my foot on top of the porch, leaning forward. "Take me through it," I said. "What happened, exactly?"

The man with the cigar, whose name I regretted not yet having learned, started to speak again, but choked up. One of his pals laid a hand on his shoulder, and commenced with his own version of events. "They arrived midday, about lunch time. Not all at once, though. Chuck Fletcher says he seen them trickling in, a couple at a time. Harmless-like…"

Another man nodded enthusiastically. Chuck Fletcher, presumably.

"One of them stopped to shoot the breeze with Miss Kingery. Made her laugh even."

"She a real friendly type?" Wade asked.

"Hell, no! Not even on Sunday," said a fourth man, and a small ripple of amusement passed through the men.

"She's pious as they come," Chuck offered a tad more generously. "Very serious. A woman of God, you know."

"Besides making Miss Kingery's acquaintance," I said, "did any of the others do or say anything strange? Anything that might've given away what they meant to do?"

"It's like I keep telling Leonard here," Chuck said, referring to the man who'd spoken on behalf of his friend who couldn't, "them that got here early were real casual. Another one spent some time getting his shoes repaired over at the tailor's. We just thought they were on their way to Newton or Wichita."

"Is that what they told you?" Dempsey asked. The kid was eager to feel like he was contributing in some meaningful way to the inquiry.

"No, but we get a fair amount of folks from Arkansas and Missouri headed that way."

I nodded, and Leonard took the opportunity to bring the conversation back on track. "Anyway, Dick"—he flung his thumb out at the fourth man who raised his hand in wordless introduction—"and me was just finishing up with some customers over at the general supplies when we heard shots. Dick was sure it was Indians come up from the Territory, and he grabbed some rifles from the stock."

"So you weren't there when the shooting started." Dempsey looked down his nose at the man. "You didn't see what started it."

"I was there," said the cigar smoker. He dropped his smoke on the ground and crushed it with the heel of his boot. He continued to grind it long after it was out. "In the bank. Me, my wife, and son. Three of them came in, packing pistols. One watched the door. The other two started throwing down with me and the other customers. Wanting to make sure we knew our place, I guess."

"Bastards," Dick said.

"Agreed," Wade said.

"I ain't normally a violent man, Marshal," the man continued. "But they was scaring my family."

"Did you draw on them?" I asked gently.

He nodded. "When their backs were turned. Thought I could put an end to it, nobody getting hurt."

"That's noble."

"No, Marshal. It was stupid. It was so goddamn *stupid*."

I took a breath, feeling the weight of the other man's guilt like a physical thing. "What happened, friend?"

"They was hassling poor Jim Frame, our teller. Jim was dragging his feet, probably hoping someone would take notice of the situation. One of the outlaws threatened to break his hands if he didn't hurry it up. I should've let it alone, but I stood up and pointed my pistol at them. I told them they best get on out of here now or I'd put some new holes in their head. I was just so angry... my wife, she was crying... what else could I have done?" His face was long and his expression, mired in deep regret, said, *anything else, I could've done anything else.*

"All three of them turned on me. I remember one had a nose that looked like it'd been broken a couple times. I thought he was going to challenge me, make me a man of my word. But he didn't say nothing. He just raised his own gun and shot my Sally in the chest. Well, I shot back." His lips twitched, considering a smile. "Fruits of my labor are laying outside there."

"Once they ran outside, Dick and I helped," Leonard said. "Sheriff, too. 'Till they gunned him down, poor bastard."

"Half the town turned out when we heard the shots," Chuck added.

"So the outlaws were defending themselves," I said. "Is that how it went down?"

The widowed man gave me a dirty look, like I was defending the outlaws. I wasn't. Just trying to understand how a common bank robbery had left so many dead. "At first. But I think they always meant to kill some of us, Marshal. They took hostages as they left the bank—took Jim and a few other customers. Soon as they had their horses, they shot 'em in the back. Some survived, thank God."

"I remember," added Chuck, "they rode through the town, shooting every which way. Killed Stanley's son right there on the corner. Boy was only nine. And worse than that, they were *laughing* as they did it. Imagine it. Whooping and hollering like it was all a game."

I ran my hand over my face. The depravity in some men's hearts never ceased to surprise me. "Did you recognize any of the men who did this?"

"The men? No…" said Leonard, and he looked around at the others. They shook their heads. "We didn't know a soul among them."

"That's because they didn't have souls," the widowed man murmured, clenching the railing with pale knuckles, as if he'd break it in half, given the strength.

"But there was a woman with them," Leonard recalled.

My chest tightened. "A woman? You sure about that?"

Leonard nodded. "Yeah. I think she was the one in charge. They all looked to her, anyway. Followed her lead and such."

"Can you describe her?"

He scratched the gray plucks of hair on his head. "Not well, no. Her hat covered up her hair, and a bandana hid most her face. With all the firing going on… can't say I got a very good look at her."

"Did you happen to catch the name of this woman?"

Leonard opened his mouth, then shut it, looking puzzled and helpless.

Dick came to his friend's rescue. "Now that you mention it, I think I remember them calling her something. Gulliver, maybe? Gregory?"

"Guillory?" I offered.

"That's it." The man snapped and pointed at me.

Wade turned his back on the men, affording us small privacy. "You know this woman?" he asked me discreetly while Dempsey looked on with curiosity.

I rubbed my jaw. Sighed. "Yeah, I know her."

"She's the one who got away from you in Asher, ain't she?"

MAKE ME NO GRAVE

I nodded.

"Well," Wade hooked his thumbs in his pockets, "that's some shit luck."

"Might be I'm wrong, but this…" I looked down one end of the street, then down the other, making note of the many alleys, entrances and potential exits, how very easy it'd be to case the bank and rob it without anyone in town being the wiser. "I don't know, Wade. This don't seem like her work."

"The dead don't lie," he said.

"No, but the living do."

Wade's forehead pinched. "You think someone's riding under her name?"

"I know, sounds crazy…"

"Excuse me," Dempsey said, stepping in close to me. I'd noticed him giving Wade a wide berth, but didn't think much of it. Wade hadn't bathed in good-Lord-only-knows how long, and after our last ride, the man smelled like hot leather and pits. Dempsey, Yankee that he was, probably thought he was being polite by not commenting on it. Like Wade didn't know. "I know I'm new to this whole hunting-violent-criminals business, but shouldn't we be going after the outlaws instead of standing around talking about them?"

"We're not going anywhere on those horses," Wade said, glancing back at the animals.

"So we get fresh mounts."

Wade raised an eyebrow. "And how're you planning on purchasing those? With your good looks?"

Dempsey had a habit of pushing his bottom lip out with his tongue when he was annoyed, and did so now as he glared at Wade.

"Wade's got a point," I said. "And besides, the outlaws would've had fresh mounts of their own stashed somewhere close by." I shook my head, squinting at the sunset with its sweaty streaks of pink and yellow sky. "They'll be hours ahead of us already." Dempsey looked about to object, but I cut him off. "We need to rest up, or we're like to get ourselves shot for our trouble."

"All part of being a good lawman, son," Wade added with a smile. "You need to know when to hold 'em and when to fold 'em."

Dempsey didn't look happy about the decision, but accepted it with a short nod.

"I'm also thinking we might need more guns," I said as we headed toward the George Brothers Undertaker's Parlor. The boy they'd called Grat lifted one of the dead outlaw's hands and waved it at us as we went. Wade smiled back at the gesture, tipping his hat.

"You want to put together a posse?" Wade asked me.

At this, Dempsey perked up.

"They said seven rode in, maybe eight," I explained. "Four are dead out there; that still leaves three. Including Guillory."

"Yeah, I did the math."

"But a few of the gang could have been hanging back. Or they might be hiring out from an outlaw town in the Indian territories. You add that to the reports we got from the other towns that were hit, and we don't know how many men—and women—we're dealing with. Might be a good idea to bring reinforcements."

Wade nodded, but said, "That could get pricey. Unless we had us some volunteers…"

I thought about the men on the porch, their faces carved in grief, their fingers itching for a trigger, noses dying for a sniff of gunpowder. And their blood, icy cold with hate. They'd come if we asked. Wouldn't need to pay them a penny; the reward was in the doing. But it felt wrong to take advantage of their pain, to manipulate their grief into more violence. It wouldn't bring them the peace they were after.

"I have some savings," I said at last. "It'll have to be enough."

Wade shook his head but didn't bother arguing with me.

"We'll stay here for the night. Tomorrow we'll swing up toward Columbus, see if anyone's willing to help us there, and then double back toward Coffeyville. Town's become an outlaw haunt as of late. Wouldn't be surprised if Guillory's gang has taken up residence there."

"Why not just have the men here join us?" Dempsey asked. "They have more reason than any to want the outlaws dead, and they've already proven good at killing them. It'd save us time and money."

"Because they're angry," I said.

"So?"

"So, an angry man's not a man who'll watch your back in a gunfight. He sees ahead of him, and nowhere else. I'm not arguing their ability, but there's no knowing what they'll do in the heat of the moment. Understand?"

Dempsey frowned. I swear the boy was always frowning. "I'm sorry, but just to clarify, we do mean to kill the outlaws, don't we? That's the whole point of hunting them down, isn't it? To put an end to their… activities."

Wade got to an answer quicker than me. "Oh, you and me, we want to plant them in the ground all right. Those men back there? *They* want them dead, too. But you're traveling with the West's own Gentleman Marshal, the great *hu-man-i-tarian*." He spread the syllables so far apart you could've seen between them. "Apostle here likes to take criminals alive, you see. He's funny like that."

"Don't have to pay burial costs that way," I pointed out, wanting to avoid any accusations of being soft after what had happened with Jed. Maybe the appearance of being hard would avoid open conflict again.

"Right. That's why you do it. Burial costs."

"Wait," Dempsey interrupted. "You have to pay out of your own pocket to bury a criminal you're forced to put down?"

I nodded. "Unless the warrant says dead's acceptable."

"My favorite," Wade said with a sharp smile.

"Unbelievable," Dempsey said.

Wade clapped him on the back, catching the younger man off guard. Dempsey pitched forward a little, but found his footing quickly enough. "Welcome to federal work, son."

CHAPTER SEVEN

Sometime around midnight, unable to find a quiet space in my head long enough to rest my eyes, I journeyed down to the saloon.

At this late hour, I expected it to be populated by the usual characters. Town drunks and the like. Men without good sense, gambling away their savings at the poker table, chewing and spitting and screaming, or red-faced and laughing, and behind them the ladies. Tired beauties in hard colors, red and blue and yellow, like raging sunlight, hovering just outside the dense circle of cigar smoke, waving their fans and smiling with only their mouths, eyes tearing up from the smoke.

But there were no gamblers in the Baxter Saloon, nor even a table looked suited for play. In fact, there was hardly a soul in the place, with the exception of the proprietor sleeping on his fist behind the counter, and a lady sitting all by her lonesome. An untouched glass of something gold and murky sat on the table in front of her.

I took my hat off and motioned with it to the seat across from her. "Mind if I join you?"

She must not have been all there, because when I spoke, it

seemed to give her a start, though she recovered quickly, face hardening like granite. Her shoulders stiffened into the back of her chair.

"Are you one of the marshals everyone's been talking about?" she asked me. She had a unique way of looking ahead without making eye contact. Made me wonder if she were putting on airs for my benefit, or if she acted this way with everyone. Like she was seeing past them.

I looked at the drink. *Or maybe it's got something to do with what happened today.*

"Yes, ma'am," I answered, smiling hesitantly, and leaning into her line of sight. "Though I can't speak to what's been said about me."

She didn't smile back, but she didn't object to my taking a seat either, so I sat.

"I'm afraid we haven't been properly introduced." I reached my hand over the table. "Apostle Richardson."

Her eyes cut to me. They were neither blue nor green, but some kind of middling color. A defeated shade of spring. Reminded me of my home back in North Carolina, before the war had its way with the countryside.

"Apostle?" she repeated, and for the first time, there was some evidence of life in her voice and manner. She pushed a straight curtain of black hair away from her face. "Like a disciple of Christ?"

"Well, I like to think so. Then again, some days it's just a name."

A smile shivered on her lips but was gone almost as soon as it appeared. Driven out by discipline, I wagered. This was not a woman accustomed to making light. She gave my hand a quick, fragile shake—as if it were a snake that'd bite her—and introduced herself as Ruth Kingery.

Well, that explains it. I recalled Dick and Chuck's earlier commentary on Ms. Kingery's humor. Or lack thereof.

"Nice to meet you, Ruth."

"Miss Kingery," she corrected. It sounded tired and rehearsed, not defensive. Apparently not wanting to offend, she added more gently, "That is, if it's all the same to you, Marshal, I prefer going by Miss Kingery."

"Apologies, Miss Kingery. Meant nothing by it."

"I know," she said and went back to watching the still surface of her drink.

I was about to get up, supposing my company wasn't welcome and not wanting to impose on the woman, when Miss Kingery asked, "You're here about the outlaws, aren't you?"

Relaxing back into my seat, I answered with a simple nod.

"Then why weren't you here sooner?" The area around her mouth was tight, lips pulled in against her teeth. Before I could reply, defend the tardiness of myself and my colleagues, it was like the pressure escaped her, and she shook her head. "No, I'm sorry. You don't have to answer that. It wasn't a fair question."

"No. You're right, Miss Kingery. We should've been here. We should've stopped these men..." *and woman,* "...weeks ago. But it don't always work out that way. Time and distance ain't always on the law's side." I rotated my hat by the brim, turning it around a couple times, running my fingers along the loose edge where the fabric was starting to peel back. "Honestly, ma'am. I would've prevented the bloodshed if I could, and I do regret we weren't here in time to help the folks of Baxter Springs."

She watched me intently, her face softening. "You speak well, Marshal. I appreciate the sentiment. Though it doesn't change what's happened, does it?"

"No, ma'am. Sadly, all the words in the world can't reverse a bullet once it's been fired."

"No…" she agreed slowly, a frown dragging down her features. She was the kind of woman a man called handsome, being not quite pretty and not quite ugly, and him trying to be polite with what words he's got. Even with her square jaw and underbite, she was still attractive in her own way, though she didn't seem the type to take much pride in her appearance, given the rags she wore and the makeup she didn't. Not that it was my place to judge.

Over at the counter, the owner snored loudly enough to wake himself. He looked around in sudden alarm before remembering where he was and seeing there was no cause for concern. As he settled his cheek back into his palm, I lifted a hand to catch his attention. He perked up, cleared his throat.

"What can I do you for, Marshal?" he asked from across the room.

"Sarsaparilla, if you've got it. Water if you don't." I was tempted to order something stiffer—a whiskey, say—but each time I considered alcohol, the ghostly prospect of my father loomed tall and ugly in my mind. A wretched shadow of failure. I feared the same weakness for drink nested somewhere inside me, just waiting. My father wasn't always a lousy drunk, after all. There had to be a time before the bottle.

The owner ambled over and set the sarsaparilla down in front of me. When I went to pay him, he just shook his head. "On the house, Marshal." I nodded my thanks, and he went back to the bar where he pretended to clean some glasses for a while, made a lame attempt to polish the counter, all before finally dozing off again on one of the stools.

"You don't drink?" Miss Kingery asked me while I tipped the sarsaparilla bottle back.

I thought about all the times when I was younger, my mother shifting me from one side of her hip to the other while trying to appeal to my father's sense of responsibility, surrounded by the other patrons' lurid stares. *For heaven's sake, Nathaniel,* she'd say, sometimes discreetly and sometimes not, *this has got to stop. Can't you see what it's doing to you? Can't you see what it's doing to your family?*

I wiped the corner of my mouth, swallowing quickly to answer. "Not if I can help it. And by the look of it, you don't either."

"Oh." She peered down her stubby nose at the full glass. "I wasn't going to drink it."

"I gathered."

"I find the taste revolting."

"Why'd you order it then?"

She shrugged, the most human gesture I'd seen from her thus far. I think she was starting to warm to me. I took another swig while she thought about her answer. "I don't know. I guess I just wanted to know what it felt like to have the option."

I furrowed my brow. "Option of doing what, you don't mind my asking?"

"The option of sleeping. Forgetting myself. Just for a little bit. I just need—" She stopped and picked up a thought from somewhere farther down the trail. "Anyway, that's how liquor works, doesn't it? You drink it, and the whole world goes away."

"Afraid it always comes back, and never kindly. Besides, what's got a gentle lady like yourself so desperate to forget anyhow? Can't imagine you've many skeletons cluttering your closet." She wouldn't meet my eyes, boring holes into the top of the table. "This have anything to do with what happened today? With that fellow who talked you up?"

Her lips parted, but it was another few seconds before any words came out of her mouth. "How do you know about that?"

"Everyone's got a story when you've got a badge," I said with a brief smile.

She ran a single finger along one wooden crevice in the table, going over it enough times that I began to worry she was going to pick up a splinter. "You may not have noticed, but I'm not a very personable person. I know what they all say about me when they think I'm not listening. They call me cold."

"Pious was the way I heard it."

"Pious," she repeated with fake surprise. "Funny how something that's supposed to be good can be made into such an insult."

"I'm afraid I'm not following. What's this got to do with the outlaw you spoke to earlier?"

"*I liked him.*" I saw it then: the passion in her eyes, the embers of some deep feeling. Wasn't love, of course, but given time, might've become it. "He was the first man to treat me like I was a woman of flesh and blood. Not some stony gargoyle on a church —architecture to be ignored. He made me feel like I could be something other than walking scripture. *Charm is deceitful, and beauty is vain, but a woman who fears the Lord is to be praised…*"

"Proverbs 31."

"You know your Bible." She nodded approvingly. "But I haven't been praised, Marshal. I've been condemned. Isolated. Cast out. People look at me, and they think I'm judging them. All the time, judging. And who wants to constantly be reminded of their sins?"

"What'd he say to you, Miss Kingery?"

"What'd he say to me? He said, 'God surely broke the mold with you, Miss.' I told him, 'If you're trying to appeal to my sense of vanity, sir, you're wasting your time and mine.' You know what he said to that? He said, 'Actually, I was appealing to God's vanity, and His good taste, but you go on and take the credit, if you like.'"

She laughed—the sound bursting suddenly from her like a sneeze, and she was too slow in clapping her hand over her mouth to stop it. Tears clung to her lashes, about ready to fall.

I didn't know what to say, or whether I should say anything, but I was starting to think maybe she needed that whiskey after all.

"The first man," she said again, hiccuping dryly, "I've *ever* given consideration to, and he turns out to be a damnable outlaw. Wouldn't it figure?"

"That's surely some bad luck, ma'am," I said, heart hurting for her.

"Bad luck or poor judgment?"

Her eyes were shining, wet and dark. I patted my vest pocket instinctively, but I wasn't carrying a handkerchief on me. I'd stopped that habit around the time my wife left me. Hadn't needed one after that.

"Sometimes there's no difference. Did he say anything else?" I was hoping for some nugget of information that might lead my band to discovering the bandits' base of operations. It felt a touch dirty, given the poor lady's state of distress, but the best way I could help Miss Kingery was to make sure something like this didn't happen in Baxter Springs ever again.

Pressing her thumb into her sleeve, she used it to touch the corners of her eyes, her breaths coming and going in quick little gasps. I was reminded of the way my mother tried to stop herself from crying in front of me after my father leveled some particularly mean or nasty epithet at her. When she stood in the square of light coming from our front door, watching him storm out and disappear into the dark fields, heading to God-only-knows-where.

"Ma'am." I reached over, taking her free hand. It was the only thing I could think to do to help comfort her. Miss Kingery looked down at my hand, but without the same suspicion as before, and she didn't remove hers. "Please, this could be important. Did he say anything else?"

"He liked my bonnet." She rolled her eyes, as if even she recognized it as a line.

I smiled. "I bet he did. Anything else? Anything about where he was headed to, or coming from?"

She thought long and hard, moving her eyes along the ceiling. "I remember asking him whether he meant to stay in Baxter Springs long. He said he'd love to, but that he had some business with the railroad that was taking him north."

Might've been a story to look upstanding and professional. But it also could've been an indication that the gang meant to hit a train. I held the Kansas geography well in my head, so I knew how far it was to the first junction. Wasn't a stretch to imagine them heading up toward Emporia, Peabody, or Walton, or swinging harder west toward Wichita. It'd take some hard riding, but they could do it if they'd a mind to.

There was no lack of railway to prey on. The Santa Fe had most of the territory in Kansas platted out, and as of the beginning of this year, its main line had made it as far as the Colorado border, pushing to meet up with the Central Pacific out of Sacramento and unite the coasts. The *Best Enterprise in the West,* as the papers toted it, was moving ahead full steam, spreading across the face of the country in a spiderweb of steel. It was a fine, marvelous thing by all accounts, but it made it damn near impossible to predict where a robbery might take place. Everyone expected the marshals to keep order, but we were already spread thin. Simple reality was we couldn't be everywhere all of the time.

Still, it was something. More than we had to go on before, and it gave me an idea about the route the gang might take. I thanked Ms. Kingery for her help, and placing my hat back onto my head, I stood to leave.

"He's dead now," she said, looking straight ahead again. "Chuck and the sheriff shot him as they were leaving the bank. You probably saw him out there on the street, all full of holes."

"Yes, ma'am. Along with the others."

"The bullets didn't kill him immediately, not like the one shot in the bank. I was there with the doctor. I remember the look in his eyes, as he was dying. He was afraid, Marshal. He was so afraid."

Most men are at the end.

Ms. Kingery stared up at me, and I was afraid she was going to start crying again. There was something desolate about her expression, like a man in the desert who can only go five miles more without a drink of water, and just realized he needs to go ten in order to reach it.

"I can't get that image out of my mind. Him lying there, pawing at me with his hands caked in blood and dust, begging me to save him—pleading for his life—and me sitting there, helpless as a fish." She shut her eyes and shook her head. "I know it's foolish. We'd only just met. But it feels like I watched an entire future drain into the dust. Just a few hours earlier, I'd imagined what it might be like to live in the light of that cowboy smile, day after day. And now I'm never going to see it again. It feels like God gaveth, only so He could taketh it away. How does a person reconcile with that?"

I thought about my ex-wife. The way she'd wear her hair up when it was hot, and the way she'd playfully swat at my hands whenever I went to move away some of the strands glued to her neck. I thought about the way she smiled at me without ever showing her teeth, sensitive about a snaggletooth she had. And how I took for granted that that was how it would always be, just me and her. I thought about the man with the fancy suit, the black derby, and bright liar's eyes, who smelled like the city and came with money and promises I couldn't make.

I might've gone by Apostle now, but I was no preacher. I didn't know what words of advice or consolation to offer the lady.

"You just do," I said, a dull ache beginning in my chest that I knew would eventually float to my head, making it hard to think. I hoped sleep would head it off.

"You make it sound easy."

"Then I'm not saying it right. It sure ain't easy. There's no trick to it either. Just takes time. But look: that man made his choices, and he answered for them. You're still alive to make yours. That's something."

I wished Ms. Kingery a good rest of her night and took off. Last I glimpsed the poor woman, she was slamming back her glass of stale whiskey and making a face.

CHAPTER EIGHT

W alking into Coffeyville with a badge was tantamount to walking into a storage room full of black powder with your hair on fire. You'd find out what was in there all right, but you were just as likely to get yourself blown away for the trouble.

Wade knew as well as I did that nobody in Coffeyville was going to roll over on their fellow outlaw, not on account of any marshals. I considered going in under the pretense of being a couple of cowpunchers, but it was a bit early for driving season, we had no cows, and there was a good chance Wade or I would've been recognized, besides.

So I came up with a different approach, though nothing so fancy as to be considered an actual plan.

"I have to say, Apostle, this has got to be the most brainless, idiotic, *stupid* idea I've ever heard of, let alone participated in," Wade complained from the seat beside me, holding the coach gun in his lap. He smiled suddenly, a bit of breakfast still lodged between his canine and another tooth. "And I *love* it. Hah! How long now, do you think?"

Above us, the Kansas sky was a wrinkled blanket of grey, and behind us a fierce wind was blowing up from the south, plastering my coat to my back. I'd already had to give up wearing my hat, lest I lose it to a sudden gale. "Could be another few hours," I said, watching the road, "Or it could be another day. Hard to judge."

Wade banged on the roof of the carriage in a quick one-two with the side of his fist. "How you holding up, son?" he hollered to Dempsey inside.

There was a weak bang in reply.

"Maybe we should pull off, let the poor kid out for some air," Wade said.

We'd discovered early into our trip, not long after our departure from the first stage near Coffeyville, that Dempsey suffered from coach sickness. Maybe it was the constant rocking motion— up, down, and around, like a baby bounced on a knee—combined with the tight interior of the coach that did it for him. Whatever the case, Dempsey needed out every few hours or else he decorated the thorough brace with vomit. Each time I was sure he didn't have anything left in his stomach, he surprised me by poking his head out past the heavy curtains and heaving onto the wheels. Poor kid.

"You want to switch off?" I asked Wade.

The man frowned beneath his whiskers, eyes going dark and humorless. "I didn't say that."

Wade shared Dempsey's hostility toward the inside of the coach, but for a different reason. He didn't like being shut up whatsoever. I think it had something to do with an event in his childhood involving a cabinet or a trunk, but he wouldn't talk about it. I'd learned not to ask.

"We can't keep stopping," I said. "They catch all three of us out in the open…"

"Yeah, I know. Just feel sorry for the kid."

I flexed my fingers which were going stiff inside my gloves, losing circulation from holding on so tightly to the reins. "So do I, but being comfortable ain't always in the marshal's purview. Best he learn that hard fact now. Might help him get over any romantic notions he has of the job."

"Well, if that ain't the pot calling the kettle black."

"How do you figure?"

Wade exploded with laughter. "Apostle Richardson, you've got to be the most damnably romantic man I know! What with your god-fearing and your Southern graces. You look at an outlaw and you see a man who's made a few bad choices in his life. A man whose life's worth sparing merely by virtue of his being alive, and I'd wager you think about *saving his soul. Turning him back to the light.*" He held his arms up in a fake gesture of worship, his voice booming with pulpit fervor.

He dropped his arms back to his lap, shaking his head. "Want to know what I see?"

I smiled tolerantly. "What do you see, Wade?"

"Job insurance. Money to get me a nice new hat." He fingered a bullet hole in the high crown of his black Stetson. I thought the hole gave the hat some character. Wade didn't share my sentimentality.

"Well, I ever find myself on the wrong side of the law, I'll be sure to remember that."

"You ever find yourself on the wrong side of the law, I'll be too busy admiring the flying pigs and enjoying the nice breeze coming up from hell to bother with you."

We rode in silence for a time. The measured clops of the horses, their snuffling breaths, and the sound of the wind rushing over the grass was enough to put a man to sleep, and I was just beginning to wonder whether or not Wade had succumbed to slumber when his entire body rumbled. Took me another moment to realize he was chuckling.

"What now?" I asked him.

"Nothing," he said, a toothy grin spreading beneath his moustache. "Just imagining the look on those bastards' faces when they ride up on us, expecting an easy take."

I glanced back for the twentieth time this trip.

"Won't have to imagine much longer," I replied, slipping my revolver from its holster and resting it on the inside of my thigh, just behind the flap of my coat. "Looks like we're about to have company."

Wade angled around to get a better look past my shoulder and the empty luggage piled high on the top of the coach.

The strangers were cutting through the field quickly. With the bottoms of their animals submerged in the grass, it almost looked as if the bandits were gliding toward us on boats, moving with the wind. The horse heads bobbed like the prows of Viking ships. I counted four riders all together, though they rode in a broken line —some gaining at times, others falling back, like they were racing each other, eager to be first to the prize.

I banged three times on the roof of the carriage, warning Dempsey.

His responding knocks were more solid than before.

"Now, remember," I told Wade who was double checking that his gun was properly loaded, "It won't do us any good if they're all dead."

Wade snapped his break-action shut with a business-like *click*. He made a noise I hoped meant he was in agreement. He wasn't smiling anymore, and without that smile, the lines around his face made him look old and grim, like all those portraits of Union and Confederate officers taken during the final years of the war. It was a strange thing, seeing a man age before his time, watching the grizzly effects of a decade crammed into the span of a few short years. Wade hadn't even hit forty yet. I couldn't picture him at fifty.

"I mean it, Wade. Watch yourself. Won't do us any good you getting yourself killed neither."

Wade's burnsides lifted some. "Managed all right so far."

No more could be said on the subject. The thieves were upon us.

Two of the riders reined up in front of the coach, forcing me to pull my team to a stop. Another rider circled round the back, eying some of the boxes in the rear boot before taking an interest in the coach's passenger. The man swung around a couple times, trying to get a better look inside, but was unable to see past the drawn curtains. Instead, he spat on the ground and kept his animal moving, slinking like a coyote among cattle.

The fourth, presumably the leader, sat back in his saddle and smiled at me. He was dusky, maybe Italian, and I think he meant me to take his stillness as non-threatening. "Where are you folks heading to?"

"Cherryvale," I told him, allowing a nervous glance at the man's companions, letting him think he had us on the ropes.

Every few seconds, the wind pushed a few strands of the man's dark hair across his forehead. "In this weather?" His eyebrows bunched together in a convincing look of concern. They were patchy, like someone kept plucking at them, and I noticed a thin line that bisected the left one, a scar where the hair wouldn't grow back.

"Our passenger here's got family there. Sick uncle or some such, I was told."

"Of course, of course." The man nodded, staring down at the ground thoughtfully. Some of the horses threw back their heads and stepped in place, scenting a storm in the air. The riders themselves looked glib, excited. When their leader looked up again, all pretenses of friendliness were gone from his pale green eyes, something sharp and greedy replacing the kindness. "He wouldn't happen to be a Du Pont, would he? Your passenger?"

"We don't want any trouble now," I said.

The man was already indicating that one of his men should

check inside the coach. The remainder had their hands near their leather, closer than I'd like. I clutched my hidden revolver, feeling my vision narrowing to a fixed point. Wade had a joke he liked to tell when he was in a mood, especially after indulging in the hospitality of a barkeep. *How do you kill outlaws?* he'd ask, and before you could answer, he'd hit you with the punch line. *One at a time.*

Wade raised his shotgun at the rider ahead of us, freezing the man's hand on the butt of his piece. He didn't say anything, but then he didn't have to. Staring down those massive twin bores, the outlaw understood what was required of him.

The rest of it happened about the same time: The leader pulled his gun—an older model of the one I carried. I recognized it immediately as an officer's weapon from the war.

I revealed mine from the flap of my coat.

It began to rain.

The man sent to investigate the coach started to move the curtains aside with the nose of his gun and the coyote-looking fella restlessly steered his horse around in the background.

I had just opened my mouth to announce we were federal marshals when the air rattled with the sound of thunder. It might as well have been a gunshot.

Dempsey opened fire through the slit of the curtain, killing the investigator point blank. The rider ahead of us decided to take his chances and drew; Wade blew him out of his seat with a single pull, and whether by accident or intention, also caught the horse's flank with the buckshot. The animal went down, falling backward in panic and rolling onto the already injured man.

The sudden percussion startled our team, and the horses bolted—with us still attached.

Both the leader and his surviving man fired at us as we tore off, but it took them another minute to catch up, given the objections of their own animals.

I ducked as balls splintered into the wood around me, a couple punching through the cheap leather luggage. Throwing the reins at Wade, I turned to return fire, hoping to catch one of the men in an arm or a leg. Somewhere that would slow them down, but not kill them outright. This was going bad fast.

I must've hit the coyote because he reined up, clutching his shoulder and cussing me all to hell. The leader was still coming on when Dempsey opened his door, hanging partially out of the coach, gun in hand. He still looked a bit queasy, especially from the present jostling, but I admired his determination.

"Hold your fire!" I yelled back—to both him and the outlaw.

Wade finally managed to get the team under control, pulling us to a sudden stop. The outlaw overshot the coach, and I expected he would turn back for another run at us—but instead, he kept on going, bending low over his saddle in a full gallop.

"Shit," I muttered. "He's running!"

"I see him," Wade said, entirely calm as he reached back for a Sharps rifle nestled between the ripped luggage. One of many guns we'd brought along for just such an occasion.

"Think you can hit him from here?"

The man was already two hundred feet away, at least. It'd take a hell of a shot.

Wade raised his iron sights, settling the stock in the crook of his shoulder for balance, making himself comfortable. "I can get him."

"Better hurry," Dempsey said.

The outlaw was three hundred feet now.

I covered my right ear as Wade fired.

And missed.

He cursed and reloaded, closing the breech with a sharp *snap*. Fired. Missed again. The bullet bit the dust. By now, the man was a shrinking dot in the distance, and I knew there wasn't any way a bullet was going to reach him. Wade lowered the gun and straightened back up. "Huh," he said, looking more confused than angry. "Guess I'm a bit rustier than I thought."

Meanwhile, I could still hear the plaintive moans of the coyote coming from a ways back. He couldn't seem to get his horse to cooperate, no matter how he kicked its flanks and urged it on, cursing desperately.

Maybe today wouldn't end up a complete wash, after all.

CHAPTER NINE

The storm proved a boon. The sudden deluge of wind and rain cleared Coffeyville's streets and pushed most of its seedier element indoors. It was practically biblical, given the town's evil reputation. Between the press of bodies in the dance-halls and the slurring calls for more whiskey in the saloons, no one was going to pay much mind to a couple of cowpunchers coming in out of the rain. Especially when they were in the company of one of Coffeyville's own.

A few precautions never hurt, though. Only me and Dempsey followed our coyote friend into Coffeyville. Wade waited outside town with our poor pockmarked stagecoach and some grumbling words about Kansas weather, wet and miserable when we left him. Of the three of us, Wade was easily the most recognizable with his burnsides and his habit of putting holes in any man whose name followed the words, *WANTED DEAD OR ALIVE.* For better or worse, news traveled fast on the frontier, and Wade was a legend in the outlaw community for all the wrong reasons.

I wore my hat low as we passed a general supply, dancehall, feed store, and a handful of saloons. The doors of the drinking establishments were all open, stopped by either a large rock or chair, each ejecting a blade of saffron light into the gutter. All the hooting, hollering, and laughter freely advertised the grand times being had inside, while the rich aroma of good smokes hovered like a fog near the entrances, smothered only somewhat by the musty smell of rain and earth. I couldn't help peering inside every saloon we passed, each time feeling a peculiar stab in my gut. That sensation of being an outsider looking in. It was stupid, knowing the sorts that visited these establishments, but still. Sure looked warm and friendly.

Dempsey didn't seem to share the attraction. He was too busy skirting puddles and watching out for the occasional cow pie in the street. The complete lack of concentration in his expression made me wonder if he was aware of how ridiculous he looked, taking such dainty steps like it was the most natural thing in the world for him to avoid getting his boots dirty. Maybe it was, given his background. I tried not holding his wealthy upbringing against him, though I must confess to intentionally distracting the poor kid once or twice with a word or sudden gesture so he would misstep. I held back a smile as Dempsey frowned and shook chunks of mud and slime from his boots, never once complaining. I liked that about him. He might've been moody, but at least he wasn't a grumbler.

"You know where you're going?" I asked, keeping close behind the coyote. He'd given his name as Owen Fairly only after Wade threatened to give him another friendly pat on the shoulder where he'd been shot. With his lanky frame and jittery gestures, I thought coyote suited him better.

Fairly nodded. His hair was a sloppy mess of black, growing long around his ears. The rain matted it against his face, which was white with strain. I couldn't tell whether it was from the blood loss or a healthy fear of Almena Guillory. Probably a mixture of both.

"Shouldn't we be checking the saloons?" Dempsey asked,

glancing back just as piano music exploded from one of the open doors. I immediately recognized the jaunty tune of "The Old Chisholm Trail." My instincts were confirmed by a chorus of saloon goers, all singing along: *coma ti yi youpy, youpy yea, youpy yea, coma ti yi youpy, youpy yea.*

"I hear they sometimes have gambling rooms in the back," Dempsey went on, ignoring the music. "I'm no criminal, but it seems like the kind of place a fugitive would be drawn to."

"My friend's got himself a point," I said to Fairly. "Mind explaining where we're headed?"

"The church," Fairly said.

"The church," I repeated dumbly. "You sure she's there?"

"You know that fellow I talked to when we first came in? The one outside Kellerman's Goods? Well, *he* told me she was up at the church. So we're going to the church. That all right with you, Lawman?"

"Hey," Dempsey said. "Don't get testy."

Fairly blinked more times than nature required, and his hand went to the area of his shoulder. "Your beau here put a fucking bullet in me," he hissed. "How am I supposed to be?"

"We took the bullet out," Dempsey said. "Now it's just a nice hole. Maybe next time you'll think twice before robbing someone."

"Or next time, I'll just fire a whole cylinder into the coach, no questions asked."

"That kind of talk's not going to earn you the chance for a next time," I told him, pressing the mouth of my revolver against his back. "Mind yourself."

"What?" he scoffed, trying to appear braver than I knew he was. "You going to shoot me again?"

"I might. Or I might just package you up and send you off to the district court with a bow attached. State judges don't normally take kindly to men threatening their marshals—and you tried to shoot two of them."

A barroom brawl spilled into the street a few feet in front of us. Men swung at each other, barely connecting, too sluggish with drink. A few others who possessed the better sense to stay out of the fight sat back on their heels and slapped their thighs, hawing about the scene from the warm doorway.

Dempsey looked at me for a cue, resting his hand inside his coat on a gun I couldn't see but knew was there. I clicked back the hammer on my own revolver, keeping the gun close to my vest, out of view of the brawling men. I continued to watch Fairly. If he started caterwauling, he could draw serious attention, especially if the words he shouted were "marshals!" they'd be on us in seconds, and I didn't fancy a gunfight with two dozen drunk outlaws.

But Fairly didn't say a word. My estimate of his character paid off. Sometimes there was honor among thieves, and a man would sacrifice himself for the survival of his friends. Fairly was not one such man, judging by the way he'd abandoned the friend Wade'd shot and trapped beneath his horse, and hadn't bothered trying to catch up with his gang leader when things started going south. He could've cried out an alarm just now, but only at tremendous personal cost. He genuinely believed I'd shoot him.

I wouldn't have done. Course not. I'd never fire on an unarmed man, but Fairly didn't know that, and I let him think what he would.

Dempsey remained tense the whole way, keeping his hand low and near his piece until we finally reached the steps of the church. No more than a few feet from the bottom steps, Fairly stopped cold, planting his heels like a donkey on the edge of a cliff.

I placed a steadying hand on his good shoulder. "Easy," I told him.

"You don't get it, do you," he said, staring at the entrance to the Lord's house with wide eyes, his expression ashy and afraid. "She's going to kill me."

The rain continued to fall. Due to the wind, it cut in at just the right angle to hit my face. I squinted at Fairly, holding my arm up in a vain attempt to block the weather. "Look, I'm not going to let her shoot you. You have my word on that."

"Your word?" Fairly repeated, voice climbing in pitch. He laughed, hysterical with fear. "Your *word?* Well, thank goodness for *your word.* You know what? Fuck your word. Your *word* isn't going to do fuck all when you're dead. And that's what you'll be, you step foot in there."

"That there is a house of worship, in case you haven't noticed."

Fairly laughed again. "You think that'll stop her from drawing blood?"

"I trust it'll give her pause."

"The hell it will. I thought you said you'd met her."

I told him to get on, nudging him with my foot.

"Come on, Marshal," he whined, turning around completely to face me. He held his shoulder gingerly but talked animatedly with his other hand. "I haven't made a fuss. I've kept my end of the bargain…"

I raised my brow.

"I've shown you where she is. Why don't you just let me go? Bygones being bygones, and all that."

My hands found my hips, and I sighed, looking at him from beneath the brim of my hat. "I apologize if I gave you the impression that letting you go was ever going to be an option, Mister Fairly. It ain't. The only thing your help has bought you is my gratitude, and a recommendation that you not be hanged. That's more than most marshals would give you, and maybe more than you deserve, given who you're running with. And what you all did in Baxter Springs."

"What?" he said, sounding confused.

"Boss," Dempsey interrupted, laying a hand on my shoulder. "If Guillory's as bad as everyone seems to think, it might be a good idea not to provoke her."

"What are you thinking?" I said.

"I'll wait outside with Fairly. Keep an eye on him while you go in."

"Oh, hell no," Fairly said, backing up from the younger man. He looked at me, shaking his head. "No fucking way. After what he did to Joe? He blew his damn head off! For *looking*!"

Dempsey glanced away angrily—or ashamed. It hadn't occurred to me until that moment that the confrontation back on the road was likely Dempsey's first time taking another man's life. Even if it wasn't, it was still something worth talking about the next chance we got.

"My colleague took what he felt was appropriate action at the time," I told Fairly while looking at Dempsey. The younger man continued frowning at the ground, a small line of thought appearing and disappearing between his brows. "I expect him to do the same now."

Dempsey looked up at me. Nodded.

"Looks like you're getting your wish, after all, Mister Fairly. You get to stay outside with Mister Du Pont here."

He cursed again but didn't object. Dempsey was clearly the lesser of two evils.

"You sure you're good for this?" I asked Dempsey in a private aside, just as Fairly plopped himself down beneath a small overhang beside the stairs. We spoke in subdued voices so as not to alert those inside to our presence. "Because if you're not, you need to tell me right now."

"I'm good," Dempsey promised.

"All right then. Goes without saying, you keep an eye on him. He starts giving you any trouble, you do whatever you have to."

I turned to head inside but stopped when I felt a hand on my arm. Dempsey's blue eyes were clear but worried. "Are *you* good for this? You'll be in there alone, with nobody watching your back."

Craning my neck, I stared up through the rain at the white steeple. The church wasn't big, just a one-room mission for the local population. In a town like this, I had to wonder how many parishioners it received. The windows were shuttered, though that could've been because of the storm. Some dry weeds grew in the corner of the steps, and the paint was peeling away from the wood. Gave the church a tired look. Still, the fact it was here at all and hadn't been burned to the ground boded well.

"Well, not nobody," I said with a reserved smile.

Dempsey looked stumped, no doubt trying to figure out a polite way to argue with my faith.

"Try not to hurt yourself now," I said gently. "I know what you meant." I waved my Colt at him. "That's why I'm bringing the gun. Don't believe there's any scripture that says the good Lord'll make me bulletproof, though that sure would be nice." I absently rubbed my shoulder where my old buckshot injury was acting up again. Too bad I hadn't had Almena Guillory around back in the day to fix me up with her fancy powers.

Dempsey exhaled slowly. "If you're sure."

"One more thing," I told him, even more quietly, hand resting on the door. "You hear any shooting, you don't stick around for the blood. You get the hell out of Coffeyville, hear? Forget about Fairly; forget about Guillory; forget about me. I want no heroics from you. Understood?"

Dempsey gave me a mute, obedient nod. I didn't believe for a second he meant to honor our agreement, being young and hot-headed, galvanized by the idea of a West that could be won, like it was a game or a friendly competition. He hadn't seen any fighting during the war, or else he would've realized the hard truth: a good man could still die even when he was fighting on the side of right.

The door opened suddenly beneath my hand, almost causing me to lose my balance.

I recovered just as a preacher appeared, draped in the customary black of his position.

"I'm sorry, friends, but the chapel is closed right now," the preacher said, an unexpected lion of a man. His shirt strained to contain him, the muscle in his arms congregating like cannonballs beneath its tight sleeves. I didn't notice until he hobbled out from the black gap of the door a little further, but one of his trouser legs was pinned back behind his thigh. He held on to the door frame for balance. "You'll have to come back another time."

I scanned his face quickly, searching for any sign of stress or anxiety. Had Guillory somehow caught on to us? Was she holding hostages in there? The preacher's face did seem drawn, like he hadn't slept recently…but he didn't appear frightened either. If anything, he looked annoyed by my interruption, impatient to get me gone.

"Preacher." I removed my hat out of respect, despite the weather. "I've traveled a long way, and it'd be a great relief to spend some time in the presence of the Lord."

"The Lord is all around us," the preacher replied. "There's a hotel down the street. Spend some time with Him there."

He started to close the door, but I pressed my shoulder into it, keeping it open. Listening, I could hear breathing and movement, the sound of a fairly large crowd. There were also voices, but I couldn't make out what they were saying. "Sounds like you've got a few friends in there."

"This is my church, and as I've said, it's closed."

I removed my badge from the pocket of my coat. "Might be

your church, but this is federal business. With all due respect, preacher, I'm going to need to come inside."

The preacher's eyes were pale bores, trying to blow me away. I half-expected him to take a swing at me.

"I have a right to offer sanctuary to whomever I please," the preacher said defensively.

"There a problem, James?" a female voice asked from the shadowy room behind him. The preacher craned his neck to look back at the speaker. "You need me to run off some more drunks again?"

I immediately recognized the voice as belonging to Almena Guillory and shoved my way inside, gun drawn.

CHAPTER TEN

The moment I stepped inside, half a dozen Osage turned to look at me. Two men, four women. Upon my rude entrance, many of the women reached for weapons—not just daggers or bows and arrows, but old rifle models, too—and began yelling at me. I didn't have to speak their language to know it probably wasn't anything nice.

The men, on the other hand, were too badly hurt to move or speak, if they were even conscious. Their tall, lean bodies barely fit the pews, legs hanging off the ends. The Grizzly Queen of the West stood among them, looking out of sorts, her skirt messed with dark blood and a smear on her cheek where she must have thoughtlessly tried to clean away some dirt.

I didn't know what to make of the scene, especially in the context of the church setting. The preacher grabbed my gun arm, as if he thought I meant to start shooting wildly, waking me from my stupor. Try as I might, I couldn't initially free myself; the man was as strong as he looked, and his grip functioned like a clap of irons.

He forced me to pistol whip him. Wasn't very Christian, I'll grant, but the preacher didn't give me a choice. Without two good legs for balance, he collapsed against the wall, hands pawing for something to catch himself on. He eventually righted himself by climbing up the door frame.

I quickly looked back at Guillory.

She had a gun trained on me now. *My* gun, actually. Same one she stole off me back in Asher. *She kept it?*

"Apostle Richardson. You're like a bad itch. You just keep coming on, don't you?"

"You keep killing, the law'll keep coming after you, Miss Guillory," I replied. "That's how it works."

She tilted her head slightly and parted her lips for a rebuttal, but the preacher cut in.

"How dare you barge in here and wave that gun around? This is a *church*." The preacher held his nose, blood running through his fingers. For that reason, his voice arrived muffled, resembling a sound like thunder.

"Calm down, James," Almena said. "Don't you know this man here's a *bona fide* U.S. Marshal?"

"I don't care if he's Ulysses S. Grant himself. No guns in my church." He rounded on Almena. "Same goes for you. Of all people, Mary. You should know better."

"Mary?" I said, recalling our conversation back in Asher. "Like the queen?"

She smirked. "Sure as shit not like the virgin."

Guillory didn't pardon me from her sights, but a small smile played in the corners of her lips, and her gray eyes were soft. Actually, fatigued was probably a better description. She was slouching a bit.

I moved deeper into the church, maintaining eye contact with Almena while backing toward the wall so no one could get the drop on me from behind. From the corner of my eyes, I glimpsed Dempsey outside, trapped at the bottom of the church stairs, gun in hand. His frozen posture didn't betray fear so much as indecision, undoubtedly torn between joining me, like he wanted to, and continuing to guard Fairly, like I'd told him to. The outlaw was currently pressing his spindly frame against the wall like a spider trying to disappear into a crack.

"Preacher," I said, "I'm not here to cause trouble." He made a skeptical noise. "I realize it may not look that way at the moment, but I'm not here to bother the natives, if that's what you're worried about. My business is with Miss Guillory."

"Who?" he said.

"Mary."

"Can we do this another time, Marshal?" Almena asked wearily, like this was all a mild inconvenience. An Osage woman stood next to her, holding a rifle, and looking mean enough to use it. The other native women had since retreated to their men, attempting to soothe them with quiet words and gentle hands. "I'm busy. In case you haven't noticed."

"Maybe you ought to explain what's going on here first," I suggested. "And lower that gun while you're at it."

"You first," she said.

"Last time I gave you the benefit of the doubt, I got shot."

"Not by me."

"No. You just *threatened* to shoot me."

"*House. Of. The. Lord,*" James said, his face cloudy with annoyance. "Both of you holster your weapons, for God's sake."

"Yes," Almena said. "For God's sake, Marshal."

I chewed my bottom lip. "On the count of three, we both lower. Agreed?"

She nodded. "Agreed."

"One."

"Two."

"Three."

Taking one of the stupidest risks of my life, I rolled the

hammer back into a resting position and sank my revolver into its holster.

Almena held out a second longer, no doubt waiting to see what I'd do, and then lowered hers, though she didn't put the piece away entirely. It was a compromise I was willing to accept.

"Now we can talk," I said. "You can start by explaining this here… powwow."

"We were attacked." The Osage woman's voice was quiet, but she spoke in clear English. Her face was round and honest, coming to a slight point at her chin, and her hair was tied into a practical braid at the back of her head. As I recalled, she was the only person, apart from the preacher, who hadn't gone for a weapon when I burst in. She knelt beside one of the men—they appeared close in age—and held a wet cloth to his head while he shook with pain or fever.

"Who attacked you?" I asked.

"Soldiers on horseback," she said. "They wore blue coats. They accused us of smuggling whiskey into Indian Territory."

"There's your so-called *federal business*," the preacher added, giving me a dirty look. I tried not to take it personally. Man was probably a greyback, born and bred. Still fighting the War of Northern Aggression in his heart, if not in reality. It explained the attitude and the leg, anyway.

I divided my attention between Almena and the Osage woman who'd spoken, glancing frequently between them. "Forgive me, ma'am, but I have to ask. *Were* you smuggling whiskey into Indian Territory?"

Selling spirits to Indians on their lands was against the law. If they wanted the liquor, the government encouraged them—forced, more like—to trek into Arkansas or Kansas to purchase it from a respectable merchant. As with most things in the West, the fact that it was illegal didn't stop a few enterprising souls from smuggling barrels of John Barleycorn across the border in the dead of night. It was a victimless crime for the most part, so the marshals usually left the problem to local sheriffs. The only time I'd ever caught a smuggler myself, it was along the Shawnee Trail, and he'd been carrying food and medicine in addition to the whiskey, headed into Cherokee territory. I let him off with a warning and slept just fine that night.

To my relief, the Osage woman didn't look offended by my question. She held my gaze a moment, before answering with a simple "Yes."

"Is that why you're helping them?" I addressed Almena. "For the money?"

Almena flattened herself into a pew, resting her arms along the top. It seemed a touch too orchestrated—every movement planned, every posture thought out. She was working too hard to look casual. "Think what you like, Marshal."

I rubbed my forehead and looked back at the Osage woman. "Ma'am... you do understand smuggling is against the law?"

"But we are not citizens of your United States," she said. "Or is that not what we have been told, again and again, by the actions of your government?"

I suspected I'd insulted her, after all, and now we were trading barbs. Much like a rose in a Texas song, somewhere beneath the woman's sweetly expression, she was hiding thorns.

"What's your name, if you don't mind my asking?"

She gave me her native name, but when I struggled to pronounce it, added, "You may also call me Footprints-in-the-woods." She said it in a way that sounded like she was used to white folk being unable to get it right, and was too tired to listen to me butcher it. "The whiskey was not for drinking. We use it for medicine, as well as to barter with the other tribes. The rations your government offers us are..."

"Shit," Almena supplied. I expected Preacher James to chide her for her language, but he didn't. "They're starving," she added.

"They could send in a request for more goods and supplies," I said. "If things are as bad as you say, surely the government will do something."

Almena shook her head. "I knew you were naïve, Marshal, but I never took you for stupid. The government's not going to do anything contrary to its interests, and it's got no interest in Indian lives. It's like a stubborn mule. Only way to get the damn thing to go is by threatening to crack a switch across its back. And the only way it answers to that threat is by making good on it in the first place."

"Stealing whiskey," I supplied, frowning.

"It isn't stealing, not really. Consider it a form of redistributing the wealth to those who need it the most."

Looking at the Osage in the church, I couldn't deny the sense of injustice. If what Almena said was true. But it was still breaking the law, and I was still a lawman. Wasn't my place to adjudicate, only to enforce. "So I'm to add smuggler to your repertoire. That about the cut of it?"

"Where's that rank on the list?" Almena asked. "Above or below cow rustling? Or maybe just south of a hold-up?"

"You angling to swing again, Miss Guillory?"

"Why? Am I getting on your nerves?"

"Enough," the preacher said, though I could see by the confused look he was giving Almena that 'Mary' never divulged all the sordid details of her past life. Smart of her. "These people weren't smuggling when they were set upon. The blue coats attacked them with no provocation."

I wanted to find that hard to believe, but truth was I didn't. Former soldiers of the Union Army were notorious for their bad behavior out here, unleashed by the war and far from the eyes and judgment of Washington. "Why come back here, then? If it was U.S. soldiers who attacked you?"

"Because of her," Footprints-in-the-woods said, meaning Almena.

Almena stared at her lap. Her finger had stopped bouncing.

"How's that now?" I asked.

"She's a healer," Footprints-in-the-woods answered. "The soldiers killed ours." I wasn't sure whether she meant some kind of medicine man or someone with the same powers Almena possessed. It hadn't occurred to me until then, but it stood to reason that more fleshcrafters like Almena existed, though they likely went by another name in the Osage community. "She can help them." Footprints-in-the-woods gestured toward the men.

Just how many times had she performed her healing trick for others, I wondered? For the Osage to have known they could find her here, they must have had prior contact, and for them to take such a tremendous risk in reaching out, they'd need to trust her. Almena Guillory, a woman famous for shooting, killing, and thieving. A woman often compared to a beast for her brutality. The woman who saved my life. And the same woman who'd shoved a pistol under my chin, at the same time carrying my bullet hole in her belly.

"Yes," Almena answered after a long moment, standing. "I'll help. That is, if it's all right with Mister Richardson here."

"You're full of contradictions, aren't you?" I said, and Almena smiled like I'd landed on a secret. I shook my head, feeling more than a little uncomfortable. "I won't stop you from helping these people, but after that's through, you'll need to answer for some things."

Almena gave a short nod. "Isn't that always the way?"

———

While I watched the Osage women gather in a tight semi-circle around Almena, Dempsey came in out of the rain, shaking the wet out of his brown hair like a dog, and dragging a reluctant Fairly by his shirt collar. I nodded to Dempsey as he pushed Fairly down into the pew just a few rows ahead of mine.

The Osage women made Almena look small, each being a height comparable to any man, including myself. Their brown skin looked like dried parchment, full of bloody scratches, which angered me almost as much as their gaunt faces. Something should have been done to help these people. Instead, they'd been attacked for merely trying to survive the conditions the government had created. Wasn't right.

I suspected Almena felt the same. She presided over her little court without the pomp I'd come to expect from her. There was no theater, nothing speaking to her reputation as a killer or a thief. She appeared simply as a woman, although not like one of those reluctant creatures spun out of their family's good intentions, all lace and loveliness. She looked like Eve must have to Adam when he first woke: a fearsome thing, made from bone instead of dust. A beautiful alien.

I could imagine Almena's response to my romanticizing. *You remember how that story ends, don't you, Marshal?*

It ended in death. But all stories do if you follow them long enough.

Almena stood in front of the first injured Osage man, arms resting at her sides, breath nice and regular. She might've looked a little bored even, except for her eyes, silver bullets alive with purpose. A peek inside some people's heads wasn't worth the imaginary penny you'd spend on the expression, but increasingly, I found myself wishing to know what Almena was thinking. What made her tick.

"She has a gift, you know," James said from his seat on the pew beside me. Up close, I could better see the age in his face: the tops of his cheeks where his greying red beard didn't reach were darkly freckled by the sun, and he had severe crow's feet around his eyes, which I found strange, given the man's prickly disposition. He didn't seem one for laughter and merry-making, but maybe they were relics from another time. A time before the war. Maybe he'd lost a lot more than just his leg in the fighting.

"That's a generous way of putting it," I said, feeling the jury was still out. Almena called what she did *bruising*, so I hesitated to name it a good thing, but I couldn't deny that it'd given me a second chance at life. "Can't imagine most men in your position would see it that way. But then, most men also wouldn't risk their hide for a couple of natives, so I'm not sure what to make of you, Preacher."

James snorted, a sound that reminded me of a bull in a pen. "World's a changing place, son." He adjusted what remained of his leg, cut off just above the knee.

I stood, trying to get a better angle on Almena's activity. After one of the Osage women removed a bandage drenched in blood, Almena placed a hand on the injury—a diagonal cut, thin and neat, probably from a saber—and pressed her fingers into the red mouth of the wound, as if she would pull it from his flesh altogether. I grimaced instinctively, recalling the cold pinch of metal tweezers the local doc had used to pick out every piece of buckshot from my shoulder back in the day. This looked worse.

"Did you fight in the war, Mister Richardson?" James asked me.

"No, sir. Not directly."

"What's that mean, not directly?"

Almena's face changed, becoming tight. She swayed, causing one of the other women to grab her by the shoulders. She shrugged the woman's hands off, shaking her head, and adjusted her footing. I watched, incredulous, as the man's wound began to disappear before my eyes—quickly, almost in flashes, the meaty inside repairing itself first, and the skin finally stitching closed over the top. It happened in a matter of seconds. I was so busy watching the miracle on his body, it took me a full minute to notice the dark spread across Almena's chest.

Meanwhile, nearby, Fairly sat complaining about his shoulder, but his warden wasn't listening. Dempsey looked visibly enamored by the Osage, eyeing their buckskin tunics, buffalo robes, and hair pipe beads with interest. He sat so far forward on one of the pews, he might as well have been standing. I suspected he didn't want to appear nosy, but he was doing a poor job of pretending otherwise.

"I dealt with the consequences of the war in a different capacity," I answered the preacher. "I was in Missouri for most of it. There was some trouble there with citizen soldiers, men loyal to the idea of secession, and determined to bring the state into the Confederacy. You hear of Quantrill's Raiders? The Lawrence Massacre?" James nodded. "That's the war I fought. Weren't no Gettysburg or Sharpsburg, but it meant something at the time."

James stared straight ahead. "You fought for the North, then?"

I gripped the back of the pew in front of me and looked down, as if the past could be found somewhere on the dusty floor of the church. "At the time, I confess I never gave much mind to North or South, Union or Confederacy. For me, it was only about keeping the peace. I wasn't fighting for anybody or anything; I was fighting *against* men like Bloody Bill Anderson and William Quantrill. Men who were making the state bleed, and needed to be stopped."

Almena moved on to another bad cut close to the Osage man's neck, where the flesh looked raw and angry. Her patient suddenly groaned, half-wailing, tears squeezing out of the corners of his eyes. He swung helplessly at his perceived attacker, connecting with her arm.

I expected Almena to swat him, but instead, she caught his hand and held it a moment. Keeping silent, she let him bluster weakly at her in his native tongue. If she understood what he was saying, her face didn't show a response, though she didn't look unsympathetic. Her mouth moved for a brief instant, but I couldn't hear what she said, and I was no good at reading lips. After another moment, he finally calmed, and she lowered his arm back down to his side, gently. His female companion received his hand like a gift, cradling it to her cheek.

"But you sound like you're from the South," James said.

"North Carolina," I agreed.

"Virginia," he said for himself. "And you had no opinion about what was happening to your home?"

"Well," I said, backtracking some. "Not exactly none. I was young, about twenty when the war broke out. I was full of opinions—about everything. My state, the war, slavery. And I'm sure most of them were stupid."

The preacher smiled for the first time. It was a thing to see, like the sun coming out in the middle of a hard winter. I noticed he had very small teeth—an odd detail, but one of the things I still remember about him.

Not sure what provoked it, but I found myself telling the man things I'd never told another living soul. Thoughts I'd never given voice to suddenly stumbled free.

"My family never owned slaves, but that don't mean I wasn't complicit," I admitted quietly. "That I didn't benefit from the institution in ways unseen. Looking back now, I can see how much easier it was for me, moving through life without having to worry about someone putting me in chains and others insisting I deserved them."

James nodded, looking thoughtful. He rubbed the stump at the end of his thigh and was silent for so long that when he did speak, it sounded like some long-awaited rock fall. "I fought for the South. Lost my leg trying to protect a way of life that I now know wasn't worth saving. Be thankful you came to wisdom sooner than I did, and at less cost."

Almena gathered several more injuries, holding them inside her body somehow. I still didn't know all the particulars of her bruising, and I guessed I might never know, unless she had a change of heart and wanted to tell me. I watched minor cuts and bruises appear on her face and on her arms, only to blend into her skin moments later, almost as if the wounds were evaporating at her will. A hundred years ago, this sort of thing would've gotten her burned at the stake or put through one of those river ordeals to see if she would float. Today... well, I wasn't sure the same couldn't still be said. You get enough people together and show them something new, they'll call it the devil's work every time.

Dempsey leaned forward, resting his arms on the back of my pew. "How is she doing that? I mean, *what* is she doing?" Wonder livened his blue eyes, and his trademark frown was absent. The kid looked enchanted. "Is it some kind of Indian ritual? I've heard stories of their magic, but I never imagined..."

"Oh, it's magic all right," I agreed. "But hers, not theirs."

He leaned in closer, speaking more quietly. "How are we going to take her when she can do—*that*?"

"I plan on asking nicely."

Dempsey gave me a funny look.

I rolled my eyes over to him, before dropping them to my holstered gun.

"Okay," he said. "Just checking."

One of the Osage women cried out, grabbing my attention like a whip. I shot to my feet, and saw the woman's hands captured in Almena's. What in blazes was she doing to make that poor woman scream?

"Guillory," I said in warning.

Almena ignored me, eyes on the Osage woman. "You want to save your husband?" The woman nodded, lip quivering. "Good. You know the price. Now hold still and keep quiet. It's not going to kill you."

Footprints-in-the-woods, with a kind expression, placed a hand on her companion's back, rubbing small circles between her shoulder blades. The woman's lip stiffened.

"What's going on?" Dempsey asked. "Is she hurting them?"

"I'm not sure," I answered.

"Shouldn't we do something?"

"Not just yet…"

The circle suddenly made sense as I watched each woman extend her hand to Almena. Dempsey wasn't far off: it did look ritualistic. Almena was trading her pain to the other women, and they accepted the wounds with straight backs and staunch expressions, as though they were receiving high honors.

The second Osage man was worse off, having taken multiple shots to his front and back. It looked like someone had spent an entire wheel on him, keeping on even when he turned to flee—but whoever it was, they weren't a very good shot. Depending on how long ago the attack took place, I thought it impressive he'd lived this long. Good physical shape couldn't account for it, so it had to be will.

After a short but heated exchange with Footprints-in-the-woods, Almena turned to me. "Marshal, a word?"

A moment later we stood together at the front of the church, off to the side of the pulpit.

"He's in bad shape, ain't he?" I guessed. "That other fella there."

"He's going to die," Almena told me. I noticed she was still wearing the worst of the previous man's wounds—the saber cut across the chest. Her face was drawn, and I found it odd she wasn't bothering to do anything about the pain.

"Nothing you can do?"

"Something. One thing. But you won't like it. *I* don't like it," she added, glancing back and meeting the steady gaze of Footprints-in-the-woods. "We took out the bullets, but the shots weren't clean. He's taken with fever, and I can't do anything about that. He might, *might* recover if I take the wounds, but... they're already infected. It'll kill whoever takes them on, me included. Even if I gave one gunshot to each of the women, it wouldn't matter. It'd poison them each like it's done him."

"Why are you telling me all this?"

"Because she's volunteered." Almena indicated Footprints-in-the-woods. "That's her little brother, The-traveling-star. She feels responsible for what happened to him. It was her idea to go out yesterday, and her whiskey operation."

"Hell," I muttered.

"That's right, Marshal. Not always so black and white in my world, is it?"

I gave her a dark look. "Nothing grey about what you did in Baxter."

She looked genuinely puzzled. "Baxter... Springs?"

"That's right."

"I don't know what you're on about, Marshal. I haven't been to Baxter Springs in over a year."

I shifted my weight from one foot to the other. Arms folded across my chest, I stared down the Grizzly Queen of the West, trying to get a read on her.

"Why?" she asked, suddenly suspicious. "What's happened in Baxter Springs?"

"A conversation for later. Let's get back to the issue at hand."

Almena rubbed her face, leaving streaks of red that looked like claw marks. "I'm only telling you this so you understand: when she dies, it's not my fault."

"Surely you're not thinking—"

"I surely am," she interrupted, perhaps more loudly than she intended. The Osage women looked over at us, and Almena lowered her voice. "It's her brother. Her life. Her choice. If she wants to die for him, I'm going to let her."

I was shaking my head, but I hadn't yet come up with a good enough argument against it.

Almena moved closer, presumably so I would hear her next words. She smelled sharp and strong, of blood and flesh barbecued by the sun, and that odor made her feel wondrously real to me. She wasn't some phantom I'd been hopelessly chasing since Asher. I hadn't made her or her odd combination of vengeance and grace up. Felt damn foolish for even believing I had the kind of mind to invent a woman like her.

When she spoke, she looked more sincere than I'd ever seen her.

"Think about what her alternative is, Apostle. Watching someone she loves die a gruesome death, the whole time knowing she has the power to save him." Almena hugged herself, looking away. With her arms crushed to her chest, I could see the saber cut peeking through the cleavage of her blouse, already starting to heal up. Another reminder this woman was accustomed to being broken. No wonder she was so dry and hard; the world had bled her. "She'll be alive, but alive and living are two separate things. Every morning, she'll wake to the reality of who she is: a woman who chooses herself over her brother."

I looked at her tenderly. "You sound like you're speaking from experience."

She went rabbit-still. "Don't do that. Don't try and be my friend."

"I ain't trying to be your friend…"

"Then why do you care?"

I frowned. "I strike you as the sort of man who doesn't care about people?"

"No," she admitted. "You strike me as the sort of man who cares too much about things he has no business caring for. A man just fool enough to believe he can make a difference in the world.

That's the sort of man you strike me as, Apostle Richardson, and I want none of that. None of you."

"Who'd you let die, Miss Guillory?" I asked.

Her eyes widened, her pulse flicking inside the vein on her neck. I'd caught her off guard. "What does it matter now?"

"Just trying to get a sense of your history. It's like you've always been here, but I know that's not the case. There's always a before. And before four years ago, no one had even heard of you."

She smiled, but it was the grim smile a skeleton wears after the desert's worn away its skin. "You think you're going to find a good woman buried somewhere in my past?"

I paused a moment, trying to see past the layers of hostility, her forced persona. I suddenly felt sorry for her, though I didn't know why. "Who was it, Almena?" I repeated, wearing a gentle expression.

"A decent man." She took another step back. "A *good* man. Hell, the greatest man I ever knew."

"Strange name for a man."

She looked confused and then shook her head, a breathy chuckle bursting from her lips. "You are something, Marshal," she said, her smile a little less skeletal.

Nothing more to say, Almena turned on her heels and fell back to where Footprints-in-the-woods and her brother were waiting.

CHAPTER ELEVEN

Almena asked James to bring Footprints-in-the-woods some of the communion wine for the pain, and to my surprise, the preacher obliged. I decided I liked the man. I'd known other pastors who would've held the wine hostage on the condition of conversion. But that just didn't seem right to me; you don't hold a man over a fire, then try and sell him water.

Fortified by the wine, Footprints-in-the-woods kept stoic for as long as she could, but around the second wound, she began to cry. At the third, her mouth broke open, releasing terrible screams, and by the fourth, her keening had turned to quiet, tortured sobs. Dempsey asked to step outside for some air, and I couldn't blame him.

The-traveling-star still hadn't come around yet. If he ever would.

Dempsey wasn't outside more than two minutes before he popped back in and motioned for me, looking skittish as an unbroken horse. I grabbed my hat and fitted it on my head as I got up to join him, sensing I was about to be dragged outside.

"Something wrong?" I asked.

"Posse just rode in," he said in a rush. "Looks like some of the men from Baxter Springs."

When it rains, it pours. "What are they up to?"

"About what you'd expect from a bunch of men who've just watched their friends and family mowed down by a gang of bloodthirsty outlaws." He frowned, rubbing the back of his neck. "You were right before, Apostle. They're angry and spoiling for a fight."

"They're not going to have much trouble finding one here." I glanced at Almena. She looked up long enough to catch me staring, a question in her eyes. She looked grim and tired and in no condition to defend herself. I turned back to Dempsey. "Do they know she's here?"

"I don't know. But they have an outlaw with them, one from back on the trail—the man Wade missed. The leader."

I pushed past Dempsey, nearly cursing. "Try leading with that next time."

I jogged down the steps of the church.

"Why are we protecting her?" Dempsey asked after me.

"Because I don't believe she's responsible for what happened in Baxter."

Dempsey joined me at the bottom of the stairs, flicking a wet fringe of hair from his eyes. It'd stopped raining, but the sky continued in a threatening shade of green. I worried she had a mind to lay down a tornado.

"Guillory did everything else she's been accused of," Dempsey said. "The robberies, the murders. She *is* an outlaw. Or isn't that why we rode out here in the first place?"

From somewhere on the street behind me, the air popped with gunfire. High, panicked voices crowded the silence that followed each gunshot. I itched to check out the scene. Someone had to intercede before things got worse, and in the absence of a more qualified lawman, seemed I was left the honor.

"Whatever her crimes, that's up to a judge to decide," I said. "We just get them off the street."

He pursued me a few more steps away from the church. "You're not the least bit worried she'll run?"

"No. I imagine that's exactly what she'll do." I read the doubt on his face, and removed my hat briefly, agitating my hair. "If you're worried about it, and feel so compelled, stay back and watch her. Just—don't let her touch you." I knew enough about bruising to recognize that physical touch had its role. "You've seen what she can do, and I reckon you've heard what else she's capable of."

"No." Dempsey shook his head. "I'm coming with you."

"All right then. Let's get on."

Together, we hastened for the main street.

"Apostle. You don't... *like* the woman, do you?" Dempsey was watching me carefully.

This time, I didn't bother to slow my pace as I addressed him. "Honestly, I don't know what to make of her. She is an outlaw, make no mistake. But she saved my life once. I'd like to see her get a fair trial. She deserves that, at least."

"She saved you? When? How?"

I held up a hand, stopping his flow of questions. "Long story. No time for it now. When we come up on the posse, keep your hands away from your leather. We don't want to spook them. Leave the talking to me. If we're lucky, they'll listen to reason, turn around, and ride right back the way they came."

"And if we're unlucky? If it comes down to a gunfight?"

"Then we do our best not to place second," I replied drily.

———

Coffeyville wasn't always here. At least, a town called Coffeyville wasn't. The original settlement was closer to Indian

Territory and farther from the cool relief of the river, but about as rowdy a place as you'd find today. I visited "Old" Coffeyville once, shortly after war's end, and once was plenty. Situated smack dab on the southern cattle trail, Old Coffeyville had attracted all kinds—people and trouble alike. The usual culprits were cowpunchers, many of them honest men just looking to blow off steam after working tirelessly in the heat all day, and who found willing accomplices in the saloons. Drink and a restless frontier spirit proved, as it almost always did, the recipe for disaster. At some point, crime got so bad in the town, they started calling its main thoroughfare the "Red Hot Street" on account of all the murder.

That nickname floated back to me as Dempsey and I came upon the scene, the air already smelling warm and ashy. Unfortunately, the layout of the town made it impossible for us to hide our arrival. The main thoroughfare was a wide avenue of dirt to allow herds of cattle to pass through, flanked on either side by wooden buildings and a few plank sidewalks. The false fronts on the buildings made them look taller and more grand than they actually were. Most were squat single-story affairs. Signposts jutted out toward the street, declaring the goods available at each store in bold capital lettering—groceries, belts, tinware, and of course, liquor. I counted three liquor signs for every one of anything else. There were at least three other buildings in various states of completion, each wearing banners that announced, *COMING SOON*, but failed to say what that something was.

I eyed a few alleys squeezed between the buildings as we passed them, but none appeared to lead anywhere interesting, and anyone with experience would tell you an alley's a bad place to be in a gunfight anyhow. No room to maneuver. I always avoided alleys when I could.

Ahead, I recognized some of the posse—Chuck Fletcher and the balding Leonard, as well as the man who'd lost his wife in the bank—but there were a dozen others with them whose names I didn't know. They were saddled on brown horses: towering, shadowless figures, displaying pistols or holding rifles against their shoulders. A few used their horses to bully the men who'd just come stumbling out of the saloons, herding them around like cattle. While some of the Coffeyville variety appeared bleary-eyed and annoyed, others looked abundantly sober and furious as they fumbled for their own weapons.

I also recognized the dark-haired bandit leader who'd attacked us. He shambled behind Leonard's horse, hands bound at the wrist and a rope around his neck. A line of blood ran down the side of his face. Had he been grazed by a bullet? Or merely knocked around a bit? Either way, the man looked exhausted. Each time the horse jerked him forward, I expected him to lose his balance and accidentally strangle himself. He came very near to choking several times.

"Go and ask that fella there what's going on," I said to Dempsey, indicating one of the posse members I didn't recognize. An older gentleman with a dark goatee that stopped halfway up the sides of his face.

"Why?" Dempsey asked.

"Because we need to know exactly what we're dealing with here. Why they've come, and what it'll take for them to leave."

"No—I mean, why me? Why not ask him yourself?"

I tried to be patient, despite feeling just the opposite. "Any number of them are likely to spot me as one of the marshals from the other day."

Dempsey looked at the man, then back at me, considering. "You don't think he'll recognize me?"

"You remember seeing that man? Talk to him at all?"

"No."

"There's your answer." Dempsey nodded, but anxiously adjusted the shoulder straps of his holster. I nearly reached out and grabbed him, feeling eyes on us. "What did I tell you about putting your hands near your leather?"

"Sorry."

He let his arms drop, pouting in his usual way. He did it so often the effect had diminished. Still, I'd begun to wonder if he was even aware of his brooding. Back in Independence, I'd taken it for boredom: a talented man being forced to work as a grocer. But maybe it was something else entirely. I knew I'd have to watch him. Malcontents could breed all sorts of problems, especially if they were armed with a badge. I still believed Dempsey had a good head on his shoulders, but the truth was, I didn't yet know his heart.

I'll just have to be cautious with him. All the kid needs is a steady hand, like I had. We still needed to talk about what happened back at the coach. But that'd have to wait until later.

"It's fine," I said. "Just do what I've asked."

Dempsey started, then stopped. "And what will you be doing?"

I gave him the full weight of my stare. "I'm still deciding. Now—" I pointed my chin toward the man with the goatee, and Dempsey finally took the hint.

"Listen up!" the widowed man said, gaining the attention of the crowd. "Two days ago, the bank in Baxter Springs was robbed. During the heist, my wife was brutally shot down in cold blood." He struggled with the telling, just as before, the words crushed between his teeth. "Others were killed, too, including our sheriff and a boy of only nine years old."

I looked around. To my surprise, those in Coffeyville were actually listening. At least, their eyes were open and their mouths shut, which amounted to just about the same thing.

"We caught one of them on the road on our way here."

Leonard gave a good hard yank on the rope, bringing the dark-haired outlaw forward. He went down on hands and knees.

Leonard yanked again, and the outlaw made a strangled sound, his Adam's apple bobbing beneath the noose. The widowed posse leader looked on, not exactly pleased, but not squeamish either.

"Casella rides with Guillory now?" I heard someone ask, somewhere to my left.

Someone else answered, "Don't be stupid. Dante Casella rides for himself and no one else. Besides, the Grizzly Queen'd never put up with the likes of him."

The outlaw wheezed. "No... no! I wasn't at Baxter Springs..."

"Shut up," Leonard said, cuffing him with the leftover tail of the rope. "Go on, Gil. Tell them the rest."

Gil. Short for Guilford or Gilbert, maybe? Without the distraction of the cigar, I was able to see the man better, noting his jowly face, partially covered by a yellow beard and a scowl. The wind swept all of his light blond hair to one side like an arrangement of grass, giving him a wild look. He wore simple clothes, the bottom buttons on his vest undone. Lots of black. Good clothes to die in, if'n he had a mind for it.

The posse leader continued his spiel while Dante Casella struggled to breathe, making no effort to get back onto his feet. Wise, considering.

"I have it on good authority from a deputy U.S. marshal that the person responsible for leading this gang of monsters is a woman by the name of Guillory."

I frowned. That wasn't exactly how I remembered our conversation going.

I stepped forward with every intention of setting the record straight, but someone grabbed me back. I turned, ready to draw down on the man who'd decided to come at me from the crowd like a coward.

"Hold your horses." Almena's voice was in my ear. She glanced down. "You mind?"

I lowered my piece from her stomach, quietly sliding the gun back into its holster. To avoid drawing attention, I went back to staring ahead, watching the posse, as if their quarry wasn't standing right there beside me.

"What are you doing out here?" I asked, barely moving my lips.

"Came to see what all the excitement was about."

"The Grizzly Queen!" someone from the crowd shouted, causing both of us to damn near break our necks turning to look, though it appeared the man was only responding to Almena's name being mentioned.

"Apparently, it involves me," she said with a wan smile. "Anything you'd like to share? Like where they got my name in association with Baxter Springs?"

There was something chilly in her voice, almost angry. I don't think she liked being related to the murder of innocents, especially a child.

"Now ain't the time," I told her. "Get back to the church. This is the last place you should be right now."

"One could say the same for you."

"Whatever you call her," Gil said, having to repeat himself twice in order to be heard, "she's a murderer and I'll see her answer for it. Her and the rest of her gang! Turn them over to us and we'll leave. Simple as that."

"Don't," Almena said to me, guessing my intentions. She still had me by the arm. I recalled my earlier warning to Dempsey: *don't let her touch you.* But while there was strength in her grip and no mistaking her decision to keep me right where I was, she wasn't hurting me any.

"Someone needs to do something."

"And of course, that someone always has to be you. That kind of attitude's going to get you killed one of these days."

"Probably."

"Coffeyville's already got a sheriff. It doesn't need you, too."

"We're awful sorry to hear about what happened at Baxter," a pot-bellied man volunteered from the crowd. Gil watched him with a dark, apathetic look. His eyes shined. "But what makes you think Guillory and her crew have"—the gentleman paused, placing a fist against his chest to stifle either a belch or the urge to vomit—"taken up here?"

"Your town's a shit hole," Leonard answered. "Ain't that where outlaws like to crawl into and hide?"

All sympathy went out of the pot-bellied man's face. "What did you say?"

I looked at Almena. "What was that about a sheriff?"

She glanced down the street, chewing the bottom corner of her lip—something I hadn't seen her do since Asher. "Give him a chance. The man's put out worse fires than this. He's probably just sleeping in one of the jail cells. James went to fetch him; he'll be here soon."

"*He's coming*," I said to Almena. "Sound familiar?"

Almena blanched as if I'd aimed to strike her. "This is different."

"My friend spoke out of turn," Gil said, shooting Leonard an annoyed look. "What he meant was, Coffeyville's not exactly what you'd call a friendly, law-abiding town."

The pot-bellied man's eyes bugged, then narrowed. "Not like your precious Baxter Springs, you mean?"

Gil held his gaze. "That's right."

"So what you're really saying is, we're all criminals here, that it?"

This comment cracked the peaceful truce between the posse and the Coffeyville crowd. Some saloon-goers began to shout insults at the men on the horses.

I started forward again.

"*Apostle*," Almena hissed. Her fingers dug into my arm. "I'm not taking another bullet for you."

I looked at her, confused. "I'd never ask you to." For whatever reason, this stunned her, and I was able to extricate myself. I pointed down the street. "Get back to the church and stay there until I come and get you."

"So you can arrest me."

"Better me than these kind folks here."

"We've got no quarrel with you," Gil said, attempting to pacify the riled Coffeyville crowd. Beside him, his posse drew near on their horses, using the bulk of the animals as a defense against the men crowing threats and curses at them. *Circling the wagons.*

"Oh, yeah? Might be *we* have a quarrel with *you*," another man said, joining his indignant pal. He was quite a bit larger, being of a height with Gil's horse, and his neck disappeared into a broad chest covered in a faded black vest. One shoulder was up higher than the other, making me think he might have some problem with his spine. "Coming into our town, all high and righteous, thinking you're better than us. Accusing us of hiding murderers and what else. I think we do have a quarrel on our hands, boys. Indeed I do!"

Almena followed behind me as I approached the conflict.

"And if you get yourself killed being all noble?" she asked.

"Then I guess you've no reason to worry either way."

"*Marshal?*" another voice cried out.

A horse reined roughly in front of me, sudden enough to draw a whinnying complaint from the animal. I rested my hand on the butt of my gun, resisting the urge to pull; in a crowd like this, such an action could practically be counted as suicide. I wished in that moment I knew some of Dorothy's tricks, that magic with the match. Disappearing sounded mighty fine right about then.

The rider lifted their head. The shadow from their hat

retracted over a strong jaw and blue-green eyes with a crown of thin lashes. Eyes I remembered well.

"Miss Kingery?" I said, showing my surprise.

With her hair trapped underneath a brown derby, and her wearing trousers and a loose-fitting duster clearly borrowed, I'd initially mistook her for a man. Like Almena, both women seemed to have an uncanny ability to blend in or go overlooked, when they wanted to.

Before I could ask Miss Kingery what in the devil's name had possessed her to ride along on a lynching, I caught snippets of a dangerous conversation starting up behind me:

"Did he just call him a marshal?"

"I think he's a woman."

"Not the rider, you moron. The marshal."

"The woman's a marshal? They have those now?"

"I thought you were riding north," Miss Kingery said, ignorant of the danger she'd just put me in. She must've spotted Almena nearby, because her eyes widened. "Is that her?"

"Who?" I said, not bothering to look.

"Lying's a sin, Marshal."

"There!" said one of the men behind me. "She did it again! She called him a marshal!"

"So's taking the law into your own hands and killing a man. Or woman," I said, moving past her with an instinctive tip of my hat. "Food for thought. Excuse me."

Dempsey was waving me over. Before I could reach him, some drunkard stumbled into a set of boxes.

Startled, the Coffeyville crowd surged forward toward the posse, carrying me halfway into the street and nearly beneath the hooves of a startled horse. Above the hats and heads, the posse bobbed around on their mounts, trying to fend off the Coffeyville men with a lot of mean words and pistol waving. Someone forced me up against the flank of another horse, momentarily crushing the air from my lungs. Someone else fired a shot—don't know if it were a warning shot or not, but it split the crowd like Moses's staff parting the Red Sea. Seconds later the crowd slammed back together, and all hell broke loose with both sides throwing down on one another.

I saw the long-haired man drag Gil from his horse, and others repeated the action, laying hands on whoever they could get at. The riders either went down or stampeded over their attackers. Bones crunched, followed by mangled cries.

As I raised my gun to the sky, intent on shutting this rodeo down, someone's fist flew out of the confusion, catching me square on the jaw. White exploded behind my eyes, and I stumbled backwards, barely managing to keep my feet under me. I didn't see who'd done it, and no one came at me for a second round. Given how inebriated some of the men were, I felt it likely the man who'd assaulted me didn't even know he'd done it.

I shook my head, blinking a couple times.

The next man who came at me didn't have the excuse of drunkenness. Nor did he have the benefit of catching me off guard. His eyes were focused, and he shoved another man out of the way on approach. Maybe he just didn't like the look of me. I don't know.

I ducked beneath his first swing and came up under his arm, plowing into him and taking us both to the ground. We grappled for a few seconds before I was able to get my gun hand free, then I clobbered him upside the head. He went limp, but being heavy as all get out, I started sinking into the mud beneath him, suffocating under his bulk.

In perfect timing, Dempsey appeared and helped move his prone body off me. We rolled him to my side, making sure to leave him facing up, rather than drowning in an inch of muck. Dempsey pulled me back onto my feet, then wiped his hands off on his trousers. I rubbed some blood from my mouth and spat.

"Now what?" he asked as we drew back from the brawling center.

I'd lost sight of Almena, but I saw Miss Kingery sitting pretty above the mess, swatting at a man who'd taken hold of her foot. I was about to go over and help her when she got the idea to kick him in the nose; he reeled back, bleeding like a stuck pig, and she took off on her horse—or the horse took off with her on it. I wasn't quite sure which. At least she was out of danger for the time being.

"Apostle?" Dempsey prompted.

"I heard you," I answered, exercising my tender jaw. "Well, let's look on the bright side. They're not shooting each other yet. That's something. Might be they just need to take out a little—"

Three successive cracks interrupted the fighting, causing a pair of men to cease their fighting and cover their ears. Behind them, a man in good dress and a high-crowned Stetson stood holding a fine-looking Winchester in his hands, twin barrels pointed toward the clouds. He'd already reloaded and locked the breech by the time the Coffeyville and Baxter Springs boys peeled apart. With him were three men, deputies most like, each clutching their own piece like it might turn around and bite them. They looked jumpy, unlike the sheriff himself, who merely appeared irritated.

"Someone want to tell me what's going on here? —Ten words or less, Pete," he added, interrupting the long-haired man (Pete, apparently), just as the latter was starting to explain.

"Did you know there was a sheriff here?" Dempsey asked me, looking relieved. "Is that what you were waiting for?"

"Not exactly, though I was informed one might be coming."

The sheriff listened to Pete's abridged version of events while posse members kept interrupting with their side of the story. Gil stood beside his horse, readjusting his suspenders and fixing his coat over his shoulder. His lip was split and his face swollen. He wore a sullen expression to match his injuries.

"Almost every town has a lawman of some sort," I told Dempsey, trudging toward the front line where it seemed everything would be decided. "Question you have to ask yourself isn't, where's the man with the badge? But what's he going to do with it once he gets here?"

CHAPTER TWELVE

Sheriff Amos Jensen had a certain charm, if you wanted to call it that. Within a few minutes, he'd just about convinced the posse to turn in for the night at one of Coffeyville's establishments, free of charge, or else get themselves on back to Baxter Springs, when Dante Casella got hold of a pistol and attempted to shoot Leonard in the back.

He missed—if taking off the other man's ear could be considered missing.

Leonard howled and clutched the side of his head, initially making it hard for anyone, including me, to know how badly he was hurt. All I could see was blood flowing through his fingers, a red mudslide rolling over his knuckles and down his arm, soaking the sleeve of his buckskin jacket. Before you could yell duck and cover, the older man turned his gun on Casella and emptied the chamber at him.

Casella, the heartless bastard, grabbed the closest man to him and pulled him into the line of fire. To my surprise, I recognized the unlucky soul as one Owen Fairly.

I couldn't say I was surprised by Fairly's escape, what with no one watching him inside the church, but the last place I expected him to be was in the thick of things. He'd probably come to free Casella in a bid to earn back some of the favor he'd lost when he tried to high lope it off the trail after being shot. For his efforts, he got four rounds—that was all Leonard had left—planted in his chest. One also passed through his throat, coming out the other side and nearly hitting Casella. Which would have been ironic, if not fitting.

Shock twisted Fairly's face, his eyes bugging out. He was still mumbling *don't shoot* as he collapsed back into Casella's arms, a lather of blood bubbling over his lips.

"Oh my God! He shot Owen!"

This from a woman standing in the doorway of one of the saloons. Her smiling mouth was crooked with horror, hand positioned over her chest in a perfect display of fright. Either she hadn't had a proper view of what happened, or else she was all too happy to ignore Casella's role in Fairly's demise. I wondered if she were malicious or just simple.

"They mean to kill us all!" she shrieked theatrically, and as she turned and fled into the saloon, I saw her wink at Casella.

Not simple, then.

She might as well have cried fire in a crowded room. The men of Coffeyville reacted predictably, unintentionally supplying Casella with cover as some scrambled away and others opened up on the posse, ignoring the sheriff's advisement for everyone to stay calm and hold their fire, *for heaven's sake*—

Casella slunk toward a nearby alley, dragging his late partner's body to use as a shield. Leonard snatched a rifle from the saddle bag of a riderless horse and shot at the fleeing outlaw. He must not have had a very good grip on the gun because the recoil knocked it from his hands, leaving him exposed to take a round in the stomach from a stranger in the crowd. Leonard grunted, staggering back into the rump of the horse, causing it to shy and kick its back legs, knocking him out cold.

I shoved Dempsey to the ground as another man fired in our direction. In the same action, I clicked the hammer back on my gun and pulled the trigger, felt it shudder in my hand at nearly the same moment the man went sprawling into the mud. I wasn't sure whether he was from Baxter Springs or from Coffeyville, but it didn't much matter just then. He was a threat. And he didn't get back up.

By now the air was filling with white powder, making it difficult to see. Men suddenly appeared beside me, then disappeared into the smoke, backlit by the occasional muzzle flash. Grabbing Dempsey by his shirt, I hoisted my partner back onto his feet and was pleased to see he had his gun in hand. I was less pleased when he decided to fire past my head without warning.

Holding my ear with my free hand, I moved out of the way and, squinting, spotted the man Dempsey had fired at just as he dropped to his knees. A dark spot grew on the ground beneath the man's legs as some liquid, urine or blood, mixed into the earth.

Fool that he was, the man continued to hold the gun aloft, threatening retribution, and Dempsey shot him again, this time in the shoulder, showing admirable restraint for someone new to shootouts. I'd seen many a lawman panic in the heat of the moment, emptying bullets into a corpse, only to click helplessly at the next man who came at them. But not Dempsey. Kid had kept his head, renewing my faith in my choice of deputy. I was proud.

Also a little deaf.

As we took cover beside a general store, he said something to me I didn't catch. "What?" I yelled over the ringing in my ears. We were still close enough to the action that the sound of the gunshots reverberated inside my chest, each one almost a physical thing, like kernels popping above an open flame.

Dempsey repeated himself, motioning frantically toward the street. This time I heard the words "sheriff" and "injured." Not exactly words you want to hear together.

Canvassing the smoky street, I saw Sheriff Jensen flat on his back beneath the haze, unmoving. I couldn't tell whether he was dead or not, but the thought of leaving him out there, exposed to further harm, was sand in my conscience. "How much ammo you have?" I asked Dempsey whilst checking my own supply.

His eyes narrowed. "You're not going back out there, are you?"

"Got to. Man needs help. How much?"

"I don't know." Dempsey touched his cartridge belt. "Enough. I guess."

"I need you to lay down some cover fire for me. Can you do that?"

Dempsey nodded. He was getting that queasy look from the carriage again.

"Can you do that, Dempsey?" I wanted him to say it.

"Yeah…" He cleared his throat. His expression stabilized, and he met my eyes. "Yeah," he said, more confidently, "I can do that."

I placed a hand on his shoulder, squeezing gently. "I trust you with this. You remember how to shoot, don't you?"

"With a gun?" he replied, wearing a splinter-sized smile.

I smiled back, affectionately grabbing him by the scruff of the neck, watching his smile turn shy before I released him and returned my attention to the street. The gunfire was beginning to putter out, but still, all it took was one lucky shot. One ball or bullet, and someone would be chipping my name into a gravestone. "All right. Stay put. Count your shots. Probably goes without saying, but try not to shoot me either."

Just as I broke cover and started for Amos, I heard Dempsey reply, "I'll try not to."

———

The sheriff groaned when I tried to move him, mumbling that I shouldn't touch him, touch him and he'd shoot me. Yet it was obvious he wasn't going to shift anywhere on his own steam.

I ducked down close enough to his ear so he'd hear me. "I'm with the U.S. Marshal Service, sir. Name's Apostle Richardson." When I tried to lift him, he dug his fingers into my shoulder, pressing hard enough to force me into letting go. "I'd like to get you to safety now, Sheriff, but you can't fight me on it."

Nearby, Dempsey fired a shot every so often, provoking replies of gunfire. Several times I swore I felt the breeze of a passing bullet.

"Hurts like a son of a bitch," the sheriff said.

"Tends to." With a grunt, I managed to lift him somewhat, carrying him by the torso while his legs and backside dragged along the ground. His feet plowed two shallow lines in the mud. "Where'd he get you?"

"My back," Amos replied.

I tried not to think about the blood amassing on my boots and the bottoms of my pants as I pulled Amos toward the general supply. "Did you see the man who did it?"

"If I'd have seen him," Amos said, drawing a pained breath between every other word, "you can be damn sure he wouldn't have gotten the drop on me."

"Fair enough. Just hold on there—Amos, isn't it?"

"To my friends."

Implication being, he wasn't sure whether I fell under that category yet or not.

"Say you're a marshal," he slurred. "Where's your badge?" His eyelids drooped, and he looked dangerously close to nodding off.

"Sheriff," I called to him through gritted teeth readjusting Amos in my arms. Man didn't look it in his shapely grey outfit, but the sheriff was heavy as an ox. "Amos." I would've shook him if I wasn't so worried about loosening the bullet in his back. "*Amos!* Damn it. Dempsey!"

Dempsey shot out of cover and without needing to be told fitted himself beneath Amos's other arm, helping me drag him the remaining few feet to the alley.

"The back. He's been shot in the back," I explained quickly. "Help me turn him over."

"Apostle." Dempsey stared past me.

"What?"

I turned, catching sight of Almena assisting one of the girls from the saloon away from the gunfight. Both of the women looked unhurt, to my relief, but then I saw Gil coming up behind them, brandishing his piece. He called out Guillory's name, and she turned without thinking.

"*Shit.* Stay with the sheriff."

"Boss—"

I thrust an angry finger at him. "*Stay with the sheriff.*"

I didn't wait for further objections.

————

The smoke was starting to clear, carried off by the wind, the smell of gunpowder washed out by the sharp scent of rain and grass. *Storm's coming back.* I glanced up once while thumbing rounds into the cylinder of my pistol quick as I could, fingers slick with the sheriff's blood.

I was nearly to Almena when several men stepped in front of me, blocking my path. Each wore the slimy grin of a cat that's caught a mouse. I recognized two of them as the pair from before who'd been discussing the possibility of my being a marshal. *Why the hell not? That's the kind of day I'm having.*

"Heard tell you're a marshal," said the first man. He had a fat mole on one cheek.

My jaw still ached from where I'd been punched earlier, the point of pain traveling higher and higher into my skull, like someone pressing a needle through the bone. Not to mention I was already dog tired from having spent the past day traveling. Between that and all the gunfighting and near-gunfighting in between, my patience was at its end.

"You ought to think long and hard about what you're looking to achieve here," I told Mole. "Because it's liable to get you and your friends killed."

This earned a round of chuckles from the men, too drunk or stupid to realize I meant it.

"Big tough talk from one little bitty lawman," said a second fella, his tongue snaking out between his lips in a partial lisp. His eyes were pale and huge. Reminded me of a lizard I'd once seen sunning itself on a rock. Later that same day, I'd accidentally crushed the creature with the heel of my boot when it darted underfoot.

"I didn't kill your wife," I heard Almena tell Gill, from a few yards away.

"No. You had one of your *lackeys* do it." His tone was like someone dropping a plate on hard wood.

"No. My gang's broken up. Been broken up for a few weeks now. We never visited Baxter Springs. We never killed anyone there—not your wife, not that child. God's honest truth."

"She's telling it right, Gil," I said over the heads of my bullies.

His head whipped toward me, tears streaming down his face. "What's it to—marshal?"

"Hey!" Lizard snapped at me. "We was talking to you—"

He made the mistake of trying to reach out and grab me. I blew his hand off.

The others recoiled instantly, telling me the measure of their character. Lizard skittered back, holding his bleeding appendage with his remaining good hand, blinking more like a fish now, like he was unable to believe I'd gone and shot him. He was lucky I wasn't Wade. Prough the Rough, as he was known in certain company, always went for the kill shot. *No sense doing otherwise*, he explained to me once. *You start sparing the sons of bitches and they start getting it into their numbskull brains they can take you.* I didn't agree with this policy, but Wade may have had a point. Either I made an example here, or I'd be made an example of.

"Might be able to save some of those fingers, you get yourself to a doctor soon enough," I said. "As for the rest of you…"

"Shoot him!" Lizard squealed. "Just shoot him!"

"*Anyone*"—I spoke loudly, so as not to be misheard or misunderstood—"who makes even the slightest indication of going for their piece, I will put down. And I cannot guarantee as clean a shot as this fella here got. All I can promise is a planter's box and six feet of earth, any of you comes at me again. Now, kindly step out of the way."

Mole held his ground. "I count four of us against one of you. You think those odds are really in your favor there, Marshal?" I gave him a dark look, what said *don't test me*. "Nah," he continued with a bleating laugh. "Naaah! Don't matter how good of a shot you think you are, I know you can't put all of us down before one of us gets a shot off."

"Maybe not. But I'll make sure you're the first one I aim for." I looked at one of Mole's partners, scouting out the most nervous among them (after Lizard) by the overlapping pattern of boot prints in the mud. The man couldn't stand still. I recognized a coward when I saw him. "And maybe you after that," I added casually.

"I don't want no trouble with a marshal, sir," the man stammered, stepping again.

"Shut up, Riley," said Mole. "You're in this, now. Same as us."

In the end, the gunshot didn't come from my gun or any of Mole's men.

Everyone, including myself, flinched at the eruption of sound. Two shots.

My stomach plummeted. *Almena.*

I shouldered my way through Lizard and Riley, done with Mole's bullshitting, judging that no one would shoot me in the back. Not one of them did. They were all too busy straining to see who'd done the shooting, while simultaneously searching themselves for holes.

Gil dropped to his knees, and then folded back like a child's rag doll, his body coming to rest at an unnatural angle.

Almena stood a few yards away, on the porch of one of the saloons, gun still in hand.

It wasn't hard to put together what had happened.

I rushed to the widowed man's side, shoveling past his jacket and shirt to find a pulse, pressing my fingers against his neck, here, then there, in case I was mistaken. Finally, muttering a curse underneath my breath, I got back to my feet, giving a hard head shake as answer to the question in Almena's face.

"He drew on me," she said in a dead voice.

I chose to believe her. Given what I knew of Gil's grief and his purpose in coming here, it made sense that he'd try and kill her, cleansing himself of the guilt over his wife's death. More sense than her shooting him down in cold blood anyway. Whatever her *nom de guerre* implied, Almena Guillory didn't strike me as a casual butcher, not like some other outlaws I'd dealt with in the past.

"He had a son," I told her.

As she lowered her gun, Almena answered, "Then maybe he should have thought about his boy before coming against me." The woman who was sometimes outlaw and sometimes not stood straight and proud, but there was quiet devastation in her eyes.

She wasn't looking at me, but past me—to the men watching her, sizing her up.

"And what do you think you're doing?" she snapped at them, stepping down from the porch and into the muck. "Threatening what's mine like you've any right to him."

If I weren't so exhausted, I might've been able to show more offense. *Hers?*

"You think you own the place?" Lizard said, sweating with pain.

I thought Guillory might shoot him then, just to prove a point. Mole probably saved his life by slapping him upside the back of the head. He closed his eyes in frustration, or possibly embarrassment. "Don't you know who that is, you stupid fuck?"

"No," Lizard said, blinking.

"That's *her*. Almena Guillory in the flesh." Lizard did a double take, while Mole scrambled to remove his hat, crumpling up the brim in his pale fists. "Apologies for my friend, ma'am. He's got a big mouth and not a whole lot of sense…"

"But that man—he's a *marshal*!" Lizard said the word 'marshal' like a lady uttering a swear in polite company.

"Of course he's a marshal," Almena said, rolling her eyes. "*My* marshal. He's on my take. Or did you think I just talked my way out of a hanging?"

Almena took care never to make eye contact with the corpse near my feet as she came and stood beside me. She hooked an arm through mine, the warm press of her body utterly familiar against my shoulder. I tried not to think of all the times my wife had pulled a similar move, usually when she wanted something, a stylish hat or material for a new dress, trading on my weakness for her.

Almena, on the other hand, didn't seem motivated by what she wanted *from* me so much as what she wanted *for* me. Her presence felt like a shield against the hostile gazes of the other men. More were gathering every moment. Some seemed attracted to Almena's fame, while others drifted in from the street now that the posse—at least those who'd survived—had ridden off. What I couldn't understand was why. Why was she protecting me?

"You're saying he's with you?" Mole asked.

"That's what I'm saying."

I watched Almena's finger rolling wrinkles into my sleeve. Nerves, maybe?

"Prove it," Lizard said, looking ever paler. I nearly suggested he get himself to a doctor but thought better of it. Wouldn't help Almena's play to look too concerned.

"She don't got to prove nothing," Mole said to Lizard. Then to Guillory, "You don't got to prove nothing, ma'am." And back to Lizard in a low, threatening voice, "She's the Grizzly fucking Queen, you moron." He swatted him in the shoulder with his hat. "Haven't you heard what she did in Abilene?"

"I think you mean Topeka," someone else said.

"I heard it was Ellsworth." Another man. "It was definitely Ellsworth, with the clawing and—and the gun—thing…"

Yet another fella, defended by the bodies in the crowd, remarked in no uncertain terms how much he'd enjoy seeing what a grizzly she was in bed. A few wheezed with laughter. For some reason, it bothered me: them exchanging crude words about Almena, like they knew the first thing about her.

"Not her," Lizard hastened to clarify. "Him. *He* shot me. And he sounded an awful lot like a lawman when he did it. Maybe he's lying to you, trying to get you to drop your guard, Miss Guillory. Planning on catching you with your drawers down."

Almena let go of my arm. "You think so?"

What's she up to now?

Mole shifted his gaze around, searching. "Actually… you might have a point there. Wasn't he with another fellow earlier? Tall, fancy sort…"

"Could've been another marshal!" Lizard jumped onto this idea like a drowning man reaching for a rope.

"Hey! Isn't that him there?"

Dempsey must've read my frown as a call for help because he pushed toward the front of the crowd, gun brandished. With their blood up from fighting off the posse, the crowd had no trouble redirecting their anger toward the newcomer. If Dempsey noticed his fresh peril, he wasn't taking a whole lot of precaution against getting a knife in the back.

Almena angled her body toward me, just enough to hide her face from the crowd. She ran a finger along the edge of my jaw, real casual-like. But she whispered, "Shoot him."

"What?"

"They need to know he's not with you." There was urgency in her voice. "You have to shoot him."

I gave a hard shake of my head. "Not going to happen."

"Shoot him," she repeated, taking a moment to smile back at the crowd, "to save him."

I had my teeth pressed so tightly together, felt like I was going to break my jaw.

"I'll kill him."

"Not if it's a clean shot. But you have to make it look good, and you have to do it right now." Almena squeezed my arm, enough to hurt. "They'll kill him, if you don't. I know you don't want that boy's blood on your conscience. I certainly don't need more blood on mine."

Someone grabbed Dempsey. As he shook their hands off, another man shoved him from behind, making him stagger forward. They berated him with questions: how's it feel playing second fiddle to a dirty lawman? Who did he think he was? Did he have a death wish coming to Coffeyville? Dempsey held his fire, but I didn't know how much longer his restraint would last; all it'd taken back on the road was the sound of thunder, and it was thundering now. Or maybe that was just the blood pounding in my head.

Assuming Guillory had every intention of following through with her threat as she drew my Colt from her holster—same one that'd killed Gil, and whoever else since she'd taken it off me in Asher—I caught her wrist, and lowered her hand, taking back my gun. Her eyes stayed with mine the whole time, and there was no doubt in my mind that Almena allowed me the liberty of disarming her. She wasn't the type to let a man command her, unless he was doing what she wanted done. I tried not to dwell on the implications of that.

Before I lost my nerve, I shoved through the crowd, crossing the short distance to reach Dempsey. My stomach turned at the relief I saw in his face as he caught sight of me, believing I was coming to his rescue. The men around him paused, though they still clutched fistfuls of his shirt in their hands, the skin of their knuckles stretched tight over bone.

They need to know he's not with you.

She was right. Didn't make what I had to do any easier.

Dempsey's lips had just begun to reflex in a smile when I cracked him across the face with my gun. His head snapped back from the force of the blow, but he recovered more quickly than I'd hoped, and gaped at me. He looked confused and hurt and—

I hit him again, this time using my fist.

Then I collared him and said loudly enough for everyone to hear, "For the last time, you go back and tell your boss, whoever he is, I'm not for sale." I held Dempsey's lopsided gaze, his right eye already swelling like a grapefruit in June. *Find Wade*, I was trying to tell him, *Explain I haven't sold out to Guillory.* "What I gotta do now, it's just business." *I don't have a choice.*

He opened his mouth to say something, and I threw hard into his gut. His legs nearly gave out, and as he buckled forward with a groan, I leaned down to whisper in his ear, "next time I hit you, stay down."

But soon as I let him go, he came at me with a half-growl, half-cry, using his shoulder as a battering ram against my chest. Knocked the wind right out of me. We went sprawling into the mud, locked in a brief struggle, until the men, without being asked, rallied on either side of us and pulled Dempsey off of me. He was still swinging madly.

My new "allies" held Dempsey, inviting me to attack him. If I was going to make this look real, I'd have to go harder at him than I'd planned. I had no option for gentleness. All eyes were on us, and too many hands were still where I couldn't see them, hidden inside coats. Waiting, I suspected, for any sign of conspiracy. Any excuse to shoot us both and have done with it.

I couldn't give them that excuse.

The men pinned Dempsey's arms to his sides for the first few punches, but let go as I really started to lay into him, sensing their assistance was no longer required. Once freed, Dempsey put his arms up like we were engaged in friendly fisticuffs, clearly unaccustomed to real fighting. He kept his hands high, in front of his face, though his nose was already split open in a meaty gash and his mouth was all bloody. His one good eye shined red.

It was hard, not wincing each time I landed a hit. Fearing the crowd would catch on to my reluctance, I arranged my features into a more appropriate expression, one from my childhood. When I was younger, people always remarked with smiles how much I took after my mother, with my blond hair and angular cheeks; but I had my daddy's eyes. They liked to say that, too. *And what is it people always say about the eyes being the windows to the soul?*

I shuttered my feelings behind my father's glare. My name, after all, wasn't really Apostle, it was Nathaniel, same as his. I let the devil do for me as he'd done for my father.

Wasn't so hard.

Eventually, Dempsey ended up on the ground, curled around himself while I kicked. I finally caught him beneath his ribs with the toe of my boot, flipping him onto his back where he lay panting like a wounded creature, holding up a hand at me filled with broken fingers.

"P-please," he said, dribbling blood from his mouth.

I snapped back into myself so suddenly, I reckoned I'd be sick. I managed to hold it together long enough to say, "Remember what I told you before." Any gentleness in my voice could have been explained by exhaustion, which was good because I wasn't in the mood for pretending any longer. The storm overhead was passing, sun was coming out, and everything seemed garish in the light. I had a headache. "You just go on and take that message back to your boss, when you're feeling better."

"To hell with you," Dempsey said in a low, pained voice.

"Well, there you have it," Almena said, rejoining me while the rest of the men exchanged theories on who Dempsey was working for, and what madness had made him think he could take on Guillory's marshal all by his lonesome.

Guillory's marshal, I thought incredibly, but tried not to worry about my new reputation; be plenty of time for that later. As well as time to correct the record and make amends. I hoped.

"I hope that's sufficient evidence for your inquiries, gentlemen," Almena said. "Now someone go fetch the doctor before that boy bleeds to death on the street."

AMONG THE WILLOWS

CHAPTER THIRTEEN

It was Almena's idea to ford the Verdigris river on horseback, insisting it would be faster. I was less than enthusiastic about the idea for a multitude of reasons, chief among them being the risk of drowning—or, more specifically, *being* drowned. Not that I counted myself among the overly superstitious, but after everything I'd seen in the past few weeks, I was starting to wonder how many other frontier myths had some truth to them. If magic was real, then maybe the ghost woman of the river was real, too. La Llorona, the Mexicans called her. The weeping woman.

I'd heard various tales about her, the story mostly coming up whenever a child drowned or went missing along the shores of a river. The ghostly legend must have made its way up from the border, attaching to every body of water along the way, so that it seemed every river in the West had its own ghost or two. While the Verdigris wasn't known specifically for a weeping woman, it was all too easy for me to imagine her at home in its waters or standing on its banks, shrouded by early morning mist.

"Did you hear that?" I asked at one point, swearing I heard crying through the reeds. "Sounds like a woman."

"Don't tell me you believe those old stories about La Llorona," Almena said.

"Not sure what I believe these days."

"And here I took you for a strict man of faith."

"Faith's a funny thing," I said, still watching the river. I was seeing figures in every gnarled tree and overgrown shrub, my tired mind inventing faces in the shadows. "Easy to lose, hard to get back. Kind of like trust."

"Good thing I'm not asking you to trust me then." Almena laid a Winchester rifle across her lap, and I took it for the warning it was.

Back when I first asked Almena where we were going, she told me to wait and see. *Not ominous at all.* If she was worried about me getting a message off to one of my partners or other law enforcement persons and staging an ambush for her along the way, she was right to worry. That's precisely what I would've done, except she made sure I wasn't given the opportunity.

Almena eventually led us off the beaten path toward a trailhead obscured by a mountain of dry brush. She ordered me down to clear the way, and I set about the task, eager to stretch my legs. I forgot all about the open cuts on my hands until I met thistle. I yanked my arm back like I'd encountered the fangs of a snake, suppressing a curse. Blood welled from my careless contact with the bush, red lines spreading into the valleys of my knuckles.

"What's the holdup?" Almena strained to see over my shoulder, where I held my hands in front of me, waiting for the sting to die down. I wondered how Dempsey was faring with his injuries but quickly shook off the thought. *Best not go there.*

"Marshal?"

"Nothing," I answered, shaking out my hand. "Just being stupid is all."

"Well, don't be stupid for too long." Her lips curved in a thin smirk.

I was so busy dwelling on my guilt over Coffeyville and hiding my infirmity, I didn't notice how uncomfortable Almena looked: her waxy complexion, or the way she sat hunched forward in her saddle, like she might go to sleep against the horse's head. Only later would I recall these details, as you do with dreams, the fog burning off after a while.

I sucked on the back of my knuckles, nursing them as I mounted up. Almena led the way, urging her animal into the nighttime quagmire. Ordinarily, the Verdigris was a thick color any copper prospector would recognize on sight, hence its name. Sometimes it was more green than grey, other times a barren brown, depending on where you were seeing it and what time of day. But it wasn't a changeable river, as far as rivers in Kansas went. Even under the best conditions, staring into its depths wasn't likely to return much, certainly no insight into what lay beneath. On a clear day, might be you got back a shivery reflection looking in, a wobbly version of yourself, but that was it. The river kept its secrets.

I waded in less confidently than Almena, taking it slow, unsure of either the river or my mount. I spoke in a gentle manner to my partner—the horse, not Guillory—as she navigated the moving current, and allowed the animal time to pick her steps. The water was just high enough to wet the tops of my boots. I kept my eye on natural debris, logs and branches mostly, bits of shadow floating downriver. Any serpentine shapes what might spook the horse. Thankfully, the river crossing proved uneventful apart from a couple close calls with some uneven mud. I didn't hear the crying woman again.

As we climbed the opposite bank, pushing over the nose of the hill, I looked back. It was doubtful anyone from Coffeyville— or Baxter, for that matter—would be able to follow us now. If the hidden path didn't throw them, then our fording the river would. Made sense now why it'd been so damn hard to find Almena the first time around, and so easy to lose her afterward. The outlaw knew her geography and Kansas provided ample space to disappear, never mind the surrounding Territories. She'd already proven her good relations with the Osage.

It was the sort of thing made a man—a marshal—wonder what he was doing out here, being led into the wilderness by a killer. Even an old dog had the sense not to follow his owner out back when he held a gun in his hands and already smelled of blood.

I reined up suddenly. Took Almena a few extra seconds to notice. She frowned, looking none too happy to be stopping.

"What?" she said.

"I think we need to have some words, Miss Guillory," I told her, polite as I could manage under the circumstances. My knuckles chafed in the cool air, and my hands ached from holding the reins for so many hours. We'd left in such a hurry, I hadn't had time to pick up some riding gloves to replace the ones I'd left with Wade and the coach.

I flexed my fingers, feeling blood rushing back into them. That hurt, too. A fuzzy sort of pain. But it was still preferable to the stiffness, and that sense of holding still for too long.

"Ride and talk, marshal."

"No, ma'am." She looked back at me, eyebrow cocked. "I'm not going another step with you. Not until we've settled some things."

I swung my leg over the rump of my horse, climbing down from the saddle. I took some pleasure in the look on Almena's face, frozen in surprise. She'd let me keep my gun, thinking we might need my talent against any stragglers from Coffeyville or vandals on the road. Imagine she regretted that decision just now, though I was careful not to make any indication of going for my piece. I didn't intend on using it, anyway.

"Get back on your horse, Apostle," Almena said, raising the

Winchester between us as I came closer. Twin bores stared me down, each one as large and mean as a buffalo's eye.

I felt tired and reckless. I reached up and grabbed the Winchester by the barrel. Shoved it out of my face. "Come on. Enough of that."

Instead of shooting me, Almena leaned back appreciatively, eyebrows raised. "You've got some balls on you, Marshal!" She let the gun stay where I'd pushed it aside, the barrel resting against her saddlebag.

"Let's get something straight," I said to her, trying to keep my temper. "Only reason I'm here is on account of you helping rescue me back at Coffeyville. I'm grateful for that. I'm *less* grateful for the way you did it, but that's splitting hairs. I'm not fool enough to think you did what you did out of the goodness of your heart, or because you fancy having a marshal for a friend. You want something from me. Fair enough. But unless you intend on knocking me out and tying me to my horse, you're going to tell me where we're headed right now."

"Don't tempt me." Her breath misted in the cool air, reminding me of slow-curling smoke from a cigarette. I wondered if she smoked. "Fine. I guess it can't hurt. Not like you'll be talking to anyone anytime soon. We're going to my house, if you must know."

"Your house?"

"What? You thought I lived on my horse? Yes, my house. I own some property, some miles from here. That's where we're headed."

"For what purpose?"

"I need some...things."

"What things?"

"Personal things. I told you where we were going. Now get back on your horse." I stood my ground, wanting to know more, until she added a resentful, "Please."

After another moment, I climbed back into my saddle. "All right. Just know this conversation ain't finished."

Almena made a small noise of acknowledgment, and on we went.

I thought back to this conversation several times afterward, while we traveled in darkness and silence. I noticed she'd only referred to her house. Her property. Never once calling it home. There was a difference; I think she knew that. After the things she'd done, the man she'd lost, and the man who'd lost her, Almena Guillory no longer had a home to come back to.

Worst part was the sense she knew it, too.

CHAPTER FOURTEEN

We were still a good ways out from Almena's house when she fell from her horse. Just before it happened, I observed her looking woozy and steered my horse closer to hers. I sat forward in my saddle, trying to catch her eye. "You feeling all right there, Miss Guillory?"

She cut her eyes toward me. "Fine."

"We can stop, if you need to take a moment—"

"I said I'm fine. Leave it alone, Marshal."

I left it alone.

Next thing I knew, she was on the ground.

I climbed down from my horse before the animal came to a complete stop, pedaling the ground before letting go of the saddle. The sudden drop in speed was jarring, but I managed not to trip over my own feet as I hurried to Almena. She was already making an effort to get back up but I could tell by the way her arms shook beneath her that she wasn't having a good time of it.

She didn't object to my helping her, which surprised me. I expected at least a swat or a sharp word—something to indicate I wasn't needed. Instead, she gazed blankly at me as I leaned over to check on her.

"I think I passed out," she said. There were creases of wonder in her forehead.

"You never passed out before?"

"No. Plenty of times." She accepted the hand I offered her. I situated my other around her shoulder, and got her back to a standing position. "Never fallen from my horse before, though. That's a first. I must be more tired than I thought…"

"Kidnapping U.S. marshals can be pretty tiring."

She smiled thinly. She was in some pain, even if she wouldn't admit it.

We took a couple steps. She moved slowly, and her arms felt cold beneath my hands, even through her coat. "You sure you can ride?"

"Guess we'll find out." Her eyes slid to the hand gripping her shoulder. "You can let go of me now."

I did as she suggested. Lady had a right to her space, of course. If she didn't want me touching her, I wouldn't. I took a few steps back but kept my hands somewhat extended, ready to catch her if she started to fall.

Almena smiled at me almost fondly before coming back into herself, an indifferent line taking place of the smile. She must've remembered where we were, and more importantly, *who* we were. A lawman and an outlaw. An old story, always ended the same— with one or the other buried. But I saw it in her eyes, that spark of hope. And the thought, *maybe*.

Almena cleared her throat. "You're making me nervous. Standing there like that."

"Only want to make sure you're not hurt."

"I'm not glass."

"Just say thank you and move on, Almena." I went to fetch my horse who'd wandered a short distance away to get at some fresh thistle.

"Thank you," I heard her say.

I turned back. "What's that?"

"Don't push your luck, Marshal."

Following this incident, and seeing as her property was yonder still, Almena decided we should find other accommodations to pass the night. I may or may not have made some remark about how I'd be interested in seeing her pull a hotel out of a hat.

"Oh, ye of little faith…" she replied.

———

The rancher's house smelled of beans and smoked wood, rich and friendly. As I followed Almena over the threshold into the sparse living quarters, I removed my hat in the presence of the missus who immediately offered me a seat at her table and rushed to feed me. Seeing as I was half-starved and barely able to keep upright, I didn't object.

Such kindness toward a stranger wasn't unheard of on the frontier, but it still took me by surprise, especially when she didn't ask to know my name or bother me about my business. While I suspected this had a lot to do with who I'd shown up with, I was still grateful for the lady's hospitality and told her so.

"No one goes hungry under my roof," she said and smiled.

I thanked Mrs. Cortez kindly as she set a wooden dish in front of me, a mountain of baked beans land-sliding into a fat square of cornbread. One bite, and I was back on the trail, that long summer I spent in Texas herding cattle with a cousin of mine and his boys up the Shawnee. For a year after, I couldn't look at a bowl of beans without feeling a stitch in my side and being reminded of the smell of sweaty cows and leathery men. Or maybe it was the other way around. This fare was better than most of what we'd eaten on the trail. The bread was moist and didn't immediately fall apart in my hands, and the pintos had a sharp kick that surprised me at first taste. I didn't even mind the beans being a little cold. Beat having to compete with a bunch of starving teenagers. Some nights in Texas, if you tripped on the way to the chuckwagon when dinner was called, you might as well have gone right back to what you were doing.

Mrs. Cortez went over and gave her husband three quick slaps on the back, chastening him. "Ai, Salvador. Don't keep our friend standing at the door. You're letting all the warm air out."

Mr. Cortez invited Almena to come in, and he closed the door behind them.

"How are those sprouts looking, Sal?" Almena asked, addressing the man of the house. Sal was short and stocky but capable looking, just like his wife whose strong grip I'd felt on my shoulders when she directed me to the table. It was dark when we arrived, but judging by what I'd seen of Sal's property—a pair of fine horses, some milking cows, wheat, and lanes of vegetables —he was doing all right out here in the middle of nowhere. Making his own way. That was enough to make me respect him, even outside of his giving us a place to hang our hats for a time.

Sal took Almena by both arms. I was surprised she allowed the contact, given her thing with touching. "Better than before, thank you. Please." He motioned to the table. "Come. Sit."

"I appreciate you letting us intrude on you like this," she said, eyes on the floor. Her swaggering posture was gone, that clench of bone that made her seem taller and larger than she actually was. Something else I noticed: she stood openly toward Sal and his wife, whereas with me and others, she often angled herself to a narrow profile. Until now, I'd mistaken the indirect stance for sloppy confidence. Thrown into such sharp contrast with this new figure, however, I recognized its true purpose.

Almena had been making herself a harder target to hit.

"Actually, Sal, there's something else I wanted to ask you about…" Almena turned back to him. She spoke low, so I couldn't make out what she was saying, but I watched her face.

She glanced at me once or twice uneasily, kicking the dusty floor with the toe of her boot. Something strange lingered in her expression.

She'd worn a similar look in Asher, right up until she stood on that scaffold, braced by rope. It was the look of a woman corrupted by hope.

She's still waiting for him. Despite everything she'd done, I felt sad for her. I knew what it was like waiting on a person who wasn't coming back. I dug into my beans before the memory of smokestacks and red lipstick railroaded my thoughts any further.

A little while later, I heard the legs of a chair being dragged across the wooden floor and when I finally looked up from my half-eaten plate, a little girl was there seated next to me. She had maneuvered the chair right close to mine, and sat on the seam between them so our shoulders almost touched. Being that it was so late, I was surprised to find her there at all, wide-eyed and bushy-tailed, dressed in a child's sleeping gown. She swung her legs back and forth, her brown toes missing the floor by an inch. The chair knocked unevenly against the floor in line with her fidgeting, the result of one chair leg being shorter than the others.

Though I wasn't feeling much for company at the moment, I mustered a smile for her. She smiled back without showing her teeth, and began to play with the end of a thick braid of dark hair. She couldn't have been older than nine, and was probably closer to six or seven.

"How do you do?" I said. "Hope we didn't wake you."

Her dark blue eyes blinked steadily at me. I wasn't sure how much English she knew, but she kept on swinging her legs, smiling. Then, wordlessly, she pointed at my hands.

I looked down at my fists, which still looked like the bruised insides of an overripe apple. "Ah, that's nothing to worry yourself over. Just got into a fight is all."

She twisted her hair around her finger, flicking the ends against her nose. "Hurts?"

"A little."

"Mama," said the little girl, calling her mother's attention, and then following the inquiry with some rapid-fire Spanish.

Mrs. Cortez appeared not long after with a wet cloth. "That's not necessary," I started to say, not wanting to be more of a burden on this family. She just clucked at me. I winced as she applied the cloth to my battered knuckles, nearly pulling away for the pain of it. "Thank you," I managed, meaning it even if my strained expression didn't suggest gratitude.

She recommended I keep it on for a few minutes, at least to help the swelling go down and prevent it from getting infected.

"Could you do me a favor?" I asked as Mrs. Cortez was going. Almena was still deep in conversation with Salvador. She screwed her mouth to the side, unhappy with whatever he was telling her. He looked sorry, and a little helpless. "Could you... could you just check on Almena? Make sure she's all right? After she's done talking, I mean. She needs some tending to, I think. Just won't admit it." I smiled weakly, wincing again as I pried the wet rag off. "Not to me, anyway."

Mrs. Cortez nodded. "Of course."

"Thank you."

"I have to say, I like you much more than the last man she brought around. Far better manners. Cleaner shave." Mrs. Cortez patted my cheek.

"Does Almena come by often?"

"Often? No. She visits maybe once, twice a month? I think she gets lonely living in that house by herself. No husband, no children."

"Imagine that would be lonely." In fact, I didn't have to imagine it. Spent as much time away from my own home for the very same reason. After Lilah left, the place took on an empty feeling. "She help out around the place?"

Mrs. Cortez smiled politely. "She… has other gifts." Which was either a nice way of saying Almena was useless at farming, or an implication that Mrs. Cortez knew about her bruising.

I decided not to query further, in case Almena intended to keep her powers secret, and instead, went back to my meal. It wasn't long before my shadow returned. The girl inched closer when I looked over at her.

"You want some?" I offered, bending my plate toward her.

She shook her head.

"All right then."

"Gunman," she said after another moment.

"What's that?"

She pointed at me. Her gaze dropped briefly to my holstered piece, the polished handle reflecting tongues of yellow candlelight. "*Gunman*," she said again, and this time I realized it was a question.

"Yes. Suppose I am."

It wasn't a reputation I liked to encourage. Having a title like that invited a bad element. Men heard you were quick on the draw… well, they just had to test it themselves. Once in Topeka, I had a man come up to me in the middle of a meal, and ask me to pull on him. I asked him if he'd mind I finish my portions first. He said he'd wait. I went back to my lunch, asking between a mouthful of pudding whether he'd eaten himself. By this time, the man was already sweating bullets and either the postponement of our gunfight or my question, however innocent, seemed to rob him of his remaining nerve. He ran. I counted that a good day. There were other days weren't so good. Like the time I had to shoot a man dead in front of my wife and more than a dozen other bystanders after he confronted me on the main thoroughfare in Atchison.

I didn't know what the little girl's idea of a gunman was, whether he was a man with blood on his hands or someone who merely carried a gun, but I didn't want to leave her with the wrong impression of who I was. "I'm also a lawman. See? I catch bad people." Unsure whether she'd understand me, I pulled my badge out to show her, thinking she might recognize the star.

Boy, did she! She pulled her arms up to her chest, as if trying to contain herself. Two little fists vibrated beneath her chin, and her knees bounced harder. "For *me*," she said, eyes full of stars over the rusting piece of silver.

I chuckled. "Are you asking me or telling me?"

She tried to snatch the badge from me, but I pulled my hand away. She giggled and tried again and again, each time finding it more hilarious when I moved the prize out of reach.

While I continued playing keep-away with the little girl, Almena snuck up behind me.

"Don't be fooled by that one," she said, snatching my leftover piece of cornbread from over my shoulder before slouching into a chair across from me. It all passed as casual, but I saw the calculated look in Almena's eyes, the little glimmer of mischief on her lips as she chewed; she wanted to see if the theft would get a rise out of me. Almena was one of those people who liked to push. Push until she was pushed back. Test a person's limits.

I slid my plate across to her, offering what was left of the beans.

Almena declined, sliding it back to me and giving a little shake of her head.

She ripped off another large bite of bread with her teeth, chewed and swallowed. "Little Mireia here pretends she only understands Spanish in the presence of strangers. Especially white strangers. Isn't that right?" Almena winked and the little girl smiled shyly, twisting her braid. "Sal did the same thing when we first met."

"Why's that?" I looked to Salvador.

He shrugged. "People speak more honestly when they think you do not understand them. But my family has lived in this country since before the war against Mexico. And Rosa Maria's family are from Alta California. We are less new to the West than most like to believe, and no strangers to English."

"I should apologize," I said. "I assumed, and I shouldn't have done."

Salvador rubbed his nose. "As I said, you are not the first. But thank you."

Mrs. Cortez didn't bother asking before dumping another spoonful of beans onto my plate on her way to serving Almena. I already felt the previous round coming back up on me, having scarfed it down too quickly, but not wanting to offend, I lifted my spoon again. As I did so, Mireia saw another opportunity to get at my badge. Even with my eyes on my plate, I was too quick for her. She didn't laugh this time.

"Oh, just give it to her already." Almena spoke with her mouth full. Her plate was almost entirely cornbread, lathered in some kind of brown syrup. I hadn't been offered any syrup, or near as much bread. It was clear who the favored guest was. "Not like you're going to have much need for a marshal's badge anymore."

My brows gathered together. I stopped eating. "What's that supposed to mean?"

Without warning, Mireia tugged hard on my arm and let out a high-pitched whine, earning a sharp rebuke from her mother. Mrs. Cortez came and lifted her daughter up from the chair.

"No, no." I hurried to the little girl's defense. "It's all right. It's my fault. I've been teasing her."

Mrs. Cortez smiled wearily. "It is past time she was in bed, anyway."

Mireia buried her face into her mother's shoulder and

continued to whine. Mrs. Cortez patted her daughter's back in an attempt to calm her. I could tell she was a little embarrassed by the helpless glances she gave me, the universal expression among mothers of, *what can you do*?

When Mireia's head finally came back up, I caught the last part of her plea: "—the star."

I pushed my chair back and stood up. "I think I can fix this," I said. Leaning over, I addressed the little girl at eye level. "Miss Mireia?"

She turned towards me, angling around in her mother's arms. Her eyes looked terribly bright, even inside a face puffy from fussing. Her bottom lip held a respectable pout. She was still a bit upset with me for bringing the wrath of bedtime down on her.

"This here star's not just a piece of fine jewelry. This is a marshal's star. You know what a marshal is?"

Mireia remained silent for a moment, probably so I'd know her displeasure. But in the end, she couldn't help wanting to prove how smart she was. "A lawman. He catches the bad people and puts them in the prison."

"That's right."

"He also shoots them dead." She held her hand up, closing one eye behind her thumb and firing an imaginary pistol at me.

"Mireia," Mrs. Cortez said, her tone holding a warning. "I'm sorry, Marshal. She has such an imagination…"

I smiled so she'd know I wasn't offended none. "I believe it. Unfortunately, she ain't wrong. I have had cause to shoot a man or two"—*Or nine*—"in my time."

Like one of those fifty-cent picture shows my wife used to give me a bad time for going to, my mind showed slides of dying men. Men howling, cussing. Crying. All of them bleeding, but not all dying immediately; that was the worst of it, the look that entered their eyes at the end when they knew they were going to their reward, but weren't sure what it entailed. Often they reached out, groping blindly for someone, something to hold on to. Took years of perfecting my aim to avoid killing a man outright, and even then, accidents happened. The bullet punched through something it ought not, and the son of a bitch unraveled in a pool of blood and agony. Mercy, I'd learned, usually meant not drawing at all.

Still, I tried holding the faces inside my head. Seemed only right. Some were crisp and clear, while others had moldered in my memory, the details gone all blurry. For those, I had other ways of remembering—whether I wanted to or not. The smell of dust was sometimes enough to summon a ghost, or the feeling of my fingers rubbing up against my leather. Every now and then, even something as universal as a man's eyes or the shape of his jaw reminded me of some criminal I'd had to put down, and pressure would build inside my chest. I didn't want to call the feeling guilt, since I was operating within the law, but I didn't have a better word for it.

Mireia smiled, satisfied with being right, and pretended to shoot me again. Normally, I might have clutched my chest and staggered back, playing along. But this was important. "Listen now. Killing a man ain't fun, Mireia. You try and remember that when you're older."

The little girl lowered her hand, nodding soberly. Trying to appear serious. Failing some.

Out of the corner of my eye, I think I saw her father smile.

"Anyway, I'm telling you this because I want you to know how important this star is to me."

"Does it give you powers?" she asked.

I smiled, charmed. "In a sense. This star gives me the authority to keep the peace. Best power there is." Mireia smiled, but I don't think she was impressed by my answer, since it didn't include the ability to fly or produce ponies on command. "All right, hold your hand out there."

She did so—even closed her eyes, though I didn't ask her to. Her toes wriggled against her mother's hip.

Carefully, laying it down so the pin wouldn't prick her, I placed my marshal's badge—my most prized possession in the world—into Mireia's little sun-kissed hand. Almena was right. After what happened at Coffeyville, I didn't need it. Didn't deserve it. Not until I made things right again.

Mireia sucked in her breath and her eyes flew open. She squeaked and held the star to her chest. "My marshal," she said dreamily. I took her to mean the star. Though it was also true, in the short time I'd known her, the little girl had captured my heart, too. I'd always wanted kids, and she reminded me why.

"I'm not giving it to you for keeps, mind," I told her, and she leaned away from me, removing the star from my sight, as if I might take it back, which made me chuckle. "Now, now. A star is earned. Takes hard work and dedication. Proof of character. There's also a messy bit of bureaucracy involving a judge, but that's neither here nor there." Her face softened in confusion. I'd lost her. "I need someone to hold on to it for a while. Someone brave and honest."

Mireia lifted her chin. "I'm brave and honest."

"Yeah. I was hoping you might be." I smiled, straightening up. "You keep that nice and safe now, hear?" Mireia nodded vigorously, turning the badge over in her hands. It was a little strange, seeing my star in the hands of a child. But it also felt right. She was sure to get more pleasure out of it than I had of late, and who knew? Maybe in the future, the marshal's service would enlist women. It seemed less farfetched now than it had before the war. "If anyone who tries to pick a fight with you, you just tell them Marshal Richardson lent you that star on account of how tough you are. That'll surely send them running for the hills."

"What do you say to the kind marshal, Mireia?" Mrs. Cortez prompted.

"Gracias," Mireia said, not bothering to look up from her gift.

I went to tip my hat, only to find it missing from my head, so I just smiled at her instead.

Without much thought, I glanced over to the table where I'd set my headwear down only to find Almena missing, too. She and her plate of food were gone, and the back door was open, a shot of blue-and-black night captured between its splintering frame.

CHAPTER FIFTEEN

I rushed outside, expecting to catch sight of Almena's back as she thundered away on her horse. It was dark out. The moon, trapped behind a drifting prison of clouds, couldn't be relied upon for seeing any great distance, nor were the stars much use, too small a congregation, as though most of them had blown away with the storm.

"Going somewhere?"

I snapped to attention, turning back, although my forward momentum took me a few steps farther than I meant to go.

There was no porch behind the Cortez's house, so Almena sat on the ground just outside the warm glow of the kitchen window, legs drawn up against her chest, back to the wall. She looked awful small. Grass filled the space around her thighs and back, almost like she'd been here so long, nature had grown in around her.

She didn't smile, but remarked, "Shoot, Marshal. You look like you've seen a ghost."

"Don't believe in ghosts," I answered reflexively, though that was perhaps no longer true.

"Oh, you don't, do you?"

"Almena, what're you doing out here?" I asked, a little more harshly than I meant to. My heart still hammered against my chest, punishing me for the mistake of having let the Grizzly Queen out of my sight. Good Lord only knows what trouble she could've gotten up to, and me being responsible for her. Me being responsible for all of this.

"Not running, if that's what you're worried about."

She was aggressively crushing cornbread in her hands, leaving a mess of crumbs on her lap. Either she didn't notice or didn't care. I thought the latter more likely. A faraway look in her eyes made me think Almena was visiting the past. Or trapped in it.

"You could've said something," I told her. "Rather than just disappearing like a... a thief in the night."

"Wasn't aware I needed your permission to come outside and relieve myself."

"That what you were doing?"

"No, but I could've been. I don't see how it's any of your business what I'm doing out here. It can't be less important than that."

"In case you haven't caught on yet, *you're* my business, Miss Guillory."

"I wish you'd stop that."

"Stop what?"

"Calling me *Miss Guillory* like I'm some lady whose delicate sensibilities you need to protect. I'm afraid that horse was let out of the barn a long time ago." She dusted the crumbs off her hands and started attacking the grass, ripping the blades out by the roots. "You don't need to coddle me."

"You sure have a funny idea of what it means to be coddled," I replied drily. "If I'm not to call you Miss Guillory, then you could try using my name, too. I think we're past titles. In that, you may have a point."

"Apostle." She shook her head. "I know that's not your real name."

"It's what I go by."

"Out here, where you could be anything, anyone, you still let others name you. Why is that?"

I scratched my ear. Never really thought about it like that. "I think you're placing a little too much importance on a name. Name isn't who you are."

She smiled wanly. A thin strip of moon appeared. I knew the two weren't related, but there was still something haunting about her face, grim and lifeless in the moonlight. "That's where you're wrong. A name you're given at birth, maybe that's not who you are. A name you take on afterward, though. That's exactly who you are."

"Jed—Sheriff Strickland, he told me they called you Killin' Al Guillory during the war. Is that who you are?"

"It's who I was."

"And now you're a grizzly bear, on account of that's what they call you."

"Careful, Apostle. That sounded almost testy."

I sighed rather than answer her and leaned up against the doorframe. As an afterthought, I closed the door to the Cortez's behind me, affording us some privacy. A chance to finally hash things out. But first, I took a few seconds to prepare my thoughts, watching Almena stare at the middling distance, where the long, jagged surface of the grass was the only thing separating the dark shade of the earth from the infinite black of the night sky. Amazing how something so empty could still be so beautiful.

I finally broke the silence. "What're we doing out here, Almena?"

Thought she might try and be clever about answering my question or dodge it entirely, but instead her response was straightforward. "There's a woman out there riding under my name. I'm planning on killing her. You're here because you're going to help me do that."

"You need *my* help to kill someone?"

She finally looked at me, smiling with her eyes. "Probably not. But I'd have a hard time passing up an opportunity to have a former marshal for a mascot. Especially one so pretty."

"Beg pardon?"

The smile migrated to her lips in a wicked curve. "Not ever."

"No, that's not—I mean, you said former."

"As in, not anymore."

"I know the meaning of the word, Almena."

Standing, she didn't bother to brush the dirt from her trousers. It clung to the shape of her rear and the curves of her thighs like a sooty fingerprint—not that I was paying special attention to those areas of her person. I kept my eyes up, much as I could.

"It's pretty simple, but since you seem to be struggling to understand, allow me to clarify. You *were* a U.S. marshal. You're not anymore." She came toward me as she spoke rather than raising her voice to be heard. Hadn't noticed before, but she was talking very gently, maybe on account of how quiet the night already was. "You crossed a line at Coffeyville, and you know it. Or isn't that why you gave Mireia your badge?"

"I'm surprised you saw that exchange, given how quickly you fled outside."

Being this close, even the subtlest change in Almena's face was obvious to me. I couldn't make sense of the contradictions I found in her expression. For example, the injury in her eyes didn't match her scowl. "It was getting a little too warm and sentimental in there for me."

"You don't have kids, I take it."

"No."

She looked away, but I heard the hesitation before her answer, that painful second suggesting some deeper truth. There was more to the story, but if she didn't want to talk about, well... it wasn't my place to ask. I recalled my wife's face, every time someone asked her about us having children—that lean, annoyed look. Her gold-brown eyes, almost catlike in the evening, daring the inquirer to press the issue.

"What about you?" Almena asked. "No pitter-patter of little marshal feet back at the old homestead?"

"No." My answer held a similar hesitation. Maybe if I opened up, though, Almena would, too. "It's a nice idea, but my wife, Lilah... she didn't want kids."

Her eyes held sympathy. For me—or for Lilah? "Did she tell you that?"

"Not in so many words, but I knew. I knew and I didn't care. I was in love. Suppose I just assumed she'd change her mind after we were married." I frowned at my boots. "That was wrong of me, saddling her with my hopes. Not believing her when she told me no. Kept telling myself she just wasn't ready, but she knew her own mind. Always did. I should've accepted that."

Almena was quiet a long moment, then she said, "You shouldn't blame yourself. Actresses are known for being fickle."

My hands went cold.

"What did you say?"

"You're not the only one who's done their homework. I did a little checking up on you after Asher. Figured it'd be good to know who I was up against. Imagine my surprise to find you divorced. And you seemed so solid, too. Loyal."

"I was faithful to my wife," I defended, feeling like a hot brand dipped in icy water.

"Then what was it? All the pressure of you wanting to put a baby in her? Or maybe she just got bored. Is that why she left you? For another man?"

"Watch yourself."

I stepped toward her, but she only angled her face up to mine in challenge.

"So the masterful Apostle Richardson shows himself to be human at last. Good. I was starting to worry you really were an apostle. I don't think that would've earned me any generosity from the big man upstairs. Not that I have much credit with Him to begin with."

Almena smirked coldly. I was suddenly reminded of something told to me when I first began my hunt for Guillory: *there's a reason they call her the queen. She enjoys seeing men on their knees.* Over the course of the day, I had forgotten who I was dealing with.

"You having a good time with this?" I asked her. "Dredging up my past?"

"She kept your name. Did you know that?"

I hadn't. Lilah wrote me a couple times after she'd gone— maybe out of guilt, I don't know—but after watching her board a train and leave home with another man, a big city broker who swore he knew all the right people to make Lilah famous, I wasn't feeling charitable. Took me a while to write back, and when I finally did, it was to beg her to reconsider. Laying aside my pride and exposing myself to her scorn and ridicule, I asked her to come home. *Just come home, Lil.* The letters stopped coming after that.

"Lilah Richardson of Richmond, Virginia. Formerly one Miss Lilah Inghram of St. Louis. Currently employed by a small theater company based out of the city. I don't remember the title, but I'm sure my associate in Richmond could find it, if sufficiently motivated."

"If you're trying to make your point, best get to it."

All trace of mockery disappeared from her tone. "I'm telling you this so you know I'm not lying when I say I can get to her."

"Are you blackmailing me?" I was pleased by how calm I

sounded. No, not calm. Tired. I just sounded tired. "Threatening to hurt her if I don't go along with your plan?"

"I'm glad we understand each other."

I shook my head. "Don't do that. Don't piss in my eye and call it rain."

"You know when you're upset, a little muscle jumps on your jaw. Right here—" She reached a finger toward the spot in question, but I pulled my head back. Almena took my recoil in stride and let her hand fall back to her side.

Too late I thought to downplay the feelings I had for my wife. Still, I couldn't help trying. "What makes you think I even care what happens to Lilah? She's my *former* wife. As I was reliably informed just recently, former means not anymore. There's a reason for that."

Almena folded her arms across her chest. "Enlighten me."

I felt the muscle on my jaw twitching, just like she said. Whatever my grievances with Lilah, it didn't feel right airing our dirty laundry to a stranger. An outlaw at that. I couldn't publicly condemn her, even now. Even when it would've been to my advantage to do so.

I looked away. "You'll forgive me if I'm not exactly feeling forthcoming at the moment."

"Right," Almena said, like she expected as much. I hated how predictable I was to her. "Well, I'll tell you what I know. Everyone has a weak spot, Apostle. Apply the tiniest amount of pressure to it and you own them. For many men, it's vice—drinking, gambling, whoring. More commonly, it's a person. Someone they love, maybe against reason and sense. Like you and your ex-wife. Don't bother trying to deny it. I watched your face just now; it went soft when you talked about her. Some part of you, however small, is still in love with her."

I had nothing to say to that. After a moment, Almena went on.

"Virtue's what condemns men like you. You have this insane

idea that the world is a fair and just place and everything'll work out if you just have faith. If you just *believe* hard enough, then good is rewarded with good, and everyone goes home a winner."

Her tone implied she was not one such person. *But maybe*, I thought, trying to see past the vitriol to its poisonous source, *she used to be*. My mama always said the worst people in the world were those who'd loved, and been hurt for their loving. I'd encountered too many bandits without a conscience to believe that was true all the time—some men were just born mean—but in Almena's case, the jury was still out. Something told me I was only seeing the part of her she wanted me to see, the hard outlaw. But I'd had glimpses of the woman underneath. I knew she wasn't all bad. Then again, maybe that was just a story I was telling myself to make this easier.

"And what would you know of virtuous men?"

"More than you think." Almena flattened herself against the house, letting her hands fall to her holstered weapon, absently caressing the gun. "Enough to know virtue doesn't mean a thing against an assassin's bullet. Standing on the moral high ground only makes you an easier target."

Assassin's bullet? I let it pass without comment, thinking it must have been some odd turn of phrase.

"Sometimes standing up for what's right often means standing alone," I said.

"In my experience, it usually means dying alone, too." She waved me off. "You keep your 'right,' Apostle. You keep on believing there's a man up there who gives a damn about anything that happens down here. I don't care. As long as it doesn't interfere with my business."

"How in the world did you get like this? Who did this to you?"

"If you're waiting to hear about the man who broke my heart and sent me down a path of crime, you're going to be disappointed." Almena peered at me from out of steady shadow. "I did this to me, Marshal. There wasn't anyone else. It was all me. I made my choices. And I'm living with them."

"But it ain't just you who's living with them." Surely she could see how unrealistic—I might even go as far as to say, selfish—that view was? World was a large place, but not so large that it meant we alone were responsible for what happened to us. Call it God or coincidence, our lives had a tendency to meet in unexpected ways. "None of us moves through this life without bumping into anyone else. Like it or not, your choices affect others. We probably wouldn't be speaking right now, if you hadn't gone and dragged me into this mess with all of these choices of yours, so please spare me that excuse for you behaving badly."

Aggravated, I rubbed the side of my face, feeling the scratch of a couple day's bristles. It wouldn't get much worse even if I neglected myself. I was one of those sad men who couldn't grow a decent beard. Grew a moustache once while on a lengthy pursuit, but my wife made me shave it soon as I got home. Said it made me look mangy. *Like a dog?* I remember asking her, smirking against her soft lips. *Positively vagrant*, she replied, but I felt her smiling, too.

Not sure why my mind kept sparking memories of Lilah recently, though I suspected Almena's presence had something to do with it. I sighed. "You know we're after the same thing here. I intend on finding the ones responsible for Baxter Springs, same as you."

"Except I intend on killing them."

"Right. Except that."

"Don't look at this as blackmail, Apostle. Look at it as an incentive."

"Incentive to do what exactly?"

"Whatever I say. Most of the men I work with—*have* worked

with in the past, money's enough to make them behave. I wouldn't insult you by offering to bribe you."

"Appreciate that."

"But I need insurance you won't stab me in the back the first opportunity you get."

Is that what this was about? She was afraid of me? "Guess you were right before, when you said I didn't have a choice."

Let her believe she'd licked me. Truth was, I'd already made my own choice. Whole reason I was out here wasn't on account of some misplaced sense of debt; I didn't feel I owed Almena anything for Asher or Coffeyville, not after what happened with Dempsey, which she undoubtedly orchestrated to condemn me in the eyes of my friends. I'd admit, Almena Guillory interested me on a personal level, but it went no further than that. I was focused on doing my job. While collaring the Grizzly Queen would have been a good start, it presented other problems. For one, with her men still at large, keeping her in prison would've required more money and manpower than I knew the state was willing to expense. They'd hang her simply to cut down on the cost, and that didn't sit easy with me. Not to mention the trouble her boys would get up to on their own in the meantime. Tracking them down without a name or face would be damn near impossible— until they committed another act of thieving or violence, and then it'd be too late.

I was sick of arriving after the fact. Sick of seeing faces pinched in grief, and the dead laid out shoulder-to-shoulder in the street like boardwalk planks. Even now, the familiar smell of dust mangled by the sharp, bodiless odor of blood wouldn't leave my head.

Why weren't you here sooner? Miss Kingery had asked me in Baxter.

It was a question I hoped never to have to answer again.

So here I was, on the cusp of a new plan which relied upon

Almena pulling her outfit back together, and me being there when she did it. After all, if going after her imposter was truly Almena's intention, she'd need others to do it. When it came time for a showdown between the two gangs, if I couldn't organize with law enforcement beforehand, I could always just… step back. Let them ventilate each other, and sweep whoever survived into a nice jail cell. With one confrontation, I could singlehandedly put an end to two of the worst threats in Kansas.

"Past this point," I said, not wanting to look too eager or complicit, "we might work together, and I'll go along with your plans. But we ain't friends."

Almena laughed. "Was there ever a chance we would be?"

CHAPTER SIXTEEN

The following morning we finally reached Almena Guillory's house.

Almena told me to wipe off my boots before coming inside. I didn't argue, obliging best I could by scraping my soles against the uneven lip of the front porch. When I looked up, prepared to offer the bottom of my boot for inspection, as I'd always done with my wife, Almena had already disappeared inside. Seemed we had a schedule to keep.

I knocked my boots once more against the porch and went in.

Unlike most Kansas residences, Almena's house had two stories. It looked like a New England transplant, a simplified version of a Southern plantation home. The neat façade was polished in simple white paint, with four narrow columns supporting a second-floor balcony.

I entered without removing my hat, making note of the open doorways along the hall. House had too many corners where anyone might be lying in wait, preparing to catch themselves a marshal unawares. I became more conscious of the way my gun belt sat low and heavy on my hips. It was powerful tempting, the desire to draw my weapon, but I resisted the urge. Pulling out my piece would come off badly. Like I didn't trust my host.

Which, of course, was true, but it didn't help my plans none. Plus, way I saw it, weren't no excuse for being rude in the lady's own home.

I instinctively pushed my coat behind my leather, leaving myself the option, and continued inside.

"Just upstairs," Almena hollered down.

The staircase hugged the entryway's right wall, its fat, bottom step only a little distance from an arcing scratch left by the front door swinging open and closed. Almena's hat crowned the first post, homey in a way. Also a good reminder: I was in her domain here. Best not forget it.

Without landings, the staircase provided a straight shot to the second floor where a two-shelved window gave some light, and dust motes swirled lazily. They turned into and away from some competing drafts, reminding me of partners in a Virginia reel. A pink body of sunlight fell crooked against the stairs, and I followed its trail up, ducking my head to protect my eyes inside the shadow of my hat.

At the top of the stairs, I entered a room unoccupied except for furniture, including a large bed dressed in a thick diamond-patterned quilt with blue and purple blocks. A mahogany dresser with dark brass handles squatted low against the opposite wall, beside a table positioned halfway in front of a large window that opened onto the back of the house.

I wondered whether this was Almena's bedroom, but just as quickly decided it was none of my business. As I was about to leave, however, something on the dresser caught my attention.

I nudged the door closed with my foot and walked back into the room. The dresser was back-boarded by a mirror whose edges were foggy from age. Along the top were an assortment of collected knick-knacks—a half-empty bottle of women's perfume, a hairbrush with yellowing teeth, some kind of oriental mirror, and a wooden box I guessed was full of jewelry, earrings and necklaces, maybe, things I'd never seen the outlaw queen wear.

But most interesting, and what had first caught my eye, were the portraits.

I lifted one from the top of the dresser, using the side of my fist to rub off the dust. It showed a young woman in a beautiful gown that closed around her throat, seated unsmiling. I almost didn't recognize the woman as Almena, but the eyes were a dead giveaway, hauntingly bright in the silver image as they stared ahead. Not cool or proud, but rather soft and a little shy. Her hair was done up in a chignon like the ladies in Washington wore. She couldn't have been more than eighteen when the portrait was done.

I returned it with care and reached for the next one, positioned a little behind the first. This picture didn't have the same air of formality to it. Instead, it showed an older woman with a wily, unreadable expression, seated in a large dark dress—perhaps in mourning?—while a little girl I guessed to be her daughter stood beside her somberly. The woman's gloved hand held tight to the girl's waist, the child's poof of a dress squashed between them.

Was this Almena and her mother?

It was hard to imagine the plump little thing in the picture growing into the hard, lean creature I knew, the one bankers and honest folk had come to fear. But the older woman, apart from sharing Almena's nose and jawline, also had the same formidable look about her. As if she could stomach a bayonet or shrug off a bullet. Then again, maybe she could've done. If Almena had inherited her mother's steel, kind of made me wonder what else she'd inherited from her.

There was one last frame I almost missed on account of it lying facedown on the dresser. This one had two pictures instead of one, locked in separate windows of glass. Partitioned by a hinge in the middle, it opened between my hands like a book. On the left, a lean crack fissured out over the frozen image of a young Union soldier—stoic, sitting tall, and holding a Springfield pointed at the ceiling. He was dressed in his blues, although I use the term loosely. The nature of the photograph meant there was no color, only outlines of silver when you moved it just right.

I let my gaze trail to the next picture. That of the man's regiment, I assumed, picking him out as the only smooth-faced man among the bunch.

Hold a moment.

I quickly looked back at the first picture, comparing them. Couldn't be... but it was! The man weren't no man at all, but Almena Guillory herself, wearing the attitude and fatigues as well as any man I ever saw. With her forage cap pushed toward the front, a shadow slumped over her forehead, making her eyes look beady and dark. She was younger here, much younger than she was now, and rounder, still carrying some of that childhood pudge in her face.

Of course, I'd known she'd fought in the war. Jed told me as much, and Almena all but confirmed it. But it was different, actually seeing these past incarnations. Knowing she'd been someone else at one time. Someone other than the criminal she was today. Someone uncorrupted by the war, by disappointment, by—hell, whatever terrible thing it was that had converted her into a murderer.

More than that, I felt like I'd stumbled into something intensely private. I rushed to put the frame back, but I must've set it down a little too hard because the back popped open.

"Shit," I muttered, the occasion warranting such language. My initial attempts to set it aright failed, and something previously hidden in the frame fell out and onto the floor. It looked like some kind of note or letter, folded over enough times to be housed together with the picture.

Wish I could say I was decent enough to put it back without reading it. That would've been the right thing to do. But maybe I wasn't so decent anymore. Almena made a good point earlier. I'd already crossed a line back in Coffeyville—and she would know, being the one who shoved me over it.

And heck, I was curious.

I carefully unfolded the note, smoothing it out. The paper was a mangle of creases, as though someone had repeatedly folded and unfolded it a dozen times. Maybe a hundred. Strong but spidery handwriting peered up at me. A smear here and there where the side of a hand had brushed against wet ink told me whoever the author was, he or she wasn't used to sitting down and writing letters. Or else they were angry and didn't care.

The more I read, the more I realized the latter was likely the case.

The letter began with a date—April 20, 1865—and a curt, anonymous address:

Dear Madam,

There are no words. I have searched long and hard for them, but nothing seems adequate to address the enormity of this loss. By now, the country should know how to mourn. I expect it will do a better job than me. But you are owed some consolation, some tendering of affection in this black time, however poor, and so I offer you this lonely sentiment from one grieving woman to another, should this letter ever find you amidst greater correspondences.

I am sorry. Your husband never aspired to be a great man, only a good one, but in so doing became great. Of course, you already know this, having loved him longer than I. Having loved him longer than anyone in this ungrateful country, this arrogant collection of States. I expect that number will only grow with time as future generations learn of his enduring courage, his inimitable compassion. For my part, I considered him a friend, a very great friend, and I regret that in the end, I was not more worthy of the kindness and understanding he showed me.

If a fault could be found in your husband, Madam, it would be this: his trust and belief in the inherent goodness of men. He believed in appealing to the better angels of our nature—but for there to be angels, there must also be demons. He placed his faith in the wrong woman. I am not an angel, except of death. Even then, I think most would agree I am more coward than fiend. I suspect I always have been, though it took this tragedy to show me the truth of it.

I let him die—

Here, she'd written those words a couple more times, the ink increasingly dark. She'd scratched them out, run lines through them so hard and with such desperation, I could feel the marks on the underside of the paper.

Then she regained herself:

I could have saved him. I cannot tell you how. You would not believe me if I did, and as with the course of history, it does not matter now. Just know that I will bear this failure for the rest of my damnable life. I wasted my chance of Calvary. I am not a pious woman anymore, if I ever was, but I am on my hands and knees now praying that my suffering satisfies your grief.

Compared to the regrets of princes and queens you will receive, I expect you will find this a poor, graceless communication, and the consolation I offer unintelligible. It will seem like the ravings of a madwoman. That is just as well. But take comfort in this knowledge: I will hunt down the man responsible for this crime, the man who murdered your husband.

I will find John Wilkes Booth, and I will show him the demons of my nature.

It was signed as a sincere friend, A. G.

As I held the letter in my hands, an obvious revelation came to me.

This letter. She'd never sent it.

CHAPTER SEVENTEEN

C lutching that letter felt like holding a gun for the first time: it came with a creeping understanding that this was a thing that could get me killed.

I refolded the paper quick as a lick, returning it to the frame the way I'd found it. I hadn't yet situated the frame facedown again when I heard the door creak open, a low, keening announcement of company.

Instinctively, I ripped my hands away from the frame. The other items rattled as my hip bumped the side of the dresser. Thankfully, I still possessed enough presence of mind to force myself to slow down as I turned toward Almena, not wanting to look any more suspicious than my being here already was.

Almena stood just inside the doorway, watching me. Her hair was mussed from some activity, loose ends of brown curling in toward her face. The effect made her look a touch out of sorts. I also noticed she'd worked the top buttons of her blouse open, showing a slight curve of breast, and smooth, unclouded skin. Appeared she'd recovered from Coffeyville already. At least physically.

"What're you doing?"

It wasn't asked with hostility, but still, it wasn't a question I could safely answer.

My eyes went to the hammer she was holding in her right hand.

I cleared my throat. "At the moment? Kind of hoping I'm not about to be bludgeoned."

"The hammer's not for you," she said before casting her all-seeing gaze to the pictures on the dresser, crooking one eyebrow. "Although maybe it should be. Find what you were searching for?"

"Is this your room?"

Her eyes shown hard. "Sometimes."

I bit down on my curiosity. "I wasn't searching for anything. Just poking around. No harm meant."

She walked over and slammed the picture of herself facedown on the dresser. I thought I heard the glass crack. "There's always harm in dredging up the past. If you haven't learned that by now..." She let her voice trail off as her eyes caught on the images of her own history. I wondered if it hurt Almena to see herself in those ways—as a daughter, a lady; loved, or hoping to be. How foreign it must've seemed now, on the other side of a river of blood. Almost like a life which belonged to someone else. When I'd seen ghosts in her eyes, back in Asher, I hadn't realized a few of them were her.

Before I could broach the subject of the war, of President Lincoln and John Wilkes Booth—I could scarcely think the names without wanting to shake my head with disbelief—Almena let out a harsh sigh, as explosive as if she'd been holding her breath. She shook her head. Waved the dresser off, dismissing her phantoms.

"I don't have time for this." She started for the door.

I followed behind. "You sure you don't want to—"

"I'm sure I don't want to talk about it."

Prickly. "Then maybe we ought to talk about why we're here in the first place. Aren't you supposed to be putting your outfit back together?"

She turned onto the stairs, and we started down. "It's not as easy as that. The men I need don't work for free, and this doesn't have a lot in the way of a reward. Not like robbing a bank or a train. Unless my doppelgänger and her outfit are carrying some hard cash when we come upon them—unlikely—this is a high-risk operation without a return investment, if you catch my drift."

"And here I thought your reputation would have men jumping at the chance to ride with you."

"Oh, reputation will bring them out. In droves." I heard the smile in her voice as she hopped off the last step. "But ask any general who's ever recruited men for a war, and he'll tell you the same thing: it's not getting them to volunteer that's the problem. It's getting them to stay once they've seen what they're in for. In my line of work, that means money."

Suddenly, the hammer made sense. "You keep your money here, in your house?" I lifted my foot to peek at the floorboard beneath me, wondering where she must've stashed it. During one of her finer heists, a rather daring train holdup, Guillory and her band of ruffians had made off with hundreds of thousands of dollars. Anyone would reckon that a lot of money, but there was a lot of house here, too. Plenty of places to squirrel it away.

Almena laughed, a real honest-to-God laugh. "I rob banks for a living, Marshal! You really think I'm going to trust some simpering, pale-faced teller to guard my dollars?"

I stepped over a coat she'd left lying in the middle of the floor, exactly where she'd taken it off earlier. I imagined her striding inside, shedding clothes, anxious to get free of her outlaw trappings at long last.

"Guess I'm just having trouble picturing you stuffing bills into your mattress."

"Oh, no. I assure you, I use my mattress for other things."

This grabbed my attention from the floor. But Almena had already vanished around the corner, leaving me to suffer the limits of my own imagination. I shook my head, breathing out through my teeth, and followed the hard sound of her boots clicking against naked wood.

Klump ker-klump ker-klump. A short pause, then it resumed. *Ker-klump ker-klump.* Even before I came into the sitting room, I guessed she was pacing.

I was right. Almena was marching back and forth between a washed-out sofa and a section of cushioned chairs on the other side of the room, presumably meant for guests. The latter had fared better outside the front window's long talon of sunlight. Almena swung her hammer next to her thigh to and fro, out of sync with her agitated steps.

Klump ker-klump ker-klump. Several times, she came close to accidentally hitting herself with her hammer swings—not that the injury would last, but still. I was concerned for her safety. And mine, in her agitated state.

Supposing she might not take well to my fretting, but hoping to distract her from whatever worried her, I suggested Almena think about investing in a rug. I noticed the floors were not only bare, but unfinished, the wood bright and raw.

Almena quit her pacing and held up a hand. "Shh."

I watched as she leaned forward, put all her weight on one foot, listened until the wood groaned. Then she let up. Satisfied with whatever that meant, she kneeled down and knocked on the wood. Meeting a hollow sound, her face relaxed some.

"I take it you found what you were looking for," I said, leaning over her shoulder to see.

"There's a room upstairs you can use," she said, sitting back on her haunches. "It's got a bed. And you look tired."

I was, having not slept well at the Cortez's house the previous night. But then, I hadn't gotten a decent night's sleep since Asher. Most evenings, the moment my head hit the pillow, I was out, sure enough, but then there were the dreams. Of Jed kneeling over me. Of Almena's feet twitching above the scaffold. The bodies laid out at Baxter Springs. And now, of Dempsey, his mouth framed in horror and confusion, gaping at me the way I used to gape at my father.

I sucked in a breath, then let it out slow. I removed my hat to give my hands something to do. "Yep," I agreed simply. "But this is more important."

She blew out of the side of her mouth, heaving hair from her face. "I'm pulling up a floorboard. It's not that important."

"Almena, c'mon now…"

Instead of acknowledging my desire to stay and help, she informed me the room upstairs came equipped with a washbasin if I was of a mind to clean myself up some. She then threw me a look that instinctively made me rub my face and check my fingers for grit.

"I'd recommend it," she said.

My fingers came away mostly clean—my ex-wife would've said that meant they were still partly dirty. Lilah would sometimes make me wash twice before letting me sit down to a meal. Refused to let me get any kind of nature on her nice tablecloth. I didn't think Almena worried about tablecloths, what with the sparseness of her home, so it was obviously her way of getting me out of her hair for a bit.

"You can get water from the pump behind the house." Her stare pushed me toward the door.

If there was anything I'd learned over the years, it was how to choose your battles. I didn't see much point in fighting this one. If Almena wanted to retrieve her money alone, no skin off my nose. My mind was busy turning over other questions, anyway, like how the Grizzly Queen of the West knew our sixteenth president, for example. And whether she'd taken part in hunting down John Wilkes Booth, as she'd promised Mrs. Lincoln.

Just pondering these unbelievable things filled me with embarrassment. Made me feel a fool for even entertaining the possibility any of it were true. But then, why else keep the letter hidden away, if it were only some kind of joke? I didn't have an answer for that.

Almena was waiting.

"I'll be sure and do that," I finally said, mustering some graciousness to her offer of cleaning up. "Thank you."

I lingered around the corner for a few moments afterward, listened to her coaxing nails out of the wood, murmuring *it's here, it has to be here*, and then I headed out back through a door in the kitchen.

———

I ducked my head, receiving a splash of cold down my neck. It'd taken some time to prime the pump, the hand lever requiring me to really lean into it. Even once the water started flowing—initially warm from the metal, then cooler—the lever continued to shriek like the wail of a woman who's just discovered a mouse in her pantry. *Eeeeeeek, eeeeeek, eeeek.*

Pulling back, I pumped the handle a couple more times. Each time, the water released in a short gush, collecting below in a wooden bucket I'd found on the porch. I cupped my hands and splashed my face, then shook my head to rid the leftover drops. A washbowl was a nice convenience, but not something I needed. Besides, I thought I'd leave Almena to her business for a bit. Figured she needed the alone time to sort herself out. Maybe she wasn't the only one.

After rubbing most of the dirt from my face, I sat down, back against the pump, watching the back of the house. My knuckles still ached, the cuts on them scabbed over, but only barely. I resisted the urge to pick at them, a childhood vice I'd never been able to shake.

While I sat there, I had the opportunity to further admire the fine spread of country around the house. We'd passed some wheat fields on the way in, and being that I'd done most of my growing up on decent Carolinian acreage and had some experience with farming, I tried explaining to Almena why she needed to tend to her crop now.

See there? The way the stalks bend and snap? They'd broken in front of our horses' progress, fragile as an old man's back in a youngster's game. *Means they're dry, maybe dead.*

I showed her how the heads were starting to nod and recommended she hire someone on to harvest the plants soon before their seeds became worthless or blew away. Another storm like the one that'd passed through Coffeyville would be enough to shatter the field. It'd be a tragedy to lose what looked like an otherwise good crop, and that wasn't even counting the profits lost or the time wasted planting the field in the first place.

Funny. I never pegged you for a farmer, Apostle.

The badge throws a lot of people off.

She'd even chuckled. As angry at her as I was for Coffeyville, I couldn't help cracking a smile, too. If I had a weakness, it was a pretty woman laughing at my jokes.

This close to the house, long-haired prairie grass replaced the wheat fields. Near the back porch, a bossy orange milkweed staked its territory. With no one to trim it, the plant had begun a slow conquest of the right half of the deck, thrusting itself through the space between the wooden slats. Eventually, that location would choke its growth, maybe even kill it. But for now, it ruled the roost, the biggest and bawdiest flower in the yard. Beautiful, but ultimately doomed.

There were other, less invasive plants around, too. Owing to summer, the whole area was bursting with wildflowers—an eruption of color, leftover from a late spring bloom. Some like the bee's balm and sage lorded over the grass in dominant shoots of magenta and blue. Others, like the Black-eyed Susans—which were always Lilah's favorite—were harder to spot. The small sunflowers clung to the trailside, strangling in a net of thistle. I thought about rescuing a few for Almena's kitchen table. Maybe it would liven the place up a little. So much of the house felt haunted, its primary resident a woman living inside the corpse of her own pride.

I jammed my hat down onto my head and pushed it forward until it almost touched my nose. After being trapped in the oppressive shadow of the house, being outside was as good as a stiff drink. The sun poured warmth into my skin, relaxed my bones, and left me thinking. Why not rest my eyes for a few minutes? Just a few. No harm in that.

Someone kicked the flat of my boot, waking me with a start. Checking the horizon, I saw the sun had slipped into the dark hills behind the house, glowing red as blood. Twilight. How long had I been asleep? Hours, at least.

Almena stood in front of me. She kicked my boot again.

"I'm up," I said, covering a yawn, and getting to my feet. I adjusted my leather around my hips, but truth was, I couldn't feel my backside. "Why didn't you wake me sooner?"

"I didn't need you sooner," she said. "I need you now."

You could write those words down at the top of a list entitled *'Things I never expected to hear out of Almena Guillory's mouth.'*

I blinked, unable to hide my surprise. "All right."

She turned, and I followed her wordlessly into the house.

CHAPTER EIGHTEEN

A lmena slammed a glass down in front of me before crashing into a chair on the other side of the table with her own cup. My brows crunched as she shoved the table's center-piece—a bowl of rotten fruit—out of the way and set a bottle with no label between us. She pulled her arms into her chest, holding a finger over her lip for a few seconds. Then she pointed, indicating the bottle.

"You know what that is, Marshal?"

I leaned over to inspect the bottle. Turned it this way, then that, searching the bottle with my thumb for some kind of embossing or indication of seller. There was nothing. As I set it back down, the contents sloshed around the empty space in the neck. "I'm no expert, but I'd say what you've got here is like to be rotgut."

That was a nice way of calling the liquor 'shit.' As a way of stretching their profits, it wasn't uncommon for some saloons to cut their whiskey with more… questionable ingredients. If you were lucky, the recipe included something harmless, like cow-horn peppers, burnt sugar, or blackberries. But ammonia and turpentine were more typical of a 'custom drink.' I'd even heard of a place in Leavenworth that produced a nasty concoction of whiskey and gunpowder, of all things. Wade confirmed it, once sharing the story of how he was sick for three days after downing half a bottle of the stuff over a bad game of faro. Another saloon —this one I'd actually visited in Abilene—boasted a drink color-fully titled *Tarantula Juice*. Don't know what they put in it, but with a name like that, it couldn't have been very tasty.

In any event, this wasn't the answer Almena was looking for.

"No," she said, reaching for the bottle. Her fingers turned white around its neck. "This right here is the only thing I have left to my name."

"What about the money?"

"Gone. All of it. Every dollar. Every bearer bond; every last cent I ever stole. Even the best of the alcohol." She shut her mouth like she was going to be sick. Then a rich, dark laughter tore from her lips, and she looked away—I think to keep me from seeing her tearful eyes. "He took everything."

"Bratt," I guessed.

She nodded, still not facing me. "You were right, Apostle. He was never coming for me."

"Why'd you go to Asher in the first place, Almena? You could've left the state, disappeared altogether. Instead, you decide to hole up in a town no larger than twenty people. I know you're a big impressive outlaw, and a smart woman, but that—well, you'll have to forgive me. I can't think of any other way to say it. That was just plain stupid."

Her smile sharpened to a point, and she nodded stiffly. "I'll drink to that."

Rather than going to the trouble of uncorking the bottle, she smashed the neck against the side of the table, breaking it open. I flinched.

"What in blazes did you do that for?" I cried as she poured herself a shot and set about casually picking the pieces out of her skin. Several shards had flown into her hand, and blood oozed into the lines of her palm.

She sucked on her thumb. Spit red. "Saved time."

Shaking my head, I got up and went outside, ignoring any objections. I came back with the bucket full of water I'd used earlier. Having been left out in the sun all day, the liquid was lukewarm to the touch, but still clean, apart from a few pieces of grass, and the tiny black bodies of two insects who'd learned the hard way they couldn't swim. "You have any washrags around here?"

"You don't have to—"

"Please. Just let me do this, all right? Now, where do you keep the rags?"

She indicated a cupboard in the kitchen. I went and fetched what was needed. Then I took my seat, this time beside her.

"Give me your hand," I said, holding out my own.

"You know what I can do," she said in a small voice. "You know I heal."

"Don't mean it doesn't hurt in the meantime. Am I wrong?"

Almena dropped her gaze to the table. For a moment, I thought she might resist, but then she reached out. Settled her hand in mine. Her fingers slid up my wrist, nails dancing lightly over my veins, until my thumb locked between her pinky and ring finger, halting the progress of her touch. I swallowed. Hoped she didn't notice.

"It used to hurt more," she said.

I plunged the rag into the water and then squeezed it out over her hand, washing off the blood. "What do you mean?"

"Taking on the injuries of others used to hurt as much as if I'd experienced the trauma myself. But over the years... something's changing. I'm starting to lose feeling. Nothing hurts anymore. Not for long, anyway."

"You telling me you can't feel pain?"

I carefully plucked out a piece of glass embedded between her fingers. A red spot of blood welled in its place. Almena didn't make any indication she felt it. Her eyes stayed on me.

"I can feel it initially. Then… nothing. Maybe it's for the best. Or maybe it's my reward. For the things I've done. Or haven't." Before she went to pieces in front of me, she looked away again, biting hard on her bottom lip.

"What about right now?" I turned her hand over, smoothing the cloth over her knuckles. "Can you feel that?"

"Only a little." Her mouth lifted into a timid smile. "Feels nice."

Looking on her now, her features relaxed with pleasure, felt like I was seeing her for the first time. Not the Grizzly Queen, but Almena herself. Prey to as much fear and loneliness as the rest of us mere mortals. As she let me hold her hand, I was reminded that she, too, was flesh and blood.

"You still didn't answer my question."

"About Asher, you mean?" I nodded. She hesitated, then leaned toward me, speaking in a confidential tone. "What would you say if I told you I was in Asher looking for a dead man?"

"I'd say you found plenty of them along the way."

"Right." That was the wrong answer. All friendliness retreated from her eyes, and she sat back, taking her glass with her free hand, and downing the whole draught in one impressive shot. Then she reached for the bottle. "If we're going to do this, I'm going to need to be a whole lot drunker than I am right now." Rather than topping herself off again, she started to pour the liquor into the glass meant for me. "I hope you're a whiskey man."

"Actually, I don't drink."

"Bullshit. You live in Kansas."

I smiled thinly. "I manage all right."

She let her eyes go to the ceiling. "I don't have many rules I live by..."

"You don't say."

"But of my rules, there is one I abide by and have never broken. I don't drink alone."

"And why's that?"

"Because it's pathetic. And because I don't trust a man who doesn't drink. In most cases, it's because he's waiting. Planning on getting the drop on me in my inebriated state. Wanting to shoot me in the back or shoot something else between my thighs. Either way..."

She slid my glass back in front of me.

I shook my head. "I'd never take advantage of you like that. But I'm sorry, I don't partake."

"I can't drink if you don't drink. And I need a drink." She took her hand back, then said the magic words: "Please, Apostle."

If she'd tried to coerce me, like on the Cortez's farm, or threaten me, as she'd done in Asher, I wouldn't have budged. I'd been bullied by bigger men than her, teased by Prough the Rough, and still come out sober as temperance. But this asking nicely thing...

Damn it.

I scrunched my face up, feeling my will cracking. She began to smile, knowing she'd won even before I answered. "I'm not gonna to get two words out of you until I say yes, am I? Fine. If it'll make you feel better, I'll have a drink. One. In return, you'll answer all my questions. About Asher and... any other thing I want to know about. Agreed?"

"Whatever makes you happy, Marshal." Almena gestured to my glass with her long, slender fingers. "After you."

I gave her a decidedly unhappy look, and brought the glass to my lips.

As I did, I caught sight of my knuckles—pink and tender, but otherwise completely healed. *Almena*. She must've done it earlier when our hands were touching. I didn't even notice. I pretended not to notice now, too, allowing her to cherish her secret act of charity. Even a bad guy needs to feel like a good guy once in a while.

Soon as the alcohol hit my tongue, I stopped thinking about my knuckles or Almena's reckless moral compass, and started thinking about what horse piss mixed with seep oil must taste like. This had to be mighty close, if not surpassing in its vileness. Knocking it back quick—truly, that was the only way to stomach its foulness—brought tears to my eyes. It was like gargling with kerosene. Burned *all* the way down.

"Lord!" I made a face. "That's awful!"

Almena smirked. "That's whiskey."

———

Come to find out, Almena couldn't *get* drunk—least, not for long. Something having to do with the same reason she could stomach bullets and tolerate the violent vandalizing of her skin like it was nothing more than a temporary inconvenience. Of course, I didn't realize this until around the third glass.

Also came to find out, when she said that bottle was the last thing she had to her name, she was being a touch dramatic. Bratt had left her at least six bottles of the stuff—real champion fellow, that Bratt—and Almena was determined to drink every one of them dry. Pressured to keep up with her, and already having broken my golden rule, I figured I might as well keep going. See what all the fuss of drinking was about.

I also feared stopping up, lest Almena put an end to her stories. Seemed like the more I drank, the more she had to say. I was learning a lot about her. Valuable, important things…

"I was friends with Abraham Lincoln, back in the day."

"The president?"

"You know another one?"

"S'ppose not."

Yep. *Things.* None I could recall, of course, as I attempted to make my way back to my room, greased by the whiskey. I moved hand-over-hand, slowly feeling my way along the wall while the floor wavered beneath me, sliding all over itself like melted butter. I kept expecting to slip and fall, but my steps held, one after the other. My torso felt buoyed by nothing, but I knew my legs were there, puzzled by the movement, but doing their job.

Atta boy, Nathan. Don't let her see what a lightweight you are.

I raised a hand to one of my ears, instinctively defending against my father's criticism. But then, losing my balance, I quickly scrambled for the wall again.

No. Wasn't my father's voice in my head. It was mine.

But the words were his. The sentiment, his. In all the years living with the man, surviving all those beatings, all that pointless misery, thinking myself better, determined to be kinder, some part of his nature had still broken off inside me. Like the head of a pick lodged into a mountain's flesh, the miner left holding just the handle. I felt it in there, in my chest.

A dark, ugly knot.

I thought I could forgive him. Lord as my witness, I thought I had. Him and my ex-wife both. My religion commanded me to forgive them, and I agreed that made the most sense, being that Nathaniel Richardson had long since gone to his reward, whatever that turned out to be, and Lilah—Lilah was gone in all the ways that mattered. Still. I held fast to that knot, pulling at its threads every now and again with a thought, making it tighter and *tighter* and—permanent. Anchoring me to a past I kept trying to be free of.

All the warmth and cheap comfort of whiskey couldn't make me forget that small, thorny place in my heart. Maybe I didn't want it to. Didn't let it. If anything, the whiskey just reminded me it was still there.

Maybe Guillory and I weren't so different, after all. Neither of us seemed to be able to let go of the people who hurt us.

How about that.

Dimly, I became aware of Almena's hand on my elbow. Helping me inch along. *Nice of her.* And just like that, I rolled off the topic of my father and back into the present. It was hard to concentrate. My mind had the consistency of sludge, and my thoughts mostly bubbled up at random.

"What?" I turned toward Almena, missing what she'd said.

"I asked if you wanted to go upstairs," she repeated.

I started laughing. Not a mild chuckle, either, but raucous, side-splitting laughter. I pitched forward with tears squeezing out of my eyes, only avoiding the floor thanks to Almena's intervention. She bent underneath me, literally shouldering my weight before she could get her hands up. Her palms flattened against my chest and pushed to keep me upright. I finally managed to sling my arm around the stair banister.

"Mind letting me in on the joke?" Almena asked, smiling uncertainly. I waved her off, trying to catch my breath. "What in hell is so funny?"

"I—don't—I don't know!" For some reason, this made me wheeze harder. I couldn't seem to stop. My throat began to hurt from laughing so much. "It's just—"

"What?"

"You and me. And—this. *Do I want to go upstairs?*" I mimicked the sound of her voice. Knuckled away tears from the corners of my eyes. "I'm sorry."

"Maybe we should just put you on the couch for now."

I sobered some by the time we reached the sitting room. In terms of humor, anyway. A dreary calm settled on me, slowly easing the smile from my face. I sank down onto the sofa, relieved to be closer to the ground. Wouldn't hurt so much if I passed out from here.

"Stand up," Almena ordered.

I gave her a helpless look.

"Come on. Up." She gestured impatiently.

Once back on my feet, Almena's hands went to my holster. I clamped down on her wrists before her fingers had completely undone the front of my belt.

"Don't get excited. I'm just removing your gun so you'll be more comfortable." She had a point, but I held fast, reluctant to trust her. Or reluctant to let her go. I rolled my thumb along the side of her hand, barely aware I was doing it. She stared up at me, her eyes mysterious and thoughtful.

"If you want to do it yourself, then by all means." She stepped back, escaping my loose grip with ease. Wouldn't keep her somewhere she didn't want to be. "But one way or another, that holster needs to come off."

"All right," I agreed simply, and she came back.

Her fingers, sure and strong, made quick work of the belt. Then she set it down together with my gun on one of the end tables near the couch where it would be within my reach, should I have need of it in the night. She must've known I'd appreciate that. Sure had me pegged, but then I'd made no secret of my beliefs or behavior. I owned only a partial and incomplete picture of who Almena was, though. The images on her dresser floated back to me.

"Is it true?" I asked when her back was turned to me.

"Is what true?"

"That you knew Lincoln?" Something surfaced in the muddy run of my thoughts. "Wait a minute. Is he the decent man you let die?"

"That'd be a bold claim."

"Found some pictures on your desk. There was a, a letter

inside one of them. Letter you wrote."

She swung around, thrusting a finger towards me. "You had no right to go snooping through my things."

"You're right. I shouldn't've done."

Almena snorted. "I can see why you didn't become a lawyer." She was still breathing a little faster than usual, but I believed I'd dodged a storm. That gave me the confidence to ask my next question.

"Did you succeed in helping track down... what's his name? Booth? Were you there at the Garrett farm when he was killed?"

"John Wilkes Booth isn't dead."

She said this like I should've known it.

I squinted. "Come again?"

"Remember why I said I came to Asher? Looking for a dead man?"

"You were looking for—John Wilkes Booth? *The* John Wilkes Booth?"

"Yes."

I gave her another cautious look. "Did you... find him?"

"Don't patronize me, Marshal. I'm not crazy. I have it on good authority he's still alive. Moved out West, I don't know where. Yet. That's why I was in Asher. My cousin wrote to me, said she'd overheard some talk there from one of the men who claimed he'd run with Booth after Virginia, first south to North Carolina, then out here to Kansas. As it turned out, the man was just some ex-Confederate deep in his cups. But I know I'm not wrong about this. I know Booth's out here somewhere."

My head ached, making it even more difficult to think straight, and I sat down to avoid a feeling of spinning. "What makes you so sure?"

"Three hours."

"What?"

She sat down next to me, strangely enthusiastic. "The reports say he was shot in the neck and it took him three hours to die. Three hours in which someone like me could have saved him. Besides that, the only people to identify the body were members of Booth's family. You don't think they had mighty good reason to lie?"

I held up my hand, indicating she should slow down. "Wait. Someone like you? You mean, there are others who can do… whatever it is you do?"

"A few. Less since the war ended."

"Since the war ended?"

"I know you're drunk, but if you're just going to repeat everything I say, this is going to be a long and irritating conversation for both of us."

"I'm trying to understand…"

She shot to her feet and began pacing the room. Her boots clomped angrily against the floor. "They killed themselves, all right? You want the grisly details? You want to know how I found one after the war, starved and half out of his mind? Some former Greyback still wearing his dead brothers' wounds, who didn't know what the fuck to do with himself now that his side had lost. I found him one morning weeks later, hanging from a rafter in the barn. Because he knew, he *knew* I would save him, if I could. That I would've—I would have stopped him. This was the only way. His body healed too damn quickly for anything else short of putting a rifle in his mouth, and that would've been messy, inconsiderate. Maybe you'd like to hear how it took me half an hour to cut him down because the saw teeth had rusted and couldn't get through the rope. Go ahead, try to understand *that*. Because I sure as hell don't. I don't understand any of it."

"I'm sorry," I answered in a small voice. "I didn't know."

Tears slid from her eyes. I could tell it surprised her because she made a startled noise before wicking the tears away from her cheeks. "How could you? It doesn't matter now. He's dead. He wasn't the only bruiser to find peace at the end of a rope or a barrel, but he was one of the few I knew personally."

One of the few, seemed to me, who knew exactly the sort of things Almena had gone through during the war. Perhaps the last man who could honestly empathize with Almena, and he'd strung himself up in her barn. *Hell.*

"What was his name?" I asked her.

"What?"

"The name of this man. If you don't mind me asking."

She folded her arms across her chest, trying to look tough. It didn't work. "What's it matter to you?"

"Dead should be remembered. Good, bad, or in between. A person deserves that much. Sometimes it's hard being the only one who bears that burden."

"Jim," she answered after a moment. "James Ealer. He was from Virginia."

We spoke a short time about James Ealer, and then about others she'd known during the war. I learned Almena had befriended several men from the Colored Troops, who upon learning she was actually a woman, kept her secret out of friendship and gratitude for her help in rescuing their fellow men who had been taken prisoner following an engagement near Richmond. When I asked about her moniker during the war, she confirmed she had served under the name Alvin, or "Al," Guillory, just as Jed had claimed, but to hear her tell it, before entering the employ of the president, she spent most of the war as a glorified medic, not a ruthless killer. The nickname came after the war, when people like me started trying to make out Almena's history through the smoke of hearsay and rumor.

I asked the occasional question to keep Almena talking, but mostly I listened, watching the way her face changed when she spoke about the people she'd fought alongside and cared about. The tension went away from her mouth, and her eyes slowly brightened; her memories still moved her. I got the feeling she didn't discuss them often with anyone, and I felt honored, then guilty. If Almena knew I was still planning on arresting her, I doubted she'd be so open to sharing.

It was only when I started to nod off—not for want of interest, mind, but medicated by the whiskey—that Almena turned quiet. She lifted my legs onto the sofa as I slouched into the cushions. The old fabric smelled faintly of cigar smoke and strong coffee. The latter conjured memories of the open range, and an Arbuckle's blend to wash the dust from my mouth after a long hard day. When I closed my eyes, I could almost imagine myself somewhere else, halfway to normal.

I heard Almena leave.

A minute later, she came back.

Something wooden clanked against the floor beside my temporary bed. I opened one eye and saw it was the bucket from before, now empty.

"Here," Almena said. "I have a feeling you'll want this come morning."

I made a noise of mild agreement and gave her a small salute.

"All right. Then I guess, good night, Marshal."

"Hey," I said, as the sound of her footsteps started going away again. "Actually, I've one more question before you go."

Her silence as good as gave me permission to ask. I sat up on my elbows.

"You told me why you went to Asher in the first place, but you never said why you stayed long enough for me to catch up to you. If you had long enough to change into that dress, those gloves... pretty as they were, makes me think you had long enough to get away. And that's not even touching on what you can do with your hands. I mean, your skin. I mean"—I sighed, struggling to find the right words—"you know what I mean." *Damn whiskey.*

Almena leaned against the door frame. Even as bleary-eyed as I was, I noticed her smile cut with anguish. "I honestly thought he'd come. I know it sounds stupid, but Lloyd—Bratt, he knew where I was going. Before we split at Ellsworth—on account of you, I might add—I told him. I said, I'm going to Asher to hunt down a lead. If you don't hear from me in a day, it means I've found trouble. I'll need you. And he promised he'd come. *Come hell or high waters.* Those were his words."

She glanced down briefly, her mouth twisting. When she finally looked back at me, her expression was unguarded, hopeful and devastated at the same time. "Have you ever wanted so badly to believe in someone, Apostle? That you were willing to overlook all their faults just so it'd work? So you could be happy, if only for a little while?"

"Yes," I said without reservation.

"Doesn't everyone deserve that chance?" I heard the question she was really asking. *Don't I deserve to be happy?*

My answer was the same. "Yes, ma'am."

"I thought it'd be good for him—getting the opportunity to be the hero for once. Saving me instead of the other way around. But some men don't have hero in them." She pushed off the door, rubbing her neck where she refused to let her rope burns heal. "I was fooling myself, thinking I could change him. Thinking anyone could change."

"People do change."

"Before we got here, I searched for Lloyd. I was sure something must have happened to him. That he got held up somehow. That *he* was the one in trouble. Otherwise, why wouldn't he come for me? But, this—"

She indicated the ripped-up floorboards. I also noticed a few new holes in the walls that weren't there before.

"He gave me up for dead, Marshal. Didn't even try." Her voice cracked on the last word. One moment she looked to be fighting tears, the next she rolled her eyes, laughed, and threw her hands up in the air. "Hell! *You* did more to save my life than he did. But forget it. I don't know why I'm even talking about this. It doesn't matter."

I frowned. "Why do you say that? Why are you always so quick to dismiss the way you're feeling?"

"Because if it matters, it hurts. And I'm sick to death of hurting all the time."

I didn't know what to say to that. If she'd been standing closer, I might've taken her hand. She looked like a woman who needed to be comforted, who needed to know she wasn't half as alone as she felt. But given our history, I probably wasn't the right fella to make her feel any better. I stayed put, wisely or not.

"Are we done now, Apostle?" she asked after an uncomfortable interlude of silence.

"Nathan," I murmured.

"What?"

"My name—real one, that is—it's Nathan. Short for Nathaniel, after my old man. He was… a lousy husband to my mother. Lousy father to me. Drunk half the time, mean the rest. That's whose name I was given at birth. That's why when people started calling me Apostle, I didn't bother correcting them. It was better than hearing them call me by my daddy's name." I smiled down at myself, at how stupid it sounded now that it was outside of my head.

"Why are you telling me this?"

"Probably 'cause I'm drunk," I admitted with a woozy chuckle, "but also because you shared something with me. Seemed only fair I return the favor." She kept on watching me, so I kept on talking. "You ain't alone in having a past, Almena. Or in being hurt by the people you love. Happens. Happens to all of us. I'd hate to see you waste yourself on regret because you were too afraid to let yourself feel something other than anger."

"Chatty even when drunk. I hope this isn't the part where you try and bring me to God."

I settled back into the sofa. "Nope. I've said my piece. Now's the part when I go to sleep. I'll tell you about Jesus tomorrow, you want."

She went through the room and turned down the lamps, one by one. Darkness rushed in, taking the place of the light. I tucked my chin down into my chest and closed my eyes.

"Good night, Nathan," I heard Almena say, without mockery.

"Night, Almena," I replied, falling asleep to the sound of her footsteps retreating up the stairs.

CHAPTER NINETEEN

The following morning Almena was back to herself, maybe improved. I heard her humming—*humming!*—while she stirred oatmeal over the stove, the picture of domesticity in a blue linen dress. Her long, brown hair was fixed neatly at the back of her head, similar to the way she'd worn it when she was younger.

She smiled at me when I came in, though I must've looked a mess. She seemed lighter, somehow. Freer. When she asked me to make myself useful and look in the cupboard to see if we had brown sugar, I didn't question the task. Maybe things would be different now. Maybe we'd crossed into a new place of understanding.

We were only a couple bites into breakfast, each of us taking turns complaining about the stale oats, when I made the mistake of asking what would happen now, with us having no money to hire her old outfit.

Took Almena all of two seconds to land on the idea of robbing a bank.

On the one hand, I shouldn't have been surprised. You go to the dentist and ask him about a pain in your mouth, of course the man's going to say you need teeth pulled. My head started to pound again, and my stomach turned at her proposal, already unsettled by the previous night's adventures. As predicted, I'd gotten mighty intimate with the bucket Almena had left me over the course of the morning.

I managed to swallow my spoonful of oatmeal before saying, "I can't believe I even need to say this, but I'm not going to help you rob a bank."

"What would you prefer instead? A train?" She sipped her water, looking thoughtful. "A small two-man team *could* pull it off, and it is less risky than hitting a bank… but you should know, normally we have to kill the express agent. He's usually holed up in the express car and rarely goes down without a fight. I can't imagine that would sit well with you, given that pesky conscience of yours."

I rubbed my face. Lord above, it was too early for this.

"Come on, Apostle." Almena scraped the edges of her bowl to get at the last dregs of warm oatmeal. I winced each time the silverware connected with the china. In the short amount of time since we'd sat down to eat, she'd managed to finish her entire bowl. I was still only a few bites into mine. The woman put away food like I couldn't believe. "Don't tell me you've never thought about how you'd pull off a robbery. Now's your chance to see if you'd have any better luck than the men you hunt."

Times like these made me feel like Almena Guillory and I were on the edge of a steep cliff, and it was only a question of whether I pulled her up before she pulled me over. Worse, I felt myself slipping. Whatever my intentions, already I'd compromised for her—the drinking, what I done to Dempsey. The fact I recognized bank robbing as going too far was a good sign. Less good was the reality in which I found myself actually considering it.

"Innocent people are going to get hurt," I objected.

"That's a distinct possibility. But the odds of that happening go way down if you work together with me on this."

Almena continued aggressively scraping her bowl until finally, I shoved my own over to her, my spoon still buried inside a mound of cooling oats.

"You sure?" she asked me.

"Please."

She didn't bother checking again before starting in on the second helping.

"It doesn't have to get bloody," she said after another moment. Her eyes were focused on the contents of the bowl, but she sounded sincere.

"You sound confident."

She shrugged. "I'm good at what I do."

"So all those times people died in your robberies... that was just, what? Fun?"

Now she looked up at me. "Accidents."

With lips pressed together, I shook my head. "Why don't I believe you?"

She used a finger to clean one corner of her mouth, removing a crust of brown sugar. I found it oddly distracting. "Believe this: I never killed anyone the world would miss. At least, not after the war."

"How would you know? You stop to conduct interviews with your hostages? What about those express agents you mentioned?"

"Wow. You really aren't friendly in the morning, are you?"

Almena looked more amused by my vinegar than offended. She would. I don't think that woman has ever reacted normally to a thing in her life.

"Sorry," I muttered, massaging my temples. "Just feels like someone's pushing a railroad spike through my head. And now you want to rob a bank, and... I'm not sure what I'm doing here anymore, to be honest."

"You don't have a choice. Remember?"

Rather than harassing, her gaze was expectant, almost urging. Like she was trying to get me to put the pieces together. I thought back. Her blackmail, the threat to Lilah. Could it have less to do with controlling me, and more to do with protecting me? Was Almena giving me a way out after this whole thing was over? A way to keep my honor, even if I still lost my badge? *I didn't have a choice,* I could say, *She was threatening to kill my wife.*

But why would she do that?

I must've looked as confused as I felt because Almena smiled faintly. She got up, banged around in the cupboards for a while, found whatever she was looking for—some coffee beans, probably as old as the oats—and brewed us both a cup. Then she returned, plunked a mug down in front of me, and swung into the chair across, pursued by a small tether of steam rising from her own cup.

I drank, grateful for the strong and sobering taste.

"Now, I'll ask you once more. Bank—or train?"

Less than a week later, once all the preliminaries were in place— ammo stocked (though Almena assured me we wouldn't be using much if things went according to plan), surrounding areas mapped, exits deliberated on, and fresh mounts in the right spots —we set out for the little town of Halverson, just south of Ottawa, posing as man and wife.

Before leaving, Almena produced two rings of modest silver, which she must've had stashed away somewhere Bratt didn't know about—inside another picture frame, perhaps?—though I couldn't imagine they were worth much more than their senti-mental value.

"It'd look strange if we didn't have wedding bands," Almena

explained, fitting one on herself and handing the other to me without ceremony. I wanted to ask where she'd gotten the bands, if she'd stolen them, but something in the way she twisted her ring back and forth on her finger told me it was a story I was probably better off not inquiring about.

In addition to the jewelry, Almena surprised me with her choice of dress. While I stood waiting near the door, she came down the stairs, her figure an hourglass of dark blue. The riding habit elegantly covered every inch of her skin, including a small collar which closed around her throat, and sleeves that descended all the way to her wrists. She looked up at me from beneath a black lace hat perched at the front of her head. Despite her movement, the hat somehow managed to remain in place, invisibly secured to a high crown of brown hair. Loose ringlets slithered out of the crown and down the nape of her neck, and I felt a familiar—although, in this case, highly inappropriate—urge to interpose my hand between the hair and her neck. The idea parched my mouth.

She smiled, catching my eyes as she slid her hands into a pair of black riding gloves. "Well? How do I look, Marshal?"

"Tell you this much," I replied, "I'll never understand how you ladies manage to do all that"—I gestured vaguely toward her hair—"all by yourselves."

Almena leaned in, a conspiratorial gleam in her eyes. Her breath tickled my ear. "Don't tell anyone, but most of us make secret pacts with the devil. Saves on time and effort."

I couldn't help a smile. "That would explain it."

As she swept toward the door, I added, "You do, though. Look beautiful, that is."

Almena reacted to my compliment with a reserved tilt of her head, very ladylike, though as she turned back toward the door, I caught her grinning.

I felt like a pauper in comparison, wearing a few of Lloyd's things—a collared shirt with a few suspicious stains that might've been tobacco or blood, and a grey jacket which covered most of those stains. The shirt was too broad in the shoulders, and pants were a little too long in the legs, but seeing as I hadn't exactly had a chance to pack before leaving Coffeyville, it wasn't like I had many options. Still, it was almost worth it for the look Almena gave me when I first emerged from the guest room.

I'd expected maybe a haunted expression, what with me wearing her vanished lover's clothes, but instead she looked— well, relieved, is the closest word I can think of. *I bear much resemblance to your Mr. Bratt?* I'd asked whilst stuffing one side of the shirt into the back of my pants, and readjusting my suspenders over my shoulders beneath the coat. She shook her head. *Not remotely.* And when her eyes moved over me, they seemed to hold new appreciation.

"You always get done up before robbing a bank?" I followed her onto the porch, closing the door behind us.

"No, but if people are looking for a female outlaw, arriving in pants and a holster might tip them off, don't you think? This dress is as good a disguise as any. No one will think twice."

"Oh, they're gonna think twice. Uh, just not about you being an outlaw."

Another covert smile. "Careful, Apostle. All these compliments… I might start getting to think you like me."

"I do like you, Almena." The words just sort of came out, though why it should've been a secret—or why it felt like one—I wasn't sure. Her smile faltered. "I just don't like what you do."

"Hate the sin, not the sinner. Is that it?"

"Something like that."

She gave a breathy laugh. "What happens when you find out we're one in the same?"

"Well… the good Lord didn't say we were only supposed to

love our neighbor's good side." I smiled cautiously, hoping it might reassure her I wasn't judging none.

But Almena only replied, "We're burning daylight here. Let's get a move on."

———

The day began wet, following a brief rainstorm like the one watered Coffeyville. Thankfully, the mass of sallow clouds moved quickly, always ahead of us on the horizon, and was gone by the time we got to Halverson, though evidence of its visit to the town remained. The main thoroughfare was flooded with mud, and some high winds had removed a few store signs. One man, presumably a business owner, stood on the porch of his store, simply shaking his head, muttering about the damn inconvenience. Other men were hard at work laying down wooden planks to ferry people from one side of the street to the other. Their boots disappeared about an inch into the peat.

"Wait," I said to Almena, as we reined up outside one of only two inns in town. I hopped down off my horse, immediately sinking into the bog. I lifted one boot free, then the other, and made my way over to her. "Here, I'll carry you."

I knew the muck wouldn't bother her none, given her rough and tumble lifestyle, but it wouldn't be seemly, a husband allowing his wife to trudge through mud. In her eyes, I saw Almena make the same calculations. After a moment she maneuvered herself from side-saddle to slide down into my arms.

"I knew there was a reason I married you," she said lightly, affecting a polite accent more suited to the parlors of Northern Virginia.

Under normal circumstances, I might have made some kind of comeback. I enjoyed bantering with her; she had all the makings of a worthy adversary, quick, intelligent. But these weren't normal circumstances, and I felt tense with the knowledge of what was coming.

Almena squeezed my arm as I set her down on the boardwalk in front of the inn. To anyone else, it would've looked like a wife showing affection to her husband.

"Relax," she urged me, maintaining a smile.

"Yeah." I fixed my gaze on the bank, just across the way. "I don't see that happening."

"Try."

"I am."

"Then try harder."

"Don't worry about me…"

I felt her hand on my cheek. "I do worry about you," she said, reminding me of what I'd said earlier. *I do like you.* The warmth of her hand pressed through her glove.

Was this more play-acting? Or something else? Something… different.

Something dangerous.

At my baffled expression, Almena withdrew with all the speed of a person taking their hand off a hot plate. "I worry you're going to get us both killed if you don't toughen up," she added, and I couldn't help thinking, *ahh, there she is.* "Let's get going already."

We started toward the inn, but I kept thinking about the way she'd looked at me just now, her gaze touched with care, actual doggone concern. The way no criminal should ever look at a lawman. I recalled how she'd felt in my arms as I carried her to the clean safety of the porch: heavier than expected, but not a burden I found I minded any. I also thought about the way I sometimes stared at Almena, like the sun was behind her and I was desperately trying to make out her face. The way no lawman should ever look at a criminal. The way I was looking at her right now, as I turned back without being sure what I was going to do exactly. Something.

Stupid, most like.

Almena glanced up from adjusting a pleat in her dress, and I covered the distance between us in two steps. My hands slid up her neck, cradling her jaw for the briefest moment, thumb darting out over her cheek before I lowered my head. Her expression tensed, seizing like a wild thing that's just caught the glint of a hunter's gun, and her gaze slanted sideways, perhaps wondering whether this was for the benefit of an audience. Eventually, her eyes returned to me. Those eyes, which did equal stints of cruel and careful, now dropped every pretense, reduced to an aching grey. The crown rolled off, the armor of her reputation flaking to pieces like dry enamel, and she stood there with the soft body of Eve. An impossible temptation.

I grazed the side of her mouth, asking the question as gently as I could. She turned her head towards me, fitting our lips completely together. Every part of me tightened, my pulse jumping. Without thought to propriety, I dropped one hand to her lower back, pulling her close. Her arms wrapped around my waist, fingers sliding just inside my waistband, and for the first time, I wasn't thinking so much about my leather. She devoured every thought inside my head, and I happily let her. As we kissed, I felt her holding her breath, and when she finally inhaled, she stole the hot breath from my mouth with a smile…

No.

That's not what actually happened. Although it might've.

A moment passed between us as we stood looking at one another, when I imagined I could've kissed her—and she would've let me. I saw the same possibility in her eyes, thoughtful with lust. Felt like there was a string tied to each of our chests, pulling taut, nearly to the point of breaking, when it would snap back to catch us both in the face.

With those thoughts, I felt myself inch a little closer to the edge of the cliff. Weight shifting toward Almena's end. The devil on her side.

No, I didn't kiss her, but Lord help me, I wanted to.

As I stepped toward Almena, words thick as chaw in my mouth, two men in the middle of the street began arguing about who would step out of the way and let the other pass. Neither fella wanted to forfeit his path on the wooden planks and hop down into the mud for the other. Nor would either make a concession of going back the way he'd come or choose a different avenue. In less than a minute, the argument escalated to fists.

My good sense returned quickly, with all the kindness of a kick to the groin. "Someone should"—a moment to clear my throat—"someone ought probably do something about that."

"You're better leaving it alone," Almena said, and I couldn't tell whether she meant the fight or whatever had almost passed between us just now. She turned away, lifting her chin with imperial grace. Twisted the ring on her finger again. "But I know you can't help yourself. So go on. I have a few errands to run before our business with the bank, anyway."

"Errands?" I asked, already off the boardwalk and two steps into the thoroughfare. The men were cussing up a storm behind me.

"Just meet me back here at the inn when you're done playing hero."

That didn't answer my question, but apparently, it was the only answer I was getting. Almena sauntered off to do… heaven only knew what, and I watched her go.

Fine. So long as she stayed out of trouble. No other marshal with any God-given sense would have left that woman alone for more than two minutes, but I think it was fair to say the horse was out of the barn. Keeping a constant eye on Almena was exhausting, and after a while, it mostly just gave me a headache.

Soon as she was gone, I could think a little clearer. Without the buzzing distraction of her presence, I refocused my attention on the men in the street. By now, their brawl had moved off the wooden planks and into the quagmire they'd been trying to avoid in the first place. The irony seemed lost on the pair as they batted at one another with slippery fists.

"All right, boys," I said, hoping a voice of reason might be the only thing needed here. "That's enough of that. Come on, now; you're making a scene."

I went to grab hold of the shorter, bulkier man when his arm suddenly broke free and his elbow released right into my nose. I caught sight of a black mustache right before a dull crack resonated in my head, jagged pain spiraling out from my nose. I'd like to say I saw stars, but weren't anything half so pretty about getting clobbered in the face. I reeled back, locked into a vision of the yellow sky above, then pitched forward, watching blood drip into the chewed-up earth.

Dazed, I blinked a couple times, backing out of the way just in time to avoid getting caught in the taller man's attack. He barreled into the mustachioed man's back, pushing him to the ground, and then proceeded to drown him, holding his face down in the mud. The other man struggled, arms flailing, still trying to force his opponent off him. Bubbles popped messily around his mouth. The mud muffled his screams.

I quickly seized the taller man beneath the arms, pulling him off with surprising ease. He made like he might come at me, but the iron appearing in my hand, plus the click of the hammer which followed, stopped him cold. Smart man.

"U.S. Marshal. Don't you move." I used the title out of habit. Didn't occur to me until after the fact that I didn't have a badge to show as proof. Luckily, he didn't ask to see one.

"He started it!" were the first sensible words past the man's lips, lathered with grime and fury. He wiped his mouth and spat brown. "Fucking drunk!"

"Did I ask you who started it? *Stay there.*"

"*He* attacked *me*! You hear me, Marshal? It wasn't my fault…"

The man continued to drone on about his innocence while I holstered my gun and helped the mustachioed man to his feet.

Another voice soon interrupted, asking what in the world was going on out here, followed by, "Bart? That you? What are you doing covered in mud? Boy, don't you know that's what the planks are for?"

I looked up into the tired expression of Halverson's sheriff. He had the face of an old basset hound: long, sad eyes, and loose folds of dark, freckled skin which wobbled every time he turned his head. His gaze swung between us, lazily. No wonder Almena chose Halverson to rob. Didn't seem like the town saw much action, judging by the sheriff's relaxed attitude.

"And who might you be?" the sheriff asked me.

Ignoring him for the moment, I thumped the mustachioed man on the back a couple times, helping him cough out viscous street water. He stood bent over, hands on his knees as he hacked and knuckled mud away from his mouth and out of his eyes.

"You all right there, friend?" I asked as he started to right himself.

He waved me away. I was about to oblige when he glanced up, and I finally saw his eyes. Like magic, the rest of his features instantly snapped into recognizable angles. Familiarity sank into me like nails.

"*Jed?*"

"So we're friends again, are we?" he slurred, in between more coughing. A blast of liquor-sweet breath assaulted me, causing me to lean away. "News to me."

I hadn't recognized Jed without his beard. The thin bar of hair above his lip hardly compared. Without the thatch, his chin appeared naked as a baby's rear end, exposing a liver spot on his jowls. His hairline marched backwards in full retreat, baldness on the horizon. It'd been less than a month since I'd seen him last, but he looked years older, and sickly, to boot.

"You two know each other?" the Halverson sheriff asked me.

"Strickland started it, Sheriff," Bart said.

"Shut your hole, Bart. I wasn't speaking to you. And I don't much care who started it. This fellow here—I didn't catch your name."

"Apostle." Almena and I planned on lying about our names, but with Jed standing right there, it would've seemed suspicious had I supplied anything other than the name he knew me by.

The sheriff's sleepy gaze raised a little. "Apostle? You a Mormon?"

"No, sir."

"You know there haven't been any apostles since Christ's day." His eyes narrowed. Did he think I was making fun? Or worse, acting out some kind of sacrilege? Fact was, I'd never really given it much thought. Doubted the men who'd started the name had either. But I wasn't going to worry about it right now. After all, I'd been going by Apostle for years. If I offended God by wearing the name, I figured He'd have let me know it by now.

"Not making any claims to the contrary, sir," I answered respectfully, though I struggled to hold back a smile at the old dog's mistrust. "Just what they call me."

"What they call you... You some kind of important, boy?"

Before I could reply, Jed piped up, saying in a falsely honorific tone, "Why, Sheriff. Don't you know who this is? This here is Apostle Richardson. Big time U.S. Marshal. Thinks he's God's goddamn gift to the law."

"Jed," I started in warning.

Halverson's sheriff looked between us, blinking steadily, and then he cleared his throat. "As I was saying, I don't much care who started the fight. Mister Richardson finished it, and I'm happy to leave it at that. Bart, go clean yourself off before Mary catches sight of you." Bart went. Grumbling. "And Jedediah... this is the third time this week I've caught you starting trouble. Happens again, and I'm gonna have to point you out of town."

Whether Jed had any response to that or not, I'll never know. At that moment, he doubled over and emptied the contents of his stomach onto the street.

CHAPTER TWENTY

As Jed climbed into the tin tub—donated graciously by hotel management only once I agreed to pay a small fee for the water—the former sheriff tried for the fourth time to convince me all he needed was a little hair of the dog and he'd be fine. Right as rain. Fit as a goddamn fiddle. I told him I could look for the dog, but how would I know if it was the one that bit him? Predictably, Jed found this about as funny as an open grave.

"When did you get such a smart mouth?" he asked, grunting as he settled into the water. I'd asked that the water be heated, but on a cold day like today, it wasn't likely to stay warm for very long.

I stood with my back to Jed out of common decency. "I don't know. Bet my daddy could've given you an exact date though. He often accused me of the same."

Jed quieted. He knew my relationship with my father. Knew it'd been mostly bad. I told him the story once, after I'd shot a man up near Emporia, near Jed's town. Wasn't the first man I'd killed, but whatever his crimes, the outlaw had been a solid family man, and he'd made me put him down in front of his kid. I was all broken up about it; my hands wouldn't stop shaking. Jed had sat me down, helped me through it. Maybe that was why I felt the need to do the same for him now. Timing couldn't have been worse, but he was a friend.

Or had been. I hadn't forgotten Asher. That was also part of this.

"What are you doing here, Jed?" I took a seat on the bed across from the tub.

"Soaking."

"You know that's not what I was asking."

He didn't flinch from my gaze. Despite the fact he was buck naked where I was fully clothed, I felt more vulnerable. "Let's see now. After you took me to court and Judge Foster relieved me of my duties as sheriff, I couldn't exactly turn back home, could I? The town had suffered enough from Guillory's visit. Didn't need the added injury of a disgraced lawman hanging around its neck."

I clenched my jaw, prying it back open only long enough to say:

"I'm real sorry about that whole business, Jed."

"Well, as long as you're *sorry*." His smile was particularly nasty without his beard. Jed's lips were swollen and raw, his face whipped by dirt and sun. "Makes everything fine and dandy. Never mind the fact you let Guillory get away. Never mind the fact you chose a *criminal* over a friend. Sorry? You damn well should be!" Muddy spittle flew from his mouth, shooting over the rim of the tub.

I kept silent.

Jed's anger drained quickly, and he slumped down into the water. "I have a cousin agreed to take me in. That's why I'm here. Why are *you* here?"

"Just passing through. I didn't know you had family in Halverson."

He cupped his hands full of water and cleaned the mud from his moustache. The deep grooves around his mouth and chin provided an easy avenue for the dirty water to travel, but also made his frown more profound. "What is this, an interrogation?"

"We're having a simple conversation, is all…"

"Stop beating around the goddamn bush, boy."

"I'm not—"

"Sure you are. You're pussy-footing around like you always do. Too afraid to say what you mean. All niceties, no substance. Either say what you came here to say to me"—his voice pushed into me like a horse backing into my chest, the pressure mounting —"or get the hell out."

I shot to my feet. "Dammit, Jedediah! You nearly got me *killed!*"

Jed huffed. "You gave a whole lot worse than you got. Seeing as you're standing here, and most of my posse ain't."

Thanks to Almena, I thought. But I couldn't tell him that.

"You forced my hand. You forced me to kill those men." Their deaths weighed heavier on my conscience than I'd like to admit.

Jed pulled himself up from the tub, gripping the edges with pale fingers. "No one forces a man to do anything but what he wants to do in the first place. He sure as sin can't make him pull the trigger on another man. It's called agency, Apostle. Look it up. *You* made the decision to kill those men. You chose one life—a sorry one at that—over half a dozen others. That was all you, son."

I couldn't look at him for a long moment, and when I finally did, the reality of what I saw shocked me. Jed didn't look angry, or even righteous. He just looked like an old man in a tub—small and sad and wet. A shriveled-up changeling. This is where his hatred of Almena had gotten him. Made me wonder where I'd end up, given my own complex relationship with the woman.

Made me wonder about a lot of things, really.

I sank back down onto the bed. "How come you can't see I was only doing what I felt was right?"

Jed shook his head. "You know what your problem is, son? Pride. Thinking your fine moral judgments are infallible. Believing your truth is the only one. Face it: the only difference between you and me is I thought Guillory should swing then, and you thought she should swing later. And for that, good men died. How's that make you feel?"

A knock came at the door. A voice I dimly recognized as belonging to the hotel owner chimed in, chasing my thoughts in different directions like a hunter scattering a herd of buffalo. "Mister Richardson?"

"Yeah?" I replied, staring at my hands. They were shaking. I hoped Jed couldn't see.

"Your wife's downstairs asking for you."

Jed's glance said it all. *Wife?*

For one wild moment, I thought he meant Lilah. "Tell her I'll be right down."

"Yes, sir."

"Well? What are you waiting for?" Jed asked when I continued to sit there like a bump on a log. "Bad manners to keep a *lady* waiting." The way he stressed the word lady made me fear he'd somehow read my mind. Knew who I was here with and what I was up to.

"You'll be all right on your own here?"

Jed sniffed in offense, gesturing at his waterlogged body. "I'm not drunk enough to drown in a couple inches of bath water, if that's what you're getting at."

I headed for the door, stopping just before it.

"Jed…" There was more to say, but the words escaped me. A lump formed in my throat, hard as granite. Sometimes you couldn't make amends; sometimes when something broke, it just stayed broke. "Take care of yourself?" It came out almost a question, like I wasn't sure he could anymore.

"Course," he grumped. "Who else is going to?"

———

As I trudged downstairs, my boots felt leaden, my head a little woozy. Might've been on account of that punch I'd taken earlier —or not. Ideas darted through my brain too quick for me to catch, like birds startled out of a dense fog. *For the best*, I told myself. Reckoned my thoughts would've just proved dark and loathsome.

I was still checking my nose for a break when Almena came into view.

She stood a little out of the way of the hotel's mullioned front window, near the corner of the room, her nose in a newspaper. Her attention was wholly absorbed by whatever article she was reading, and that small, thoughtful line she got when something puzzled or intrigued her had just begun to manifest between her brows when she looked up and saw me approaching. She folded the newspaper down with a snap and met me halfway.

Somewhere between thoughts of Jed—the way his shoulders hunched, chest noticeably concave, as though when Foster took his badge, they'd scooped most of the rest of him out along with it —and mixed feelings about being summoned by a wife who wasn't my wife, it occurred to me that Almena wasn't wearing one of her gloves.

As she reached up to investigate my nose, I reared back instinctively. We both glanced around to see if anyone had noticed my strange reaction, but the only people present were a woman with a port-wine stain on her neck sweeping near the entrance, and the hotel owner behind the front desk, too busy counting something out on his fingers and tallying it in a book to be concerned with our marital affairs.

Almena drew me back into the privacy of the corner, speaking low. "What was that about?"

"I don't want you getting hurt on my account."

Her smile appeared then disappeared, quick as sunlight

between the dark leaves of a tree. "I can touch without bruising, you know. I control it. You can't hurt me unless I let you."

She tried for me again, and again I leaned away, though less aggressively than before. Part of me wanted to feel proof of her concern—proof someone else in this world cared about me. Lilah surely didn't. And while I wasn't surprised to learn of Jed's sour grapes after what went down between us in Asher, his loathing still stung.

"I mean it, Almena. I earned this."

She held me fast by the arm while she used her free hand to probe the bridge of my nose, ignoring my wishes. When she touched on just the right spot, pain lanced out in sharp branches through my head. I gritted my teeth, showing my misery, not all of it owing to my nose. She let her hand fall, but not before tracing her thumb over a cut on my upper lip, which had also been caught by Jed's elbow. I felt it vanish, the tiny edge of pain gone in a second, and watched the cut curve across her own lip. Just couldn't help herself, could she?

"The nose is good and swollen, but I don't think it's broken. Should I ask to see the other fellow?" She smiled, trying to encourage my good humor. When I gave no indication of perking up, Almena switched to a frown. "All right. What is it? What aren't you telling me?"

Hell of a lot of things. My lip still buzzed from contact with her finger. "I think we should abandon Halverson."

"Please tell me you're joking."

"'fraid not."

Probably thinking I was merely suffering from nerves, Almena tried to reassure me, which might've been sweet, leaving aside the fact she was trying to talk me into robbing a bank. She talked about how everyone got cold feet the first time, and how everything would be fine if we just stuck to the plan...

I held up a hand. "I'm going to stop you there. Almena... Jed Strickland's here."

"The sheriff?"

I nodded. "Met him in the street. He was one of the men fighting, and he was drunk. Probably went looking for it."

"Is that why you were upstairs just now?" She stepped away. "You were with him?"

"Not in the way you're thinking, Almena. I'm not conspiring, if that's what's got you fearful."

"All right," she said, seeming to accept my word. I guessed maybe I was finally earning her trust. "Well, does he know about us?"

"He knows I'm here. Wager it won't be long before he discovers you, too.

"Shit," Almena said.

"Agreed."

Almena considered the situation for a moment, before shaking her head. "We can't quit Halverson. Not until we've done what we came here to do." She unfolded the newspaper in an angry crunch and thrust the front page at me. "See there?"

I read. "'Good business suits from 15 dollars. Pants from four—'"

"No. There." Her finger stabbed the page.

"'Reward of five-hundred dollars for the capture or killing of Almena Guillory and any Association.'" I stopped, looking up with a frown. Almena insisted I continue. "'Known by many as the Grizzly Queen of the West for her part in robberies across the greater plains territories, Guillory is described as being of medium height with a fair complexion, brown hair, and steely grey eyes. Acquaintances tell of the woman's cunning nature and canorous speech—' *Canorous.* That even a word?" I tried to make light, but truth was, my bad feeling was getting worse.

"Skip to the bottom."

I noticed the woman with the birthmark had moved her cleaning a little closer to us, quietly scraping the floor with the bristles of her broom. Eavesdropping, no doubt. Couldn't blame her. The hotel proprietor probably paid her for information pertaining to his guests, or anything else of profitable intrigue. Still, I cleared my throat and gave her a polite, but firm look that persuaded her to take her chores elsewhere.

"'The Helena Daily Herald says there is no truth in rumors that Guillory has moved her operations to Montana, from the fact that Guillory is now and has been for some time in Kansas. A short time ago Guillory was credited with a bloody robbery at the First National Bank in Baxter Springs, and more recently she and members of her gang were spotted robbing a train at a pass near Newton. It is the opinion of the Wichita Eagle that she, along with other members of her gang, have taken temporary residence in the area of Newton. On behalf of the governor of Kansas, the Eagle appeals to its readers for further information regarding known sightings of the outlaw and—'"

"They're heading to Ellsworth," Almena interrupted.

"Where's that written?"

"Don't be cute. They've been moving north since Baxter. With the amount of heat on them, it's not surprising. They'll spend some time in Ellsworth, and then probably make for Nebraska or Iowa."

I massaged my jaw. "How can you be so sure?"

"Because it's what I would do. Ellsworth is basically a northern Coffeyville. If they need a place to lie low, that's where they'll go. Don't you see what this means?" She cut her eyes toward the proprietor to make sure he wasn't suspicious about our prolonged conversation, and moved closer. "We know where they are now, Apostle. This is our chance. Maybe our last chance before they split the state. The money from this… endeavor will buy a lot of friends in Ellsworth, and trust me, we'll need a lot of

friends in that town. Especially if we're going to find my imper-
sonator and bring this whole thing to an end."

"And how exactly does this end, Almena? With you giving
her the second barrel? Swell. Then what?"

"Then I'll buy myself a drink."

"Will killing her make you happy? Will it put you at peace?"

Laughter spilled out of her like I'd said something funny. That
tipped me off. I glanced over in time to catch the proprietor
watching us. He smiled at us, and I returned the expression, albeit
leanly. Still smiling, Almena said, "What business is it of yours
whether I'm at peace or not?"

I shrugged and handed the newspaper back to her. "You do
what you've always done, you'll get what you've always got.
Maybe this is your chance for a clean break. To go a different way
than you've gone before."

"Same could be said for you, Apostle. You're wasted as a
lawman."

"How d'you figure?"

"I don't let just anyone ride with me." She paused, and I could
see her struggling against the instinct to run, gaze constantly
returning to the stairs. The fact she was taking time to address my
fears meant something—to me, at least. "If you're so worried, I'd
love to hear a better idea. The way I see it, this is our only option.
There's no way we get another chance at this in some other town
and meet the deadline of Ellsworth."

She wasn't wrong, though I desperately wished she was. "No,
I don't have a better idea."

"All right then. Let's go make a withdrawal."

CHAPTER TWENTY-ONE

The bank was the only truly formidable building in town, built out of strong poplar boards, and two stories as opposed to one. A thinly-roofed porch left a solid block of shadow over the doors, while the single-pane windows were covered from within with heavy red curtains, preventing any gawking passersby, or criminals looking to case the joint.

Almena simply walked in, no fuss.

There were no guards, no officers of the law standing around providing kind incentive for customers to behave. *Heck*, I thought. *No wonder these places are getting robbed all the time. They're low-hanging fruit.* I wondered where the town's sheriff had gotten himself off to after reprimanding Jed in the street, but wherever it was, it wasn't here. That was the important thing.

While Almena handled the act, I brought the horses around to the alley beside the bank, as agreed upon. It was plain, old-fashioned good luck that the building next door happened to be a feed store. I could mill about without drawing any suspicion. When a gentleman resembling one of those greasy carpet-baggers that plagued the South after the war asked me what my business was in Halverson, I made up some excuse about needing to have my horses shod. He then tried to sell me some kind of saddle polish, but I turned him away with a firm word. The man retreated with a rictus grin and a "good day to you, sir."

I stood holding the reins, half-resting my shoulder against the wall of the bank, and waited. Wasn't much else I could do at this point. I didn't bother tying the horses to the hitching rack, not wanting to have to untie them during our getaway. One of the animals snuffled, fat lips probing the nape of my neck. I turned around, patting the creature affectionately on the nose. She snorted a warm breath into the palm of my hand, throwing her head a little and inching forward a step.

"Easy," I soothed. "Easy now. Shouldn't be too much longer."

Busy keeping an eye on my horse, I didn't see the man staggering past the mouth of the alley until he started hollering.

"They're robbing the place!" Blood coursed down the curve of his cheek from a cut beneath his swollen right eye, and he kept yelling like his leg was on fire. "*They're robbing the bank!*"

Almena! I thought. Along with half a dozen words not meant for polite company.

Wait. *They?*

I tossed the reins over the hitching rack and started for him, but the carpet-bagger met the man ahead of me.

"What's that?" he asked, grabbing the injured man by the shoulder to steady him.

"Men. Robbers!" He was breathless with fear. "In the bank—"

"Slow down, and tell it to me straight. What men?"

Before he could reply, the carpet-bagger bent him forward, crushing his stomach onto a knife. The man's mouth still hung open with a response he'd never be able to give as his body fell towards me.

Son of a—I'd been mistaken before. He was no salesman, this man with the slicked-back hair and crocodile smile. He was another gang's *lookout*.

Which meant there was already another gang in the bank. With Almena.

As the injured man collapsed at my feet, the outlaw spotted me. I saw the flash of intention in his eyes, as he surely must've seen the same in mine. We drew at the same time, but the knife in his hand slowed him down, and my hammer struck first. I only clipped him in the shoulder, but he howled like a banshee. First time being shot, I wagered. If he was lucky, it'd be his last, but he seemed the type to court misfortune, given his choice of occupation.

I leaned down to check on the man who had been stabbed, see if there was anything I could do for him. The poor fellow was shaking and clutching himself, as if he could keep his insides from spilling out. A dark spot spread out from his trousers, and I didn't think it was blood.

"You're going to be all right." I laid a hand on his shoulder to keep him from trying to sit up. "Don't try to move."

"You—you think so?" he asked, blinking erratically. I could tell he wanted to believe me.

"I've seen men recover from a lot worse."

"Have you?"

I didn't tell him I'd seen men die from a lot less, too.

"I don't feel well," he mumbled. "I'm bleeding something awful, ain't I? This is an awful lot of blood. I mean, don't you think?"

"Yeah." I gave his shoulder a gentle squeeze. I wished I had time to do more for the man, but it didn't take a doctor to see he was fading fast. The wound was clearly fatal. Wasn't a whole lot I could do, even to make him comfortable. "I'm going to go fetch the doctor now," I lied. In truth, I had to see about the bank and Almena.

He stared up sightlessly, gaze soaring past me to the clouds, all those grey crumbs left by the storm. His expression began to sag.

"Robbers in the bank," the man murmured, and promptly expired.

Wasting no time, I rounded the corner, and in my haste caught the toe of my boot on the lip of the porch. That inconvenient stumble ended up saving my life. Just as I started to regain my balance, a bullet cracked into the thin wooden pillar near my head, where I'd been not a moment before. I leaned back, turning and firing—somewhat haphazardly—at the outlaw who'd managed to reach his piece again. He kept his barrel pointed at me with one eye shut, tongue between his teeth in concentration, but couldn't seem to hold it steady with his shoulder hurting him something fierce.

I missed. He fired again, but the shot went wide.

With the thin pylon at my back—poor cover was still better than no cover—I turned over my shoulder and gave him another round. This time, I didn't miss. The lookout slumped to the ground, and though his gun remained pointed at me, there was no longer any life in his fingers to pull the trigger.

I retrieved the weapon, anyway, to be on the safe side. Quickly opened the cylinder to check how many shots were left, and snapped the gate shut before tucking the gun safely into my belt.

By that time, another robber was emerging from the bank. He shuffled forward, a sleepwalker with bulging eyes, clutching his throat. An unmistakable gush of black flowed through the canyons between his fingers, telling me everything I needed to know about his condition. He was precisely the figure in mind when one referred to someone as a dead man walking.

I heard shouting and cursing in the brief moment before the door slipped closed again.

A few seconds later, the man fell down, dead.

My mind raced. It was possible Almena had managed to get a shot off at him in all the commotion—but then, it was just as likely Almena had suffered the wound and simply passed it on to him. My stomach dropped, the same feeling I'd experienced when I'd tripped. Imagining Almena taking one to the throat—the searing pain of that—

Nothing hurts anymore. Not for very long, anyway.

I remembered being shot. The initial agony felt like a small eternity. How many of those small eternities had Almena experienced in her lifetime? How much of her memory was merely flashes of pain?

Can you feel this?

Only a little. Feels nice, though.

Couldn't think about that right now. Couldn't think about her. In there. With them. Almena Guillory may have been one of the most capable persons I'd ever met, but even capable people suffered bad luck. I once knew a fella could shoot the hat off a nit and ride with the best of them. He ended up shot and killed by a boy of nine who'd been playing with his pa's loaded Seventeen. All it took was one lucky shot.

The urge to go in guns blazing surfaced in me like an old childhood injury acting up. I dragged in a breath. Told myself to slow down. Think.

Think.

There were probably hostages inside, innocent folk caught up in all this. Not to mention the unknown number of bandits. Experience told me I could expect at least a two-man team, if not more. Much as I wanted to burst through the front door and make a quick end of it, I knew doing so would be like as to get me killed. But I couldn't just stand around and do nothing.

"What's all the commotion out here?" This from an elderly gentleman emerging from the feed store. He wore a faded green apron and was still in the process of wiping his hands off on it. He also had on the smallest spectacles I'd ever seen, like two coins balanced across his nose. "Thought I heard some gunshots…" His eyes settled on my piece, but he didn't look terribly surprised, or afraid. "Shit, son. You planning on doing something with that?"

"No, sir. I mean, yes, but I'm a U.S. Marshal. I'm afraid your bank's being robbed."

He squinted toward the bank. "Is it? Looks all right to me."

"Why don't you go on back inside, sir? Better yet, would you mind fetching the sheriff and a few boys? Tell 'em the bank's being robbed and they should bring guns."

"Sure can. *Martha!*" he hollered back into the store. I glanced anxiously over my shoulder at the bank, but no more ruffians had come out since the dying one. "*I'm going to get the sheriff!*

"*The sheriff? Why?*" returned a scratchy female voice.

"*The bank's being robbed!*"

"*The bank's being what?*"

"*Being robbed!*"

"By who?" Martha finally appeared on the threshold of Marl's Feed and Animal Supply, one hand on the doorframe for support. She wore a matching apron, though hers was decorated with little white frills on the hem.

"Hell if I know, woman," the elderly man—presumably Marl —answered, untying his apron and hanging it over the banister. "I'm just letting you know so you don't wonder where I've up and gotten off to. Tell Tim to mind the counter."

"I can mind it myself, thank you. Who's this?" Her gaze swung to me.

"Says he's a marshal."

"Is he? Did you tell him about the trouble we've been having with Arnie refusing to pay his bills?"

"Sir; ma'am," I interjected, already five steps into the alley. "The sheriff, please."

I maneuvered around the back of the building with my piece

out and ready, searching for an unlocked window, or better yet a rear exit. Most banks had one, allowing the employees a quick escape should a robbery occur. If I found such an entrance, I could get the drop of the bandits. Maybe force them to release any hostages and surrender peaceably. The dream of every lawman— except for maybe Prough. Wade liked it when they tried to throw down on him. I told him he'd like it a lot less the day they actually succeeded in killing him.

The door was there, all right, but it was locked tight. For good measure, I gave the knob a few turns and tugs, but I could tell it wasn't going anywhere unless forced. I didn't need to put my ear to the door to hear inside either; two voices were going at it, talking over each other.

The door was designed to open out, not in, meaning it was hopeless trying to bust it in. Still, I had to try something. I kicked at the area nearest the jamb, hoping to meet some wretched wood, but the door was solid as a boulder, gave not even a little, and I damn near broke my foot in the attempt.

On the bright side, I heard footfalls as someone approached the door. I stepped back, raising my gun. There was a pause. More yelling. The tumblers clicked in the lock.

The door creaked open a crack. "Jimmy?"

I aimed low when I fired, wanting to injure, not kill, whoever stood on the other side. The usual cussing ensued, followed by the sound of boots tottering backwards across the wooden floor. Yanking the door open, I slammed the butt of my gun into the man's head, knocking him out cold and clearing my way inside.

Somewhere, farther into the bank, I heard Almena laugh. "I guess it wasn't Jimmy."

CHAPTER TWENTY-TWO

My hands sweated against the cold iron of my gun as I stepped over the body of the unconscious doorman and entered the back of the bank.

I emerged behind the teller's cage, protected by a half inch of cheap steel fencing and its splintering wood frame. Never before had I given thought to how frankly useless the cage was as a defense against crime, but I considered it now. That tiny grate had suddenly become the only thing between me and a reception of bullets.

I led with my gun, coming around the door. "Federal marshal!" I announced. There was no point in being subtle now.

"*Marshal!*"

Who should be on the other side of the teller's desk but my dear ole friend Dante Casella, pacing near the windows. He greeted me with the feral grin of a cat, but I'd have to have been some kind of stupid to believe that smile meant he was happy to see me. He peeked at me from one open eye behind the sights of a Winchester. "We must stop meeting like this. It is uncivil."

"Almena," I called to her. "You all right?"

"Just shoot him," she called back from behind the counter at the far end of the bank, where the teller's cage made a hard right turn into the wall.

Casella shook his head, flinging two sweaty strands of hair from his eyes. "Is that any way to talk to an admirer, Miss Guillory? You know, I have followed your career for some time. All I ever wanted was the chance to ride with you." There was an actual note of disappointment in his voice, enhanced by his accent —Italian, I suspected. "I suppose it was not to be."

"You sure have a strange way of showing admiration, holding the lady hostage," I said.

"She killed two of my men. One, she did in with a pistol. Fair enough. She is quite a capable marksman, is she not? But the second..." His cheek twitched. Nerves. "He made the mistake of shooting her, you see."

"And she didn't take kindly to it, I assume."

Casella glancing toward Almena. "You hear rumors about the Grizzly Queen. That she once clawed a man to death. That, like a bear, she consumes the flesh of her victims." I wondered if Almena had heard that last one. I surely hadn't, and I couldn't imagine she'd started it herself. Knowing her as I did, the story seemed unlikely. Not the least on account of her being more of a cornbread-and-beans gal. "And, of course, the rumor that she cannot be killed."

"Casella, are you holding anyone else in here?" From where I stood, there were a couple blind spots, places he could be hiding more men or hostages. I needed an answer, not a lengthy monologue about Almena's peculiarity.

But Casella seemed lost in his narrative, face straining with incredulity, and he ignored my question. "Jude shot her through the throat. She merely *touched* him, and his neck exploded as if he'd turned the gun on himself. I ask you, Marshal: how is such a thing possible?"

"Almena, is there anyone else with you?"

"He's got one man crouched behind the counter there—"

"Shut up!" Casella barked at her.

"And a teller and his boy with him," she continued as if he hadn't spoken. "There was another teller, but he got away."

Casella gritted his teeth, but didn't try reprimanding her again. Seemed he couldn't decide whether to be afraid of Almena, frustrated with the woman's stubbornness, or impressed by her grit. I knew the feeling.

"Afraid he didn't get away, after all," I said, recalling the waiting gaze of the dead man lying in the alleyway. Then, to Casella, "Your lookout stuck him, but don't go thinking you have help coming neither. I took care of him."

"Meaning you shot him," Casella said.

"He gave me no choice. I'm hoping you're a more reasonable sort."

"Make me an offer."

"Put your gun down, and have your man do the same. Let Miss Guillory and the teller go, and maybe I don't let the good folks of Halverson string you up." Regardless of how this went, if he came out of it alive, I'd do my best to prevent a lynching—but he didn't know that. Didn't need to. Better he think the hat I wore was a shade of grey.

The outlaw gave a dry, scratchy laugh that made me want to fetch him a glass of water. "That's not an offer, Marshal. That sounds like an ultimatum."

"You killed a man and tried to rob a federal bank. It's the best I can do under the circumstances. Now, throw down your weapon."

"*I* didn't kill him. You said it yourself, Jimmy did. And you killed Jimmy."

"That don't make things square, if that's what you're getting at."

"You're responsible for what your men do when they ride for you," Almena added. "You know that, Casella. Don't play dumb."

I took a step forward. "I've already sent for the sheriff. In a few minutes, this place is going to be surrounded by some very angry men with guns. If you and your man lay down your weapons now, I can bring you out, under the protection of the United States government…"

"Is that right?" I wondered if Casella's arms were getting tired, holding up that rifle. Beads of sweat rested in the crunch of his brow, and he licked his lips. "I don't see a badge. How am I supposed to be sure you are even a lawman anymore? I was there in Coffeyville when you put the hurt on that boy."

I took another subtle step forward. I hoped to reach the door separating me from the service area, if only to put something more tangible between myself and the outlaw. Backward letters showed through the opaque glass at eye level: *Employees Only*. If I put a round through the glass, would it slow the bullet down? Chances were good it'd still be a killing shot—though that was true whether the bullet in question was going or coming.

"Ah!" Casella shook his rifle at me. "Ah, ah. Stay where you are. You, too." The look he threw Almena, dirty as a barn rag, made me wonder how many times she'd tried to pull one over on him before I arrived. In fact, I wondered why she wasn't making an attempt to escape now. Surely it wasn't getting shot she was afraid of.

A teller and his boy.

Someone banged on the door of the bank, causing Casella to flinch and almost turn around. He straightened out, but not before I'd taken another two steps toward the door. The knob was now within reach, but I wasn't sure how fast I could pull it open, line up a shot, and fire. Maybe not fast enough.

"Whoever's in there, come out right now," came the sheriff's voice. He sounded a little more awake than when I'd met him earlier in the day. Maybe he'd found the body of the poor teller in the alley. He surely couldn't have missed the lookout I'd left on the street.

"Seems we've arrived at an impasse, Casella," I said.

"I could always shoot you."

"Could do. But then there'd be no one to stop the mob outside from finishing the job the Baxter men started in Coffeyville." He flipped his head again to get those two strands of sweaty hair out of his face. "Come on now. You don't strike me as a fool. Am I wrong?"

"Marshal? You in there?" The sheriff again.

With a sharp nod, Casella gestured for his partner to come forward. He dragged the teller's boy with him, holding him by the scruff of the neck, a shiny derringer threatening the boy's throat. Small as the piece was, it'd do the job. The boy panted with fear, his eyes round as dinner plates. His father called out, pleadingly, for Casella's man not to harm the child.

"Please. Please, he's my only son. He's a good boy. Please—"

At the same moment, Almena shot to her feet. There was a red mark at her throat that had replaced the fading rope burn, and her cheek was swollen to twice its size just below her left eye. I clenched my jaw, easing off the trigger, if only because I was afraid I'd do something stupid.

"You touch one hair on his head, and I swear to God, Casella, I will end you," Almena threatened. Casella swung his rifle toward her, backing up a step. The muzzle waited mere inches from the point of her nose, but you wouldn't have known it by the fierce set of her mouth and the fearlessness in her eyes.

"I imagine it might be difficult with a few bullets in your head," Casella said.

"You've seen what I can do, Dante. You really want to test me?"

He continued to watch her but spoke to me. "Here is what's

going to happen, Marshal. You are going to put that pretty pistol of yours down, and any other weapons you have. You are going to come with me, and we are going to walk out of here together."

"With me as your hostage," I concluded.

"And the boy. Just as a little added insurance. Once we get some distance away, I'll release him, unharmed. You have my word."

I noticed he made no mention of my own fate.

"Bullshit," Almena said.

"How do I know you'll honor your word?" I asked.

"You can't be considering this."

"You will just have to take it on faith," Casella answered me. "So, what do you say, Marshal?"

My mother used to tell me stories about brave, honorable men, hoping it'd rub off on me. I like to think some of it did. Since stepping foot into the bank, I'd been hoping for some sudden burst of inspiration like in the stories, but seemed I was less creative than those noble heroes. Weren't no chandelier I could crash upon the villains' heads, no barrel full of gunpowder conveniently placed to explode. There was simply a boy's life, his father's life, Almena's life—and mine. I had to choose.

"All right," I agreed. "I'm going to come through the door now, and set the gun down there on the floor."

"Slowly," Casella warned while pressing the gun against Almena's chest.

"No need for that," I said in a hard voice.

"Apostle." Almena gripped my arm urgently as I went by her, prepared to step out in front of Casella. "He's going to kill you."

"I reckon he'll try," I answered, "but no man's managed yet. Or woman."

Her hand lingered—until Dante grabbed me backwards by my jacket.

"Not through the front," he said with some exasperation. "Out the back."

"They could be covering the back, too," I pointed out.

"Perhaps, but we know for certain they are out front. Now, *move*."

CHAPTER TWENTY-THREE

The saddlebags, stuffed with bonds and cash, slapped against the horse's flank as we departed Halverson. We got maybe a few miles outside of town before one of the animals threw a shoe and Casella's man was forced to stop to survey the damage.

I sat atop my borrowed horse while Casella kept behind me on his own mount, making sure I was within shooting distance as we rode. On the horse with the bad hoof, the teller's boy slouched forward in the saddle without another body to prop him up. He watched everything with a dull, tired expression, unable to maintain a constant state of fear. I gave him a small smile when he glanced my way, hoping to reassure him some, but he didn't return it.

"Well?" Casella asked hurriedly.

"Not good." The man grunted. "She's not going to get anywhere fast."

"We're far enough out," I said. We'd made a wide loop around the town to mislead any would-be pursuers before taking off at a high lope, and now Halverson wasn't even a speck in the distance. Any light you'd have seen from it at night was invisible against the harsh glow of the sun going down. "Why don't you let the boy go? Give him the lame horse, he can walk her back."

The man looked to his boss. Casella rolled his fingers along the handle of his piece, seeming to consider it. "You know how to get back from here?" he asked the boy.

It was a reasonable question, given that we'd abandoned the trail and veered into wild country almost as soon as the bank disappeared beneath the hip of the horizon.

The boy nodded. "Yes, sir."

"Go on, then." Casella gestured vaguely. "Get out of here. Wait."

The boy waited, hanging off the side of the horse, one hand still clutching the saddle horn. I itched for a weapon. From here, I had no way of defending the child if Casella went back on his word. My mouth went prickly with dread.

"Mark, get the bags first," Casella said. "Throw them onto the marshal's horse."

Casella didn't bother to hop down and lend a hand, not even when it probably would've made things go faster. Instead, while Mark slaved over the load, Casella remained on his horse, sitting comfortably above his colleague's struggles, like a plantation overseer. The comparison made me dislike him just a bit more.

Meanwhile, I was made to get down and stand aside with the boy. He was tall for his age, with light hair and a smattering of freckles that left him looking like he'd been out playing in the fields and needed to wash up. Reminded me of all the times I came in after a day spent tromping around the farm, when my mother would cluck, tip my chin up, lick her thumb, and attempt to scrub the filth from my cheeks.

"Is it true?" the boy asked me, while we watched Mark huff and puff, piqued even in the shoddy heat of the evening. Someone was out of shape.

I looked down at the boy. "Suppose that depends on the question."

"Are you really a marshal?"

"Last I checked."

He seemed skeptical. "If you're a marshal, why don't you have a badge?"

I thought about what I should tell him, the truth versus what would satisfy his curiosity. "I let someone borrow it."

His brow wrinkled. "You can do that?"

"Probably not," I admitted.

The boy moved his puckered lips around in thought. I tried not to smile. Suspected he wasn't aware of the childish tic, and wouldn't take kindly to my amusement. He seemed like such a serious child. "Are you famous?"

"There's a question. How might I qualify that?"

"Well, you can tell me your name, and I can tell you whether I've heard of you."

"Sounds fair. Name's Apostle Richardson."

He opened his mouth. "*The* Apostle Richardson?"

"You've heard of me?" Pride wasn't something I liked to indulge in, being a deadly sin and all, but I couldn't deny that I was tickled by the idea of having my name recognized in the Territories, or even just Kansas, synonymous with law and order.

The boy cracked the first smile I'd seen from him. "No, but you should have seen your face just now."

Yep. I liked this kid.

"What about you? What's your name?"

"Charles. Charles Wilmott. You wouldn't have heard of me, either, I expect." He stared sullenly at the ground.

"Maybe one day," I said, and he looked back up at me.

I tried not think it, but the thought came anyway. *He's got the same color eyes as Lilah.* Golden brown, albeit guileless, where hers had always been thoughtful, and sometimes sad, like the world was constantly disappointing her and she didn't know what to do about it. *Or maybe it was just me who was disappointing her*. Charles was far older than any child we could've had when we were together, but still, I imagined our boy might've looked something like him. A lump came to my throat. Regret resurfaced at the oddest of times.

Mark finished his task after a few minutes, not without exchanging a few words with Casella I didn't hear—I assumed it was probably less than friendly encouragement for him to hurry up. When it was all done, Casella motioned for the boy. "All right. Come on."

Charles looked at me, as if for permission that it was indeed all right. I nodded. "Go on. Get back to your father now. He's probably worried sick."

He started walking, but stopped and glanced back at me with those Lilah-colored eyes. "What's going to happen to you?" he asked in his high-pitched child's voice, full of anxiety.

"I'll be fine. They'll probably just rough me up a little. Don't you worry about me."

Mark offered the boy the reins to the lame horse, and Charles obediently took them. With growing relief, I watched the boy and the horse turn back toward Halverson. He looked back a couple times, as if we might disappear on him, or worse. But Casella just sat frowning and sweating, contemplating the back of his horse's head. Mark appeared occupied with adjusting one of the saddlebags.

I stood watching Charles the whole time, so I didn't see Casella quietly draw his pistol.

Instead, I stared, first in confusion, then in horror, as the boy was laid flat by a single bullet to the back of the head, never knowing what hit him. It almost looked as if he'd simply tripped and fallen forward, but I knew better. His hand still clutched the reins as he collapsed, yanking the horse's head down. The horse tried to rear; probably smelling the blood.

"*No!*" I yelled, or I think I did. I must've done. However, it came too late.

My ears were still ringing when I turned toward Casella. He'd already turned his gun on me, but I launched myself at him, miraculously reaching him before he fired. I took hold of his suspenders and dragged him from his horse. A sharp pain exploded in my shoulder, but I ignored it in favor of slamming a fist into the outlaw's face, as many times as I could before he started to give some back.

We wrestled over the gun. I heard the soft click of the hammer rolling back again. Slapping my hand down on the wrist holding the gun, I turned my whole body around on top of the man and took his arm with me. Pulled until a bone crunched, maybe his elbow or his wrist. Casella blasted me with such hollering as could raise the dead.

At that moment, Mark stepped back from the saddlebag, and I glimpsed his pistol.

So they were both in on the plan to kill me from the start. I wasn't surprised. Only sorry their bloodlust had involved the boy.

When Casella fired in a moment of flailing panic, I aimed his gun for Mark and put one between the outlaw's eyes before he could do boo about it. I used my free hand to cock Casella's gun and forced him to fire it once more at his partner's chest, for good measure. *He's out*, I thought, dimly aware of the carrying capacity of the revolver. Though that didn't mean he wasn't carrying spare ammunition, or that he couldn't use the empty piece as a bludgeoning tool.

Before I could rip the weapon from his grip, Casella got his other arm free from beneath my knee and boxed my ear, throwing me off of him. I suddenly found myself facedown, head pounding, and jagged grass poking at my eyes.

"I had no choice," Casella said, the same moment his hands came around my neck. "He saw both our faces, and he could've told the town what direction we'd gone—"

"He was… just a boy," I choked out.

"Rough world we live in." His hold tightened, bringing a slight fuzziness to the corners of my vision. "Isn't it?"

"Only on account… of men *like you*."

I slammed my head back, creating a new point of agony between us. But it was enough—enough to send him sprawling backwards, anyway. He held his nose and cursed me in what I guessed was Italian. Gasping and coughing, I clutched feebly at the ground, trying to drag myself away from him. Catch my breath. Just needed to catch my breath. I touched the skin at the base of my throat, fingers coming away with dots of crimson where his filthy, unclipped fingernails had drawn blood. I could still feel them digging into my flesh. I coughed a few more times.

My reprieve lasted only seconds before Casella's hands burrowed into my hair, and he yanked my head back, exposing the vulnerable line of my neck. I imagined my Adam's apple bobbing like a lure as I swallowed.

Before Casella brought his knife to my throat, I reached up and grabbed onto his shoulders, digging my thumbs into his pits, and gaining what I hoped would be enough leverage to flip him over me.

At least, that was the plan.

My gunshot filled my shoulder with white-hot pain, and I only performed the maneuver partway. I extricated myself from the mess of tangled limbs, scrabbling to my feet, and when he reached to grab me, I kicked out at his face with the heel of my boot. I'm ashamed to admit, his obscene cry gave me that same visceral jolt of pleasure you get from hearing bacon sizzling. It wasn't enough, but it was a start.

When I finally had the chance to look him straight on, I saw he'd dropped his knife. That alone filled me with the confidence to tackle him again.

"He was just a boy, you *son of a bitch*," I said. Those words, *he was just a boy*, were the only words that made sense in the whole wide world. The only truth I had. I latched onto them like a drowning man to a piece of driftwood, floating down the current of my anger.

If Casella said something then, I didn't hear it.

Too busy driving my knuckles into his jaw.

We wrestled a little more, rolling over one another, hitting and grabbing and scratching, like a pair of rabid dogs. Blood dripped into my eyes. I don't know how long this went on, us tussling in the middle of nowhere, but finally, I got the upper hand. I sat on his stomach, pinning both of his arms beneath my legs, and proceeded to pummel his face into pulp.

I kept on roaring, "*He was just a boy!*"

"Stop," he pleaded, but I didn't hear him.

No, that's not true.

I heard him.

I didn't care.

"P-please..." Teeth dribbled from his mouth, along with the blood. And as he looked up at me, I swore he was *grinning*, even with his cut lip and messed-up teeth. And suddenly, he looked so much like the man who'd come to Topeka and smiled at my wife, I couldn't bear it.

And I couldn't stop.

"*He*"—right fist—"*was*"—left fist—"*just*"—right —"*a*"—left—"*boy*!"

———

He's just a boy, Nathaniel. Leave him out of this.

He'll be a man soon enough, and I'll be damned if he grows up showing such disrespect to his father.

I wasn't being disrespectful, sir. Honest.

Nathan. Don't say another word.

I'm the judge of that, and I say you were.

Nathaniel, please. He didn't mean anything.

Get out of the way, Sarah.

For God's sake, Nathaniel! He's just a boy!

———

I watched Casella's head go back and forth with every punch, feeling nothing.

Nothing at all. Except maybe rage, which at first, felt hot and righteous and rang out in my head like a battle cry, *this is for Charles, and this, and this,* but in the end, it burned fast, like molten iron rushing into my hollow shape.

"*Apostle!*" Almena's voice tore into me like a whip, and I suddenly snapped back into myself so quickly I felt I was gonna be sick. How she'd found us, I wasn't sure. Maybe it was some magic power she'd neglected to tell me about, or maybe, more likely, she'd guessed Casella's route, given how closely it resembled the one she and I had planned to take.

Almena jumped down from her horse and silently assessed the scene, her gaze traveling from me to Casella, beaten, bloody, and breathing wetly, before finally landing on the bodies of Mark and Charles. She seemed to understand in mere seconds all the events my mind was still struggling to make sense of.

"That's enough," Almena told me, and I wasn't sure what she meant until I looked down at Casella, who'd done passed out. He wasn't dead, but had I landed a few more punches…

I lowered my fists and fell backwards, landing hard, bile lurching into my throat. I'd almost just killed a man. Almost beaten him to death with my bare hands, naked before God in my fury, Cain revisited. All that black anger I'd inherited from my father had finally unleashed, and I hadn't held back, hadn't even tried to fight it.

I heard the soft crunch of Almena's boots as she approached. "Is the boy—?" she started to ask, leaving out the crucial word. I nodded, eyes closed. "And the money?"

"Run off," I told her, my voice thick. All of this, for *money*.

"I'll take care of Casella," she said, already turning the unconscious bandit over so she could tie him up. "See to the boy."

See to the boy. Of course. *Charles.* I had to take him home.

Shakily, I rose. I managed maybe two steps before my legs buckled and I dropped back to my knees. A warm breath escaped my lips, half a sob. I squeezed my eyes shut. Not now. Not *now*. Charles was what was important here. I could wrestle with my ghoulish morality later.

"Apostle." Almena spoke my name quietly, with more compassion than I deserved just then. There was a question there, but I wasn't ready to answer, so I pretended I didn't hear her.

On my feet and holding my shoulder, I limped towards the boy. The boy's body, I should say. Charles himself—his personality, his character, everything that made him *him*—that was all gone.

I crouched and rolled the boy onto his back. There was a small hole beneath his right eye where the bullet had gone straight through. His expression still held relief, safe in the knowledge that he'd soon be back in Halverson with his father. *At least it was quick.*

I kept seeing his face, that last time he looked back at me, questioning. *Is it safe?* That's what he'd wanted to know. I'd encouraged him with my staying put, my silence, and the small smile I'd given him. I'd as good as promised him it was.

As I lifted Charles into my arms, I was surprised by his lightness. I'd moved sacks of potatoes with more weight. Even still, I struggled to get to my feet. The bullet was still in my shoulder, and I damn sure felt it. Each time I got Charles into my arms and tried to set off, my injuries acted up, sending such a wave of pain through me I feared I'd pass out. I staggered and stumbled, and sometimes had to stop entirely, lay the boy down again until the dizziness passed. Startled by the gunshots, the horses had fled, even the one that'd thrown a shoe. I could see her in the middling distance. Might as well have been all the way in California for how far it felt. Almena's horse was closer, but she was already throwing Casella over its flank.

As I ventured toward the other horse, I talked to him a little— Charles. Apologized for what'd happened to him on my watch, and for my bumbling efforts now, including my blood ruining his fine white shirt. My tears splattered his face, almost in lieu of his own. I was sorry for that, too.

"Almost there," I said, hoisting Charles up into the saddle. He immediately tipped over the side, and I couldn't catch him quickly enough. His body put up a little puff of dust when it hit.

I wanted to give up. Just give up and sit down and…

I don't know what would've come next.

Instead, I went around and picked Charles up again, hissing through my teeth as I laid him over the saddle by the stomach. It allowed me enough time to get my boot in the stirrup and lift myself up. Once seated, I had an easier job of keeping the boy in the saddle. I cradled Charles in the crook of my arm. His head lulled like a doll's, and I could almost imagine he was sleeping. How many times had his own father experienced this feeling as he took a turn rocking him to sleep as a babe, or taught him how to ride?

"Lord," I breathed, though I wasn't sure whether I was entreating him for help, or taking his name in vain.

I kicked the horse's flank and told her to walk on.

CHAPTER TWENTY-FOUR

F or obvious reasons, we couldn't stay in Halverson after that. Leaving aside Almena's tense relationship with the law, I was, you could say, a touch removed from the decision-making process, mindless with something resembling grief, possibly shock or guilt. Tears flowed over my cheeks when I thought of Charles, and for the life of me, I couldn't stop thinking about that moment right before the gun went off.

The rest of the night passed in flashes, like the hard strobe of a lighthouse. I remembered reaching town, Charles's father taking the boy from my arms, and then later, the doctor thrusting hot pliers into my wound, withdrawing a tiny chunk of lead, and depositing it with a soft clink into a metal bowl. Other moments I expect I imagined. Like Almena holding a cold cloth to my fore-head, speaking gently while I shook, feverish. The warm, soothing press of her hand on my bruised jaw. The next day, the doc expressed amazement at the rate of my recovery, but I knew it was no miracle. That same morning, I noticed Almena holding herself a little stiffly when she walked.

We left as soon as I was able, making for a town just north, a place to lie low and recover from our spoiled plan. We rented a room and took turns sleeping, though I judged by the position of the sun that Almena was letting her shifts go long.

"Where's your hat?" she asked me during one shift change.

"Must've lost it in the scuffle with Casella."

"We'll get you a new one in Ellsworth."

"I don't want a new hat, Almena." I sat on the edge of the bed, my hands dangling between my knees.

"Really? You seemed pretty attached to the old one…"

"That's not what I mean. Of course I'll need a new one, at some point. I just… it's not… I'm…" I sealed my mouth in frustration and shook my head.

Almena came and sat next to me. "You're still sore over what happened with that boy." Her hand came to rest on the mattress between us. "It wasn't your fault."

"I know."

"You did what you could."

"I know what I did. Look, I appreciate what you're trying to do and all, but with respect…"

"With respect, what?" I looked up to find her crooking an eyebrow at me. "With respect, I don't know what it's like to kill a man, or watch boys die senselessly in the mud? You forget who you're talking to, Marshal."

"You're right. Sorry."

Her gaze shot up to the ceiling, visibly annoyed. "For God's sake, don't apologize." She sighed. "Apostle. *Nathan*," she corrected and quickly looked away. Like just the act of speaking my given name was too intimate. I had to agree, her use of it did make the room feel close. "You've been so damn quiet since Halverson… it's like I'm traveling with a ghost. I hate to say it, but I miss your chatter."

I forced a smile, but instead of making me feel better, it smashed my resolve to be stoic and private about the whole matter. Almena seemed doggone determined to pry that last stone loose, the one holding back the flood.

"Talk to me," she whispered. "Say something."

I scrubbed at my forehead like it was dirty, dragging in a shaky breath. I didn't know what to do with my hands. My own gestures felt foreign and strange, awkward as when I was a boy growing into gangly limbs. "You didn't see it. Casella shot that boy down in cold blood, and I came too close to killing him for it. I wasn't myself… or maybe I was. That's the worst of it. I don't know. Maybe that's who I am underneath it all, just another brute with a badge."

"You're more than just the worst thing you've done. And besides, God forgives," she added awkwardly, "or isn't that what you keep trying to tell me?"

"Suppose it's easier being on the other side of that conversation."

"Suppose it is," she said, adopting the cadence of my speech again with a smirk.

"I just keep thinking…"

"Stop. Casella would have killed you. You were defending yourself."

"But I should've stopped sooner. If you hadn't of come along, don't know what would've happened. That scares me." I'd never wanted violence to be my way, spent my whole life trying to avoid becoming a man who spoke with his fists, yet I couldn't seem to keep from stumbling into conflict. Clearly, I'd gone into the wrong line of work.

"You're overthinking this. Some men need a bullet. That's just how it is."

"If that's how you feel, why didn't you give him one?"

"I don't know. Maybe you're rubbing off on me."

I let out a cold laugh. "Like I believe that."

It was a mean thing to say, but Almena didn't seem to take no offense from it. Instead, she rose and went to the small pack of belongings she'd brought with her from her house, which I guessed was mostly filled with ammunition. Meanwhile, I reviewed my return to Halverson, as I'd done continually since we'd left. It was a scab I couldn't stop picking at, refused to let heal.

"You know, he thanked me," I said while she rummaged.

I thought maybe Almena didn't know who I was talking about, but then she said, "I know. I was there."

"I brought him his dead son, and the man *thanked* me."

"He was grateful. You gave him the opportunity to bury his boy. That matters."

"Would you have thanked me? If it was your son I'd brought back?"

"No."

"Would you have blamed me?"

"Absolutely." Almena returned to the bed, sitting closer than before. "But I've always been partial to the rending of garments and gnashing of teeth." She was holding something in her hands, but I couldn't see what it was until she took my hand, folding my gold marshal's star into it. The sharp corners of the badge laid flat in my palm. "Grief has a way of changing the color of the world, making everything seem black and white when it's not. If you aren't careful, you can lose yourself in those shades of grey."

"My badge." I gawped at her. "But I gave this to Mireia."

"Mireia's father didn't feel comfortable with his daughter having a marshal's star. He thought someone might get the wrong idea and suspect he killed a lawman and stole it off his corpse. I promised him I'd give it back to you."

"Why now?"

"Because right now, I think you need the reminder."

I stared down at the star in my hands, dazzled by its familiar contours, and what it meant for my future. Almena's hand slid onto the back of my neck, hesitant at first, but when I didn't pull away, her fingers began to move, gently managing my tension. I had to fight the desire not to close my eyes like a dog being scratched behind the ears, relaxed by her ministrations.

"You're a good man, Apostle Richardson, but even good men sometimes have to do bad in defense of what's right," she said, low into my ear. "Be careful you don't forget that because once you start seeing yourself as a monster, it's hard to stop from becoming one."

"What happened to *you're wasted as a lawman*? Seems like the whole time we've been together you've been trying to convince me to put on the black hat."

"I changed my mind."

"About being an outlaw?"

"About you. You were willing to give up your life in that bank. Not just for me, I know, but let's be honest here. You've got too much martyr in you. I almost wonder if you're not just hunting for the right cause to die for. Or the right person."

Truth was, I'd sometimes wondered the same thing. If some part of me had a death wish. If being a marshal was my round-about way of getting out. Was I some paragon of goodness like everyone believed, or was I just very good at not being my father? If he'd been a better man, would I have been a worse one?

"It's not a critique," Almena continued. "Hell, it's one of the things I like about you. You always try to see the good in people. Sometimes that's frustrating, but other times, it's like I'm listening to someone discuss a book I've already read. Your perspective is completely different. Part of me wants to tell you you're seeing things all wrong, but the other part... wants only to be quiet and listen. The world you see is so much more beautiful than mine, Nathan. It offers hope and consolation and justice for those who deserve it. When I'm with you, I almost see it again, that world of possibility. I remember what it was like to believe in people, and I don't want you to lose that."

I was silent, listening, trying to take in what she was saying, but I couldn't keep myself from hearing what she wasn't saying, too. *I don't want you to turn into me.* Emotion pressed the silence that followed into something hard and uncomfortable, until, embarrassed, Almena finally got up. I grabbed her hand, keeping her with me a moment longer.

"You aren't locked into this lifestyle, Almena. You don't have to continue like this."

She gave me a narrow look but didn't pull away. "Sometimes you get in a thing so deep, you can't turn back. I wouldn't expect you to understand."

"Haven't you ever felt sorry?" Suddenly it was very important I know whether she regretted the crimes she'd committed. "About what you done, I mean. After the war."

"There you go again, looking for the best in people," Almena said, but it wasn't a denial. After another moment, she nodded sharply in the direction of the window. "You know, there's a small church near the miller's place. Little place with yellow doors. I saw it when we rode in. We have a few hours until we need to leave. If you want to go… I won't stop you."

The idea of being in a church right then filled me with terrible apprehension. All the more reason I knew I should go.

"Thought you didn't believe in God," I said, as a way of stalling my decision.

Almena smiled wistfully and rolled her shoulders. "I don't. But I know you. I know what you need right now is to make peace with your Redeemer. So, by all means, if it'll make you a little less mopey, go." She gave a little flap of her hands.

"I'm"—I paused to clear my throat—"thank you. Not sure a building's what I need right now, though I wouldn't turn my nose up to reading a little out of the Good Book. Don't suppose you're carrying a copy in your bag of goodies there?"

"You'll be shocked to learn I'm not, but I can go downstairs and see if the owner has one he'd be willing to lend you."

"No need. I can do it." I started to stand.

She placed her hands on each of my shoulders, pressing me back down to the mattress. "For once in your life, Apostle, let someone do something for you."

"Much obliged," I answered stiffly.

"Stay and rest up. I'll be back in a minute."

———

In fact, she didn't return for ten, but just as I was starting to worry, she came through the door and closed it softly behind her.

"I was starting to wonder if you'd gotten lost," I joked.

Almena wordlessly handed me the Bible. Its binding bore no wrinkles, and the ink on the pages was still crisp and black. There was no handwriting or personal inscriptions in it, save for a small stamp that read *Property of The Cattlewick Hotel.*

"What is it?" I asked, questioning Almena's nervous silence.

"Prough the Rough's dead."

"What?" I nearly dropped the Bible.

"Some men downstairs were talking about it. Apparently, a lawman was shot and killed in a shootout with the Guillory gang near here, yesterday in Emporia. They gave his name as Wade Prough. Prough the Rough. Wasn't he one of the men you traveled with?"

"Yes. He was my friend, but… Wade would never be so stupid as to get himself—"

What was I going to say? *Shot*? *Killed*?

I swallowed and clenched my eyes shut, bowing my head.

Except he would. Wade would be stupid. Or he'd be slow in

his old age. And we both knew he wasn't a man to render up the ghost without the help of a bullet. It'd taken more than forty years to get here, but it'd come all the same.

"I'm sorry, Apostle," Almena said, and she sounded it too, though she had no reason to shed tears over the death of one of her enemies. One less lawman could only benefit her in the long run.

No, that was an unworthy thought.

"Was there any mention of a young man with him?" I asked, looking up suddenly. "Boy by the name of Du Pont?"

She shook her head. "None that I heard."

"Emporia. That's not far from here. They're moving east, not west." Almena's mouth was tight with tension. She chewed on her fingernail. "You were wrong. They're not going to Ellsworth."

"Doesn't seem likely, no. Your friend must have spooked her. My guess is they're probably headed for Missouri now. Or maybe a train in Topeka."

"You think they'd risk it?"

"I don't know!" Almena flared. "I'm not a fucking psychic."

"But if you had to guess. If you had to stake your life on it— where would you go? *Think*, Almena."

"I am thinking! What do you imagine I've been doing this whole time? Twiddling my thumbs?"

"*Where?*"

"Topeka," she decided after another moment.

"Why?"

"There are more people in Topeka. It'd be easier to blend in. Disappear. If the marshals are looking for a gang on the run, staying put in a city as big as Topeka is the safest way to hide."

"Topeka," I repeated, looking for my boots somewhere beneath the bed. "You're sure?"

"As sure as I can be, under the circumstances. Where are you going?"

I grunted as I got up, feeling every bruise like I was receiving it for the first time. A coordinated ache crisscrossed my body. The bullet wound might have been mostly healed, but it was still an effort to lean over and pull my boots on. "I've changed my mind. I think I will go to church. You mind handing me that Bible? Thank you. And when I get back, you best be packed, because we're heading for Topeka."

A HARD PLACE

CHAPTER TWENTY-FIVE

W hen Almena told me we were going to meet an old friend on the outskirts of Topeka, I wasn't sure what to expect. Of those who might be counted among her friends, such as the Cortezes, none were folks I'd have guessed ahead of time. Almena seemed to take comfort in the company of those society preferred not to see, and I wondered if it wasn't on account of her viewing herself as an outcast. One more exile in a land of exiles.

"Their name is Song," she told me when I finally pressed her on a name for the fella we were supposed to be getting help from.

"And this Song, you think he's gonna know where to find our quarry?"

"*They,*" Almena corrected, "always manage to know a little bit about everything going on around them at any given time. If anyone's been keeping their ear to the ground, it's Song. And before you ask, nothing they sell is magical, although they might try to convince you otherwise."

Wasn't sure why she felt the need to warn me until we entered Song's shop. It was a small, single room in the back of a dingy furniture store—and it was full of mirrors. Many were about the size of my hand, but together they covered almost every square inch of the space in round patterns of light. I didn't understand most of what I saw reflected on the walls, seeing as they featured symbols I wasn't familiar with, and I supposed that was why Almena worried I might mistake it for magic.

"Chinese magic mirrors," Almena explained to me in a quiet aside. "The back of the mirror is bronze and features a design that can be seen when light hits the polished front."

"They're beautiful," I said, and I meant it. Even someone as hopeless as I was when it came to crafts could see these mirrors were skillfully made.

"We're closed, thank you," came a voice from somewhere behind the mirrors. I saw Song's reflection before I saw them. They wore their hair short like a man's, cut close to the scalp, and a bowtie clenched the high collar of their shirt, but they also dressed in a skirt that swept the floor as they moved out from behind the counter to shoo us off.

"We're not here to buy anything," Almena said, "only here for information."

"That is sometimes the costliest purchase of all." Song smiled and held out a hand to Almena, recognition lighting up their face. Now Almena's earlier correction made sense to me. At a glance, I couldn't tell whether Song was a man or a woman, and I got the feeling that was the whole point. As wild a notion as it seemed to me, existing as both or neither gender, it also made a strange kind of sense out here on the frontier, where people's assumptions about your character mattered half of what they did back in polite society. Out here, how you lived was your business, long as it didn't encroach on another's way of life. "It's been some time, Allan."

"Almena now," she said, avoiding Song's long, painted nails to give their hand a firm, and friendly shake.

Song took the change in stride. "Not the Almena Guillory I've been hearing so much about? The one terrorizing Kansas?"

"That's actually what I'm here to ask you about. There's a woman riding under my name, pretending to lead my gang. I know she's come to Topeka. I thought you might be able to tell me where she's staying."

"Quite the assumption."

"You fought. You know as well as I do, sometimes a hunch is all you've got to go on."

Song seemed to accept this answer, nodding. Their gaze drifted toward me, more curious than hostile. "And who's your friend?"

"He's nobody," Almena said.

"Somehow I doubt that." Song tilted a mirror so that its light caught me, blinding.

"Easy does it," I said, holding up a hand.

"You're a lawman, aren't you?"

I wasn't sure what made them think that. Ask a child to draw you a picture of a marshal, and nine times out of ten they'll put him in a fancy suit, bowtie perfect, hat on straight. I couldn't have looked less kempt, even in Bratt's nicer clothes. Having missed the opportunity to bathe, I smelled like a saddle. Even my face was turning sharp and prickly, showing more growth than I'd thought myself capable of.

In the end, Almena answered on my behalf. "He's with me. You can trust him."

"I don't have to," Song said. "I'm not the one working with him." They smiled brightly. "But who am I to judge? The world makes strange bedfellows. I'm just glad to see you've found a friend. Took you long enough."

I turned to catch Almena's expression at this comment, but if anything passed across her face at the suggestion of us being friends, it was gone by the time I looked.

"Can you help us find her?" I asked. "Guillory."

"This fake one, you mean? I might have heard something.

Although I think the question you're asking is not the only one you want answered," Song added with a meaningful look at Almena.

She responded with an impatient look. "Don't treat me like a customer, Song. What have you heard?"

"She *was* here, this imposter of yours. I can't say for sure if she still is, as last I heard Almena Guillory was hunting down a train. My guess would be that she and her partners are leaving Kansas." Song paused, tracing the frame of one of their larger mirrors. I watched their expression from the glass, pensive, and perhaps a little sad. "Is it true they killed a boy and a mother in Baxter Springs?"

"It's true," I answered.

Song flattened the mirror so suddenly, and with such force, I thought they might break it.

"You need a name," Song said. "To make an end of things."

"We'd be grateful," I said, before realizing they were asking Almena, not me. Made sense, them being friends and all. When Almena first mentioned going to see Song, all she'd say was that they'd fought together in the same theater during the war. At the time, I hadn't thought much about it, but now I found the possibility of their meeting passing strange, recalling that even in the Northern ranks the fighting regiments had been segregated. Perhaps that hadn't applied to the Chinese, or perhaps Almena wasn't telling the whole truth. Sometimes it was hard to tell with her.

"If we don't stop her," Almena said, "a lot more people are going to die. I have enough of a body count without adding hers."

"Yes, all right," Song agreed. "Give me a moment."

They went back behind the sales counter, and took out a large jar full of what looked like handwritten receipts, such as a grocer might keep. After unscrewing the tin lid, they reached in, selecting a strip of paper, seemingly at random. Their hand emerged a moment later covered in a thick red slime I only realized was blood when Song used a rag to clean themselves off, and I saw the flesh had been stripped to their wrist. I glanced back at the jar, but Song was already putting it away. By the time they turned back to us, their skin was already healing, covered in shiny white scars the shape of snake bites. It all happened so quickly, if I hadn't become accustomed to such acts of wonderment from Almena, I wouldn't have believed my eyes.

Almena had warned me that nothing Song *sold* was magical, but this was freely given. Song was even careful not to let Almena touch them, and instead, slid the paper across the counter to her.

"I would have paid for that," Almena said with a frown, and I guessed she meant the pain it'd cost Song to perform whatever magics she had.

"On the house," Song said. "I still owe you for Antietam."

"And here I thought your memory was flawless," Almena countered with a fond smile, and then looked down at the paper, reading the name aloud. "Ruth? Is that all? No last name?"

Ruth. Why did that name sound familiar?

Song shrugged. "You know how it works. If that's all you got, that's all you need."

I continued to spin the name around in my head, like a wheel stuck in a rut. Only Ruth came to mind was Miss Ruth Kingery of Baxter Springs. The name wasn't uncommon, but the icicle descending into my gut warned me not to dismiss it as mere coincidence.

"I can also tell you this," Song added. "There's been some grumbling about some men claiming to be companions of the Grizzly Queen of the West overstaying their welcome at the house on the corner of Tyler Street. You know the one?"

"That's a brothel, ain't it?" I said, earning a look from Almena. *Guess that warrants an explanation.* "You might not be surprised to learn that many an enterprising criminal has sought comfort in the arms of a soiled dove."

Song made a face at my terminology, while Almena said, "Only the stupid ones."

"Anyway, it's a start," I said. "Thank you, Song."

"Since you're here," Song said, "perhaps I could interest you in one of my mirrors? You know a mirror is the only item in the world that tells only the unvarnished truth, and my mirrors do even more than that…"

Almena laughed. "Not this again."

"Now, wait a minute, I'd like to hear them out," I said, feeling it was only polite after everything Song had done for us. Almena just rolled her eyes as Song gave me their entire sales pitch, including a bit where they figured out I was a dog using something called a lunar calendar. Honestly, I didn't understand everything said, especially when they started talking about true and secret animals, but I'd always liked dogs, so I couldn't see how it was such a bad thing to be one.

"All right, all right," I finally cut in with a smile. "You sold me. How much for that one over there?" Right now, it held Almena in profile, almost as if it were a portrait of her rather than a reflection of the real woman.

"Good choice," Song agreed.

"You mind keeping it for me for a little while?" I asked, dropping what little I had left as far as funds went into their hand. "Things might get rough around here, and I'd hate to break it by accident."

Song nodded. "Come back anytime—except not this late again. I sleep, too, you know."

Almena and Song made their goodbyes, teasing one another with references I couldn't begin to understand, concerning a time when they'd both been caught up in pretending to be people they weren't. I stood aside, letting them have this rare moment together, and I thought about Wade, the last thing I'd said to him, as well as his half of the memories we shared, taken to the grave. Wished I'd

Later, when we were just about to head out, Song remarked, "And here I thought you'd come to ask about Bratt."

At the mention of his name, Almena looked like she'd been struck. "Have you heard something about Lloyd? Do you know where he is?"

Song frowned. "I assumed you already knew he was in town."

"Lloyd's *here*?" I was struck by the raw nerve in her voice, the vulnerability, the hurt. Suddenly, I wanted very much to have words with Lloyd Bratt.

"He's put some of your old posse back together. They're heading out to California at first light. Bratt's convinced there's money to be made in the mountains. He bought horses, a few wagons, and more mining equipment than he knows how to use." Song shook their head. "He asked me for advice while he was here buying benches for the wagon, as if I know the first thing about gold mining. Stupid man. Thinks because I'm Chinese, I must have worked on the railroad, and know everything about mountains."

For a long moment, Almena was silent. Then she smiled and shook her head. "That son of a bitch."

It wasn't the reaction I was expecting.

"Do you know where he's staying right now?"

"That, I do not know. And I'm not planning on using the jar again to find out."

Almena waved them off. "No, you've done enough. Thank you for your help. I'm sorry it's taken me this long to come visit, and now only for a favor."

"If it wasn't you, it'd be someone else," Song said. Judging by Almena's pained look, the words seemed to hold special meaning to her. I felt like maybe the phrase was something they had passed between them over the years, like a well-worn coat.

"Take care of yourself, Song," Almena said.

"I'll start with some sleep," they replied. With that, they turned and began blowing out each of the candles providing light to the mirrors. By the time we exited through the front of the store, the room behind us had gone dark, and the mirrors only showed shadow.

————

As soon as we were outside, I turned to Almena. "That jar back there... how's that work exactly?"

"Your guess is as good as mine," Almena replied. "Song won it from a flesh witch in a game of faro years ago. I didn't realize they'd kept it. I always found the maggots off-putting."

"Maggots?"

"Why? What did you see?"

"Receipts. Little scraps of paper."

"Song said the jar looks full of cotton to them. I guess we all see what we want to."

I shook my head. "I'm never gonna understand magic."

"Maybe that's the point." Almena stopped to look behind us. I hadn't realized we'd walked so far from the store, but we were alone, easily out of earshot of anyone who might be listening. "Now, what's this about our mystery woman? And don't say you don't know what I'm talking about, because I saw your expression in there when I said the name Ruth."

"First, I need to know something. You still planning on killing her?"

She hesitated, maybe considering a lie. "Are you still planning on getting in my way if I am?"

"Probably. You know, we could work together on this. Don't you think there's been enough bloodshed?"

"Maybe. But she owes blood for what she's done. Nothing less will do."

"Kind of like you?"

Almena smiled at the sky. "What do you want from me, Apostle?"

"You ever see a circus? See one of them grizzlies in the ring trying to balance on a bicycle? I visited a circus in Missouri once, just after the war. I remember thinking, if that animal had any inkling what it could do, the sheer power and will at its disposal, it surely wouldn't be performing this little song and dance for us. But that bear was scared. It had naked patches all over its back where chunks of fur and meat had been taken off by the trainer's whip."

"What's your point?"

"Fear," I answered. "Fear kept that bear doing what it did. Fear kept it chained, humiliated, destroyed. That bear sat on that bike not because it was the only thing it was capable of doing, but because years of getting licked by a whip had dulled its instincts, made it think it was something it wasn't." Almena held her silence, looking very much like she wanted to say something but didn't know how to say it. I stepped in close and saw her breath hitch. Light from the nearby building fell over her eyes, making them shine. "Is this really the life you want, Almena? Filling buckets with blood, yours and others? Playing to an audience like some bear on a damn trapeze?"

"Thought it was a bicycle."

"Give it to me straight. Look me in the eyes, and tell me this is the life you want. Tell me revenge is all that matters to you, rest of the world be damned, and I'll not say another word on the matter. I'll let you go to hell your own way, as you like."

She sank against the wall of the saloon, mouth curving defensively. I leaned towards her, couldn't help myself. Even after all of this, after everything, I wanted to be close to her. "You asked me what I wanted," I added gently. "But don't matter what I want. Matters what you do."

She moistened her lips and tried to move past me. "We're wasting time…"

"Enough running, Almena. You don't gotta be honest with me, but maybe you ought to try being honest with yourself for once."

"You're either the most stubborn man in the West, or the stupidest," Almena said, shaking her head with a droll, self-deprecating smile. "If you stopped idealizing me for two seconds, you'd see—"

"Idealizing?"

"Yes, idealizing! You're just as bad as those who named me the Grizzly Queen, only you've invented a woman you can *sympathize* with. A woman worth redeeming, one you can understand, and feel for. One you seem to think you can lecture and *fix*." She flung the words at me like they were knives.

"That's not—"

"Otherwise, you'd have to face the rotten reality: you've taken up with an outlaw who's done some nasty things in her life, and who's just as likely to keep doing them. I *am* a murderer, Nathan. Those aren't just stories someone made up to besmirch my pearly reputation. I'm a sinner, a liar, thief, fornicator—everything a woman shouldn't be, according to your Good Book."

"Almena, stop it."

She was listing her evils almost the same way Jed had done, and the irony of that was not lost on me. Although I longed to reach out to her, I held back, not wanting to push her farther into the corner she seemed to feel she was in.

"If you just stopped and looked at me, really looked—"

"What? What are you so afraid I'll see?"

She cut her eyes away, voice falling to a murmur. "That there's nothing worth loving here, Nathan. There's just nothing."

"Is that what you think? Almena. Hey." I was surprised when she let me take her chin. Let me touch her. As I tilted her face up, she gripped my arm weakly; not sure she even realized she'd reached out for me. "I didn't mean to lecture. Just seems like you've taken up the cross for another man's sins, and don't know how to put it down."

"Booth," she said, almost like a curse.

I nodded, glad she took my meaning. "I know there ain't much I can say regarding that business. Wouldn't know where to begin, if I'm honest. I want to help, though, that's all I meant with my jabbering. I'm sorry it hit you a different way." She was tight-lipped, studying my face so intently, I felt my cheeks starting to catch. I kept on, nervous about what awaited us on the other side of this conversation. "I realize it ain't my place to pull you out of the hole, especially if you're not holding a hand up. If you don't want the rope, I can't... Ah, hell."

I gave up on words and moved my hand around to the back of her head, bringing her forehead softly to my lips. Her skin was warm and dirty, smelling faintly of horse and whatever soap she'd used back at the hotel, what seemed like centuries ago, and I waited, not exactly sure what for, smoothing her cheek with the thumb of my other hand until she finally looked at me. Then we crossed that line together. Her fingers slid up my neck, and she lowered my head to hers. I pressed her back against the building, knowing she was a woman for whom gentleness was not a virtue.

When at last we separated, she stood back, touching her mouth like she'd taken a punch.

"I do see you, Almena," I said, my breath coming a little fast. "Haven't been able to look away since Asher, and it ain't because all I seen is sunshine and rainbows. I seen a woman trying to escape the pull of her past only way she knows how. I know the darkness you're afraid of." I'd seen the same kind of darkness inside myself after what I did to Casella. Wagered she knew that.

Her lips parted, but it took her another moment to speak. "Then what? You suddenly don't care about the law?"

"Of course I care. Though I reckon you haven't done half the things they say you have. Am I right?"

"Still leaves the half that's true."

"Yeah, but you could make amends if you wanted to. You've got a gift." She scoffed. "You do. And with that gift, the things you could make right, the people you could help... but you can't do it at the end of a rope. And that's where you're gonna end up if we're not careful."

"We?"

I smiled. "I ain't here for my health. I'm with you, long as you're with me. You with me, Almena?"

She leaned in, kissing me again, this time with more desperation, holding even less back than before. I'd hoped that was an answer, but then, while my head was bent over her neck, she said, "You don't want me to kill anyone else."

"If it can be avoided."

"Then I can't come with you."

I drew back. "What?"

Her jaw looked tense as a board. "I'm going after Lloyd, Nathan."

I started to object, feeling sick, but she cut me off by placing a finger against my lips.

"No. This isn't a negotiation. You had your turn to talk, now it's mine. I need to settle accounts with Lloyd Bratt. Besides, I think we both know what will happen if I come with you."

"Not sure I can manage this alone," I confessed. Pride had started me down this path, whispering sweet nothings in my ear to the tune of taking down two outlaw gangs all by my lonesome. Being a hero, becoming a household name. Part of me wondered if my pride wasn't also the thing got Wade killed. If we'd stayed together, if I'd been able to get a message to him sooner, let him in on my plans…

Pride be damned.

"Wasn't that the whole reason we planned on hiring men once we got here?" I added. "Because the two of us alone wouldn't be enough."

"But you're not alone," Almena said. "Your marshal friends are here. Or wasn't that your plan all along?"

So she knew about my telegram, the one I'd sent after Halverson. Maybe she'd seen me stray from the path to the church, and followed me to the telegram office. Or maybe she was merely guessing. After all, I'd been out of her sight a couple times now since Coffeyville. It wasn't unreasonable to assume I had something up my sleeve.

Several heartbeats passed before I answered. "Yeah." No point lying about it now. "But plans change."

She slid past me into the long shadow of the street. "Yes, they certainly do."

"Where are you going?"

"This is where we part ways, Marshal." Her tone stayed even as a slab of pavement.

I felt dizzy. It was Lilah all over again. I was losing Almena to a man I'd never even met, to a way of life I could never compromise and accept. "Why?"

"Because you might be right about me. But I can't test it this soon." I didn't know what to say to that, so I said nothing. "Don't come after me," she added.

"Might not have a choice."

"I mean it. I'll take care of Lloyd. I'll disband the gang, once and for all."

"I'd like to take you at your word, Almena, but the men I work for…"

"You said I could make amends. Well, charity starts in the home. Unless you're planning on handholding me through the process, you have to leave me to my reparations. And I'll leave you to your job, just as soon as I have a promise from you that she'll swing for Baxter Springs and everything else she's done in my name. Promise me."

"Judge'll decide the punishment. But I'll see her to that day."

Almena nodded, satisfied. "Go fetch your marshals."

"I'm not going to see you again after today, am I?" I don't know what she saw in my eyes just then, but she swallowed, leading me to wonder if she felt the same tight clench I was feeling in my chest.

She started back toward me, then thought better of it. "You can keep the clothes."

They were the last words she spoke to me before disappearing down the street.

Not for the first time, I watched Almena Guillory go, wondering what I could've done to make her stay.

CHAPTER TWENTY-SIX

T he following day dawned bright and hot, vivid, but also hazy, like the sun coming through a dirty window. Everything felt hard to look at.

I paced the Union Pacific platform, trying to withstand the ebb and flow of the afternoon crowd. Well-dressed folk flocked onto train cars, accustomed to the smell of overheated iron, sweat mixed with perfume, and coal fumes, resilient to the nasty business of travel in a way I wasn't. I tried to keep my head down, eyes up, but it was no use. Noise pummeled me from every direction—hacking coughs from behind thin handkerchiefs, engines belching smoke. Broken pieces of conversation darted past my ears, all falling silent behind the shriek of brakes as a hundred tons of metal came to a harsh sigh on the track.

It'd been some time since I'd taken a train anywhere. Now I remembered why.

While I kept an eye on the southern end of the platform for any sign of Kingery and her ilk, I balanced one of the brothel tokens I'd acquired the previous night on my thumbnail, flipping it occasionally and watching the words *Lee's Respite, Topeka Kan., Good for One Screw* spin into a dark golden blur. Regardless of which face the token landed on, two little engraved hearts were always there to greet me.

In my pocket jangled half a dozen similar coins, friendly currency from one or more of the ladies I'd interrogated on the possible whereabouts of Miss Kingery and company after the Tyler Street brothel proved a dead end. Most of them didn't know anything. When they took a name, they said, it was usually only the first or last, never both. The women generously offered to compensate us for our time, however, hard-working lawmen that we were. I politely declined each offer as it came, but the tokens managed to find a way into my hands, regardless. Seemed rude to refuse a lady twice to her face.

After a while of waiting, the searing afternoon heat forced me into the shade of the railway office's overhang, and I chose the side of the bench seemed least likely to give me splinters. From here, I might've been able to spot the other marshals and lawmen hovering around, had I known who they were. I didn't. I'd been told a few would be stationed on trains coming and going, but seeing as they all dressed plainly and had their guns and badges hidden from view, it was near impossible to pick them apart from the mess of jackets and bowler hats. I'd given up trying to sort it out hours ago, trusting instead to the word of one J. R. Cornwell, the federal in charge of this here operation, local fella. When I'd come to him with my story, I knew there was a chance he would dismiss me—or worse, given some of the ugly rumors coming out of Coffeyville. Thankfully, he was a man of reasonable disposition and was willing to overlook my recent transgressions. For now, anyway. I knew a time was coming soon when I'd have to answer for the calls I'd made, and good intentions or not, it'd likely cost me my badge.

I rubbed the brothel token between my fingers until it was warm, and then aimed it for a slot between the platform boards. It just missed. Such was my luck lately. I watched the coin bounce once and land on its thin edge, spinning round and round until finally falling flat onto its side. And there were those damned hearts again.

A young man quickly scuttled up to the token, picked it up, and offered it back to me. "You dropped this, mister."

Out of reflex, I was about to suggest he keep it before I remembered what it bought. "Thank you," I said, accepting it back when I'd much rather have cranked my arm and sent it flying. His mother stood nearby, overlooking his good deed with benevolent pride, and I gave her a grateful nod as well.

The boy yanked his chin up and down, solemn as a soldier, and dashed back to his mother. She adjusted his small hat and flicked some dust from the shoulder of his fine attire, before marching them away from the platform, toward a man waiting with some luggage and an eager smile, presumably the father. Seemed like a nice family.

The shrill whistle of the train punched through me like a needle. Even surrounded by steam, I felt cold and removed. Wasn't just this business with Almena had me shaken. Everywhere I was seeing ghosts. Couples played out the denouement of my marriage, parting ways with an embrace or a kiss, so much warmer than the cool peck on the cheek I'd received when Lilah left me. Boys Charlie's age ran about, except with their heads still intact. A father swung his little girl up into his arms. She looked on his face with loving glee, without an ounce of the fear I'd felt for my own father. Worst part was knowing the apparitions wouldn't depart when these good folks did. All my ghosts traveled with me.

Kind of like someone else I knew.

No. I quickly wrangled my thoughts. *Let's have none of that, now.*

Every now and again as I sat watching the comings and goings, I swore I caught a face in the crowd what looked familiar.

The curve of a clever smile. Grey eyes flashing at me from beneath a fringe of brown hair. I kept seeing her. Sometimes in the upright gait of a confident woman, other times in an elusive side profile, tantalizing my imagination. Each time caused something inside me to lurch. I had to remind myself she was gone. Almena Guillory was gone, wasn't ever coming back if she knew what was good for her, and that was for the best. Had to be.

About the time I got up to stretch my legs, the 2:10 from Omaha was pulling into the station. The engine roared one last time, its stack shedding puffs of steam. The train's next destination was Chicago, though it had several stops along the way. I'd memorized the routes of every train departing Topeka today. If the brothel investigation had succeeded at anything, I hoped it'd act as a stick, startling Ruth Kingery and any of them boys she had with her out of the bushes.

A lesser criminal would've bolted the minute we started busting down doors, been on the first train getting the hell out of Topeka, earlier this morning. It spoke well of Miss Kingery that she hadn't panicked at our tactics and rushed to leave. About as well as you could speak about a woman whose gang had murdered innocent people, that is.

I hung back while the queue to board formed, scanning faces in the crowd, searching. This was the last train out today. Might be one or two more arriving, but they'd be cooling their engines overnight, worthless to a woman looking to get out of town.

This was my last chance to catch her. The finality of it dragged on my bones, making me heavy. If I failed, it'd all have been for nothing. Asher and Baxter Springs and Coffeyville and Halverson. The death of Gil, his wife, and Charles Wilmott. What I'd done to Casella. Wade's murder and Dempsey's beat down.

Just then, as if my thinking summoned him, I looked over and saw Dempsey.

At first, I thought I was imagining things. *What's Dempsey doing here? Now, of all times?* But sure enough, there he was, carrying as sullen an expression as I'd ever seen, his face a canvas of injury: his left eye and the side of his nose were bluish with bruises, the right side of his cheek swollen and if I had to guess, he was still missing a few teeth. Far from his usual upright posture, Dempsey slouched forward, as if some giant had his thumb on his back.

A woman stood beside him, and not just another stranger in line as I'd first assumed. Dempsey hadn't seen me yet, but she most certainly had. Her eyes appraised me, annoyance pooled in their murky color. *Kingery*. She crowded close to Dempsey, her hand disappearing into a shawl at his lower back.

I managed one step toward them before another man cut in front of me and before I could say excuse me, the hard mouth of a pistol pushed into my ribs, stopping me cold. I cast my eyes skyward, exasperated with my own slow-wittedness. I should've known.

"Marshal," the man greeted me, but there was a greasy arrogance to his tone that I couldn't mistake for anything other than a threat.

I moved to draw, but he shoved the gun in deeper, making me grimace.

"Ah, ah," he said, taking a moment to lift his hat and wipe his brow with the back of his free hand. "None of that now, Marshal. You be a good boy and stay right where you are."

"What say you put your gun down and we talk about this?" I suggested. Over the man's shoulder, Dempsey and Kingery were nearing the front of the line. If they got on that train and I didn't... No telling where she'd end up, but Dempsey was sure to catch a bullet somewhere along the route. "Unless you're planning on shooting me in front of everyone?"

The man glanced down at his gun, then back up at me. "Ain't plannin' on shootin' you." I watched his gaze track a woman going by—"Maybe her"—then swing left to a couple of young brothers—"or them. Or how's about that nice family over there?"

"All right," I said. "I take your meaning."

"Good. The Grizzly Queen said you were a sensible sort."

I took a step back, and he came with me, keeping his gun beside his hip, but always aimed at my chest. "Cut the act. I happen to know the Grizzly Queen personally, and I can tell you, that woman over there is no Almena Guillory. Don't even come close."

He glared at me. "Why don't you just keep your mouth shut?"

"See, if you actually knew Almena, she'd be the first to tell you, I have some trouble with that. Chatty, she calls me." I cast my gaze wider, trying to identify Kingery's other men, if they were here, or any of my own company of federals. A few men strutted about with recognizable bulges beneath their jackets, but that meant nothing in this part of the country.

"Talking like you know the Grizzly Queen." My captor snorted.

Ahead, Kingery gave Dempsey a small kick at the ankles to encourage him to move forward. When he turned to glare at her, he spotted me, surprise and then relief registering in his eyes. His mouth formed around my name, then he did something he probably ought not have.

He turned and grappled for Kingery's gun.

I sucked in a breath, expecting the clap of a gunshot.

Ruth Kingery could've dropped Dempsey then and run. Could've signaled her boys to open fire on the crowd as a diversion. My hand slid back to my gun, expecting any number of gruesome possibilities. Then Kingery up and did about the last thing I'd expect: she started screaming. Wailing like a banshee.

Her hollering attracted the attention of not only the nearby conductor but everyone else in line. Women spread apart from her like she had plague, while a couple of men who could've been my fellow lawmen or simply concerned citizens rushed to Kingery's aid. At the same time, her own stooge made the mistake of taking his eyes off me.

Using that brief diversion, I was finally able to draw, but instead of shooting, I flipped the pistol end-over-end in my hand and brought the butt down hard on the outlaw's wrist. He yelped like a kicked dog and dropped his piece. Before he could so much as reach down to retrieve the gun, I smashed him in the face with my fist.

While shaking the pain out of my hand, I looked back at Dempsey. He wore a panicked look of confusion, holding Kingery's tiny Derringer. His eyes met mine two seconds before a pair of men plowed into him, driving him into the platform like a stubborn nail. The gun popped out of his hands and landed near Kingery's feet.

I figured out pretty quick what had happened. Kingery had *let* him have the gun, let him appear the aggressor, drawing the marshals out like poison from a wound.

She was good. I'd grant her that.

Crowd was already dispersing around the scuffle as I pushed through. I kept my gun low, so as not to offend or startle, but I couldn't get there before Kingery boarded the train, hastily ushered on by the concerned cooing of fellow passengers and an apologetic conductor. The men who I assumed were marshals were so focused on Dempsey, intent on holding his face to the ground, none of them noticed the three gentlemen climbing aboard the porch of the last car.

Shit.

Now I had a true hostage situation on my hands, and my options were rapidly shrinking. No telling what Kingery would do if I put a hold on the train, but Baxter Springs had proven the fake outlaw queen wasn't a woman lamented the bloodshed of inno-cents, even kids. A better solution, I thought, was for me to slip aboard myself and try to sort things out, real civil-like, as we rode towards the next stop. One lone marshal wouldn't be too much cause for concern, not when she had her boys with her. Of course, it didn't exactly offer me much bargaining power neither. If there was a third option, I didn't know it at the time.

Lord help me, I boarded the train.

CHAPTER TWENTY-SEVEN

Once aboard, first thing I did was warn the engineer. I explained the situation plainly. We had some outlaws on board but weren't in any danger so long as nobody confronted them.

"What do they want?" the engineer asked. He glanced back across the small gap between the car and the engine where the rest of the train waited in a hush of steam. We hadn't yet pulled out of the station, but even now, I could hear the conductor bellowing "All aboard!" somewhere farther down the line, provoking the last passengers to hustle.

"To get out of here. So that's what we're going to let them do."

As we spoke, I watched the man for tremors or any other sign of nerves. The risky kind might loosen his grip on important controls at a critical juncture. Wouldn't help matters to have us suddenly careening off the track. Instead, at the mention of fugitives, his body went still as a capstone. I saw intelligence in his eyes, combating the wild gleam of fear. His head stayed dry; no sweat. Good. Here was a man could function under pressure.

"And what are you going to do, Marshal?" His expression

held that quiet mix of hope and skepticism I'd received from many people since beginning my career. I didn't take it personally. Wasn't exactly feeling optimistic about my chances, myself.

"You just worry about driving this thing. I'll worry about the outlaws."

"Sure, sure. But what are you going to *do*?"

I held on to the frame of the cab window. Damn train wasn't even moving yet, and I felt unsteady. "Whatever I have to." I made a vague gesture toward the controls. "Now let's get her moving. Don't you have a schedule to keep?"

———

I nearly collided with a man as I made my way back toward the express car to inform the agent there of the danger. I hadn't yet ruled out the possibility Kingery and her gang might try for one last heist and thought it only right to share my suspicions.

The narrow vestibule of the compartment car forced me and the stranger in close, closer than I'd have liked, given the number of times I'd had my piece stolen off me in recent weeks. He had his head down, and his hat forward on his head, so I couldn't see his face. Not until I grabbed his arm and swung him around to face me.

Weren't no man at all, as it turned out.

"*Almena*?" I could barely speak around the knot of disbelief in my throat. "What in—"

Almena dragged me into an empty passenger compartment, closed it shut behind us, and turned the tiny lock with a click. She looked tired, like she hadn't slept the night before, or any night previously. She was dressed in a manly fashion, wearing baggy trousers and a striped vest. With her hair stuffed into her hat, I couldn't help thinking how much she looked like the soldier in those pictures I'd seen on her dresser. Kind of made me wonder if she was planning on putting the "Killin'" back in Killin' Al Guillory.

Her movements felt rote as she went to the window, drawing the small privacy curtain, before checking the lock on the door again. Not that it'd be very effective in keeping someone out if they were determined to bust through. The wood was more decorative than functional.

"Almena." As she made for the window again, I intercepted her. Her gaze swooped up to meet mine, and all the toughness seemed to fall off her like chiseled stone. Her expression, rigid with tension, finally softened. "What are you doing here?" I wanted to hear her say it.

"I saw you get on the train with Kingery."

"And?"

"And," she said, stalling. "And... I couldn't sleep last night."

I blinked, scattered by the unexpected answer. "All right..."

"You don't understand. I've murdered men over money and pride and slept just fine. I watched boys go to their death in a war they had no business being in, and when I crawled into bed those nights, listening to the dying ones crying, I rolled over and found I could still disappear into sleep." She sucked in a shaky breath. "You don't know what it means when sleep's the only true escape you have from the things you've done. To have that last refuge taken away from you. It's hell."

"I'm not sure I'm following," I admitted.

"Apart from times when I feared for my life, I only recall being unable to sleep the night Lincoln was shot. Did I tell you Stanton sent a telegram to me?" I shook my head. I think she'd left that part out, the few times we'd broached the subject. "It demanded I come, fulfill the office I'd sworn myself to. I'd made a promise to Lincoln that should anything happen, I would use my power to save him, that I would trade my life for his, if it came down to it. It wasn't something he wanted or asked for, but

297

neither was the war. When I made that oath, I truly believed I could keep it, too." She paused, collecting herself. "It should've been me who died that night, Apostle. How different this country would be if I had honored my pledge."

"Almena—"

She raised a hand, the whorls of her fingers close to my lips. "Lincoln was more than my president, he was my greatest friend. He was wise and kind, and so very sad at times, I feared it would swallow him. He seemed to know my hurts before I understood them myself, and always knew just what to say in a moment of sorrow. I loved that man. Yet when he needed my help, I ran. And I didn't stop until the West was as much behind me as in front of me."

"Why tell me all of this now?"

"To help you understand. When I tell you I couldn't sleep, I don't just mean I had a bad night or an uncomfortable bed." Her eyes were full of an emotion I was afraid to name. "You'd like to know what I'm doing here? I'm here trying not to repeat a past mistake."

I couldn't help a small, disbelieving smile. "Almena Guillory, were you worried about me?"

Almena rolled her eyes, but her lips were smile-touched. She gave a shrug.

That's a yes.

"What about Bratt?" Seemed like a thing I should ask about.

"Bratt can wait," she said.

"Yeah, but what's that mean?"

"It means this is more important." I knew this couldn't have been an easy decision for her to come by, so I didn't press her further.

The compartment lurched suddenly as the coupling rods engaged the car's wheels, and the locomotive pulled out of the station. Both Almena and I reached out to steady each other.

Beyond the curtain and glass, the train whistle sounded twice, dignifying the train's departure with a cloud of steam.

"Guess this means it's too late trying to persuade you to get off," I remarked.

"Between the two of us, who do you really think is in more danger?"

I conceded the point to her. "Don't suppose you have a plan that don't consist of killing Kingery outright?"

She raised an eyebrow. "Do you?"

"I was going to try talking to her."

"Talking to her."

I gave Almena a weak smile, swallowing the need to pull her even closer. It was difficult ignoring the warmth of her beneath my hands, even knowing there were other, more important things to deal with right now. "Worked with you, didn't it?"

"It helped that you also took a bullet for me. And keep trying to take more."

I cleared my throat, finally forcing myself to release her. "I appreciate you coming, I do. But nothing's changed…"

She wrapped her arms around my neck, drawing me toward her. As she pressed in close, I shut my eyes, releasing a harsh breath, straining against every sinful urge to do more than just stand there, taking in the feel of her body.

"If you think that, Apostle Richardson,"—her breath tickled my earlobe—"then you haven't been paying attention."

CHAPTER TWENTY-EIGHT

Someone banged on the door, and Almena jerked away from me. She bent her head, so her hat covered her face once more, and collapsed into a seat, spreading her legs apart like a man relaxing after a long, hard day.

"Ticket!" came the call from outside.

I opened the door and showed the conductor my badge. "Marshal's business," I said, trying to sound calmer than I felt.

Wasn't the conductor standing in front of me, however, but a bull of a man holding a blade dripping with gore. By the time my brain caught up to this fact, he'd already plunged the knife in and out of my stomach.

The pain didn't rush me immediately. I used that time to throw myself into my attacker, knocking us both backwards into the wall. The knife rammed me again, this time lower on my side, and the shock of it woke my body to the first stabbing. Woke it screaming. A curse burst from my lips, but I didn't let go of the man's arm, trying to prevent him from goring me a third time, or from turning on Almena.

The world teetered for a short, terrifying moment.

I tried to anchor myself to consciousness by focusing on the details around me. My shirt felt slick. The floor beneath my feet quaked like the bed of a wagon traveling over gravel road. A sharp bump bounced me against another compartment door, while the wheels of the train as they clattered across old, metal tracks grew louder in my ears.

A gunshot interrupted all of it, the sound, the sensations, like a firecracker going off. The acrid smell of gunsmoke clogged my nostrils, and I glanced down to find my Colt in hand, though I couldn't remember drawing it.

The big man was still on his feet. Suppose I missed.

I staggered backward like a drunkard, my vision catching on the hard edge of the blade as it dove for my chest—and bit into my shoulder instead. The knife passed through the thin fabric of my shirt like it was water, chewing into skin. Seemed wrong to call something so painful luck, but it was. Because just when the knife would've ensured a gravedigger's next commission, the car visited some more bad track, probably warped from the sun, toppling me sideways again.

Almena was there. One of her hands seized my shoulder, steadying me, while the other wrapped around my naked wrist, skin to skin. I felt the pain jump from me to her—fast, faster than I'd thought possible, even for her. The fog before my eyes lifted. Almena's gaze darkened, and her face struggled to hold back an expression of pain. She hissed through her teeth, stepped forward, and slammed her palm flat against the outlaw's face.

The knife fell from his hand. He patted himself with an absent, uncomprehending look, fingers coming away slimy as pudding. Red spots bloomed on his shoulder and side, while he clutched his stomach hopelessly.

"W-witch," he sputtered, a second before his eyes rolled into the back of his head and he dropped. His skull thudded against the floor like a judge's gavel rendering the final verdict.

"Get him by the legs," Almena commanded, slipping her

hands beneath the dead man's arms.

I was already moving by the time I thought to ask why.

"Someone will have heard that shot," she said, grunting as we shifted him toward the empty compartment. I tried to ignore the stench coming up as dark spread around the dead man's crotch. "Marshal or no, if word gets back to the passengers that you've just killed an outlaw, what do you think happens then?"

Lot of dead passengers, I imagined.

We tried long-ways first without stopping to consider the logistics of a big man through a small doorway, traded one another an exasperated look, then rotated. Even still, the man's giant shoulders clashed with the door frame, and in my haste, I nearly jammed his knees into his face. Instead, his head slumped backward, dipping into Almena's lap obscenely. She shifted out from under him, and we finally managed to deposit him inside. Try as we might, though, he kept slipping off the bench. Refused to stay upright. His legs blocked the door from closing.

"What in God's name is going on here?"

The voice came from over my shoulder. I turned so fast, nearly gave myself a crick in the neck.

The conductor stood, mouth hanging almost to the floor. His eyes darted between the body, myself, and Almena with the speed of a ricocheting bullet. I knew that look. Seen it in men and horses alike. In a moment, he was going to bolt.

For the second time that day, I showed my badge. The star rooted him in place, buying me a minute to explain.

"This man attacked myself and my friend here." I gestured with a nod toward Almena, who kept her face angled down. "You've got a bit of an outlaw problem on this train. They're holed up in the passenger cars with everyone else at the moment. Now, don't panic. I've already spoken with the engineer. He knows all about it. He's doing his job by keeping the train moving. And now I'm going to need you to do your part."

"My part?" His eyes cut again to Almena who was still trying to fit the corpse all the way inside.

I stepped between him and Almena, blocking his view of the grisly scene. He looked up at me. Fella was short. "It's likely some passengers heard that shot. If that's the case and one of them asks about it, you need to assure them it was a minor mishap. Someone's revolver going off. All right?"

"Are you—" He pointed at the red mouths on my shirt, each knife-slit and gaping as if in surprise.

I grabbed him by the shoulder. "Did you hear a word I just said?"

"You're hurt," he mumbled again, all the color rapidly leaving his face.

"It's not my blood." Of course, it was, but try explaining that one to a man already close to dribbling on himself. I leaned over, meeting his eyes directly. "I need you to calm down and pull yourself together. Hear me? Stop and take a breath."

He did so, shakily.

"Good. Now, when you're feeling up to it, why don't you go in there and check on the passengers. Answer any questions they might have. Simple as that."

"But the outlaws..." His shoulder continued to vibrate beneath my hand.

"They won't do anything unless you give 'em cause to."

Almena kicked the corpse's leg inside and finally snapped the door shut. The conductor jumped at the sound, and I caught a smirk peeking out from underneath the rim of Almena's hat. All heart, my girl.

"What are you going to do?"

I clenched my jaw. Why did people keep asking me that?

"My job," I answered drily. "Now go do yours." Blood still leapt inside my veins from a moment ago, making it difficult to keep my voice gentle. Between Almena standing near enough to touch, and the criminals waiting just a car away, I felt halfway to crawling out of my skin.

"You might want to consider taking a breath yourself," Almena said as soon as the conductor was gone. Her voice sounded miles away, my own breath loud as an engine in my ears. Feeling unsteady at the trundling movement of the train, I anchored myself between the compartment door and the wall, spreading my arms. My stomach dropped through me, and my eyes followed its trajectory to the floor.

I shook my head. "I don't have a plan here," I admitted quietly.

"What happened to talking it out?"

I gave her a look.

"What was your plan when you got on the train?" she asked.

"Didn't have one then either. I was hoping I'd come up with something. But no such luck. I just—" I stared at the door at the end of the hall, at the patch of afternoon light on the carpet. Lines of shadow flitted across it where the sun was slipping between the cars. Almost looked like prison bars. "I don't know what the hell to do. Seems whatever I try, people end up hurt or killed."

"Oh, stop it," Almena ordered.

Her response surprised me. "What?"

"You know what I'm talking about. This whole feeling sorry for yourself business." She gestured angrily at me as if I was wearing something offensive. "It doesn't matter what's come before. All that matters is where we go from here." Her intense gaze required an answer, at the same time daring me to disagree. "Isn't that right, Apostle?"

Using my own philosophies against me. Dastardly.

"Yeah," I said. "You're right. But now I think we've got another problem on our hands."

Almena glanced around. "Oh?"

I checked my pistol and glanced again at that patch of light, the bars of shadow falling less quickly. "Train's slowing down."

————

There was no time to find out what had happened, though I had my suspicions. Damn conductor probably panicked and persuaded the lead engineer to stop and telegraph ahead to warn the next station of our outlaw infestation. But the stopping also gave me an idea, the kind Wade would've laughed and called me a fool for. In this case, he'd have been right to do so.

I ripped the dead man's neckerchief off and tied it around the lower half of my face, tugging it up over my nose so only my eyes showed.

"You're kidding," Almena said, watching me. "This is your plan?"

The material smelled like stale vomit and mothballs. I had to open the kerchief to the air once for a breath, clenching my eyes against the stench. "Train's stopped."

A normal person might've needed a minute to grapple with the implications, but not Almena. "You're going to pretend to rob the train."

"*We're* going to pretend to rob the train." Grabbing the dead man's shirt, I tore a nice, ragged slice, balled it up, and tossed it to her. She caught it without trying.

As she put it on, she asked, "You think they'll stop us?"

"Everyone wants to feel like a hero, one time or another."

She struggled to get the bandana tied at the back, the strip short and soaked through with blood. I leaned over to help her, and heard her murmur, "Not everyone." I knew she was thinking of Bratt, but I was willing to bet the boys with pious Ruth Kingery were cut from different cloth. They'd stuck with Kingery this far. Some bond of chivalry leashed them.

I placed my hands on Almena's shoulders. "I know I'm asking a lot, but—"

"Wanting me to attend a debutante ball is asking a lot." There was a smile in her voice. "This is just finishing what's been started."

A knot of tension unwound in my chest. "When we go in there, I need you to promise me you'll look after the passengers, first and foremost. Them living's what's important here."

"It's cute when you act like I haven't been through something like this before."

"Just want to make sure we're clear."

"Do you trust me?"

I glanced up from my waist, where I was checking how much ammunition I had left. Almena's steel-grey eyes watched me above her mask.

"Yeah," I said. "I trust you."

The skin around her eyes wrinkled. She nodded.

"You ready?" I asked her.

She rolled up her sleeves—more room to ply her trick with all that exposed flesh, I guessed—and I caught sight of that arm-length scar of hers, whose origins I'd never learned. I flashed back to Asher, and Dorothy's hotel room, the quiet murmur of the evening coming up through the window, and two strangers tossed together by God or fate. Truth be told, that night seemed far away now. The woman standing before me was not the same proud outlaw chained to the phantoms of her past, ready to kill to cover the pain; nor was I the same lawman who would trust her fate to the cold, timid hearts of the court. Our lives had tangled at the same crossroad, and for better or worse, I felt myself changed. I believed the same was also true for Almena, but only time would tell.

"Make sure that's on tight," I gestured to the poor man's mask around Almena's face, and then we headed for the passenger car.

———

Thought about making a swaggering entrance, the way outlaws often do. Maybe I'd holler, waving my gun in the air, and even make a few threats by firing into the ceiling.

Upon entering the car, two things made me reconsider that option. One, I already owed Dorothy for the hole in *her* ceiling. Heaven only knew how much the Union Pacific would put me out of pocket for damaging their passenger car. At this rate, even if I managed to bring Kingery and her entire gang in, the whole business could end up a financial wash.

As for the second, firing in such a small, enclosed space was like to make me deaf. Well, more deaf than the shot in the compartment car had left me, anyway. My ears still sang, the blood pulsing in them, as if someone had smashed a plate near my head. If I made it to forty with my hearing intact, I'd call it a miracle.

Almena went behind me through the doorway, per my request. If the passengers were going to focus on one of us, I'd rather it be me than her. At least I could defend myself against witness accounts later. Explaining the presence of outlaw royalty, on the other hand... That was a pleasure I could do without. So long as Almena didn't perform any miracles to set herself apart—such as taking a bullet and spitting it from her skin—she could rest easy in anonymity. For my part, I had to be the more memorable actor.

A narrow walkway bisected the two lanes of forward-facing benches, forcing Almena and myself to walk single file. The car was surprisingly empty, nowhere approaching capacity. *Small mercy*, I thought.

The passengers' attention didn't shift to us all at once, but slowly, like the heads of wild horses going up in response to danger. Those who'd been gazing out the window took longer to notice us. Eyes jerked to our masks. A quiet gasp rattled the lips of one woman who clutched her husband's arm. On her other side, she pulled her daughter close, dropping her arm down in front of the girl like it were a steel bar, capable of bulletproofing the child. I almost gave in to the urge to look behind me to locate the source of their fright.

Their unease settled into my stomach like week-old chili. I wanted to rip off the kerchief, claw it away from my face. This wasn't me.

But that was the whole point. Right now, my badge was useless. Right now, man named Apostle was useless.

This must've been how Almena had felt on the battlefield, surrounded by greasy plumes of smoke and the thunder of cannons. An invasion of calm settling on her like cold morning fog as she came upon the enemy, watching him scramble to load his rifle or flee backwards into the mud, telling herself the greatest lie of all when she touched him, repelling her own death. *It's for a good cause.*

I pointed to the mother and daughter. "You there," I said, relaxing into a deeper drawl, not necessarily to disguise my voice, but to lure Kingery's boys into coming against me. Most underestimated a man who talked like he'd just rolled out of a field. This time, they'd do so at their peril. "Stand up."

The woman quailed into her husband's side. "Please, no," she whimpered.

"Take me instead." The husband lurched to his feet. He had short blond hair, but a long, pale face and trembling lashes. I tried to gauge whether he was a fighter and would give me any trouble, but just as quickly decided it didn't matter. Best to ere on the side of caution.

"How's about I take all three of you, then?" I gestured to Almena who squeezed around me and grabbed the girl first, pulling the family into the aisle, as if they were all connected by an invisible string.

I stepped out of the way as she took them into the next car, and then followed behind.

Once the door shut, the husband began an impassioned, if stuttering, plea for his family's life. I waved him off and tugged my mask down. "I'm not going to hurt you or your family, sir. I'm with the United States marshal service. See, here's my badge."

"You're a marshal?" His brows pinched. "Then why—"

"There are three wanted fugitives in that car with you."

"Outlaws?" The little girl sounded more delighted than frightened.

I smiled at her but quickly returned to my explanation. "I'm sorry about the manner, but I needed a way to get your family out of the line of fire without the outlaws knowing I was on to them. Now, I want you to head up toward the front of the train. Pick a room in the compartment car, lock the door and keep your heads down. Stay there until someone comes and gets you. Uh, not the second room, though," I added as they turned to go, thinking of the dead body pretzeled inside.

"Is he another marshal?" the wife asked, eying Almena hopefully.

"He's here to help me," I said. I started to move between them, out of an abundance of caution. These were cramped quarters, and I feared if the wife came any closer, she might notice a thing or two about "him."

In the end, she grabbed Almena's hand before I could stop her. "Thank you," she said, and then again, "Thank you." Then her husband bustled her and the little girl off.

I met Almena's eyes. They were soft with a smile. "I'd forgotten what that's like."

"What's that?"

"Nothing. Let's go."

We returned to the car, and a pair of men sprang apart. They'd been conversing shoulder-to-shoulder. Conspiring, most like.

"Listen up," I barked, anchoring my boot on the seat of a bench. *Time for some gun-waving.* "Any of you try anything funny—and I mean *anything*—that family in there's gonna pay the price. You wanna live with that on your conscience? Go ahead, try me. Otherwise, keep still, keep quiet, and don't even think about making trouble."

If Lilah could see me now, I thought. She would surely get a kick out of my acting, especially seeing as she'd always said I didn't appreciate the theater.

My eyes swept over the benches. *Who else?*

A couple men sitting near the front sweated bullets, though that could've been owing to the suits they were wearing—probably bankers or investors. Not likely to put up much fuss, by the look of them. Neither could meet my eyes. Almost made me wonder if they'd been through this before.

"Turn out your pockets," I ordered them, the business end of my Colt providing sufficient motivation. I continued scanning the rest of the car as they stumbled over themselves to obey.

To my relief, there were no other children present. No other families, far as I could tell. Most of the passengers were working men, their faces burned, clothes clogged with dust; the rest wore clean like shame. They must've missed the opportunity for honest pay, and headed home now with empty pockets. On the one hand, the disparity of women made it easy to pick out Ruth Kingery at the back, even with her eyes tilted to the ground. On the downside, I couldn't tell who her compatriots were. I hadn't gotten a good look at them before they'd boarded, and most of the men here had a mercenary look to them. Many of the braver ones sat glaring at me.

Well, only one way to find out.

I clomped down the aisle toward Kingery, each step feeling like a mile hike. Behind me, Almena continued to mutely menace the other passengers. They leaned away, rushing to toss her wallets and watches.

A single man sat beside Kingery, close enough for their knees to touch through the green fabric of her dress. I figured it a safe bet he was one of hers. She'd never allow anyone else that close.

"What do we have here?" Shucking every instinct to keep my distance, I leaned into their row and made as if to grab Kingery. At the same time, I deliberately left my gun hanging loose at my side.

The bandit went for it. I like to think I made a decent show of wrestling for it with him, but in the end, I let him take it. There was a risk here: if his partner remained silent, or shot me from the back, I couldn't do a thing about it. But neither of those things happened.

"Give him a round, Johnny!" shouted one fella from my right.

And there was the reward. They knew each other all right. Johnny looked to Kingery for permission, which she gave by covering her ears. The outlaw's finger tightened, the hammer came down, and he grinned, no doubt expecting me to jerk back from the force of a bullet slamming into me at such close range.

But nothing happened.

"What the f—"

I grabbed hold of his wrist and jammed my elbow into his arm until I heard a crack. He got to finish his curse, after all.

At the same time, a different gun went off—Almena's— causing everyone in the car to flinch and cover themselves. The other bandit hopped on one leg, gripping the back of the bench in front of him and howling like the moon was out. Almena had shot him in the leg. *Anywhere*, I thought, somewhere in the back of my mind. *She could've shot him anywhere, and she shoots him in the leg.* Felt like progress.

Keeping one hand on the bandit's arm, I delivered a solid punch to his face. His nose broke open, but he refused to go down. Instead, he threw into me, knocking me backwards against the wall of the train. Air shot out of my lungs, then returned a moment later, right as I dodged a blow that made an ugly, crashing sound as the man's fist collided with the window.

I couldn't get around the bandit. The benches prevented it, unless I wanted to climb over them. *No way out but through.* Lowering my shoulder, I rammed the man with enough force to send him spilling over the bench. He stopped shouting, making me think—hope—his stubborn head had met with something hard enough to knock him out cold.

My victory was short-lived as arms suddenly came around me. Someone pulled me back, turned and tossed me into another man, who imprisoned me with his bulk. He forced me against the wall, pressing my head into the wood paneling. I yelled—nothing coherent, just the mindless cry of an animal in pain.

The other passengers rallied then, turning on us. I had been gambling on their cowardice, or at least their shrewd indifference, hoping they wouldn't interfere. Maybe I should've known better. The West wasn't known for its delicate flowers.

"Try and rob us. We'll show you what's rough," said the man holding me to the wall.

He pummeled my lower back, causing my knees to buckle. Almena's name nearly broke from my lips. I sought her wildly in my periphery, my view partially obfuscated by a big, sweaty hand. "Wait," I started to say, but the man boxed me again before I could fumble my badge out.

Only a gunshot interrupted the assault. My attacker jerked back to see what the fuss was, and I went with him, unwillingly. He had me by the hair. My hat had tumbled off at some point, and my kerchief had slid down, now slouching around my neck.

Having fired into the ceiling, Almena now stood beneath a tiny grate of light, funniest angel I ever saw. Her intention was clear: if anyone moved, the next one wouldn't be going into the roof. She wagged her gun in my direction, and the man released me. I staggered to my feet.

That should've been the end of it, but of course, it wasn't.

Almena casually turned her gun on Kingery, motioning her toward the rear exit of the car. Ruth eased out of her row with her chin high. She pinched her dress between her fingers, with all the solemn dignity of a nun. *All she's missing is a habit. And a soul.*

Some of the male passengers balked at the hostage-taking, but Almena silenced them by aiming her gun in their faces as she followed Kingery out back.

Finally, I managed to get to my badge. I flashed the star at the passengers, swishing it back and forth like I was attempting to drive the darkness out of a cave with a torch. "Marshal," I croaked, hurrying down the aisle, touching each bench to help support myself. "All an act. Long story." There'd be time later for a proper explanation—trusting Almena didn't lose her mind and shoot me, too.

Just in case, I retrieved my gun from the floor. I liberated the Colt's bullets from my pocket and thumbed them back into the chamber before burying the gun in my holster and throwing the flap of my coat over its deadly shape. Lord, I hoped I wouldn't have to use it.

I staggered off the train, which was still at a dead stop, emerging from the car's shadowy lip into the hard line of daylight. For a few moments, as my eyes adjusted, I couldn't spot either woman against the bright horizon. They materialized like apparitions in the desert, heat pouring over them in wavering lines.

Almena and Ruth stood several paces apart, holding one another at gunpoint. Both pieces looked dull in the sun, where I'd expected them to shine.

"Al!" I shouted, using her nickname in case anyone should overhear.

Almena's back was to me and the train, but Kingery saw me clearly. Her chest heaved, but her voice sounded calm when she said, "That was a wonderful trick on the train, Marshal."

I trudged forward through the grass.

"Almena," I said, quietly now, so only she and the lizards underfoot would hear me. I needed her to look at me.

She remained frozen, not adjusting her grip on the gun.

"Almena?" Ruth said. "Almena Guillory? Is that who you brought along, Marshal? You're even dirtier than I thought. I would say I'm disappointed, but that would be redundant."

"Why are you doing this, Ruth?" I asked, stepping closer.

"Miss Kingery," she corrected.

"That night in Baxter. Was anything you said true?"

Almena's eyes shot to me. The question circled inside her gaze like a vulture above something rotten. *Night in Baxter?*

"I don't drink," she said. "That's true."

"God. Faith. Love. Those things mean nothing to you?"

The wind caught Kingery's raven hair, sending it into her face like a shirt on a clothesline. Some strands stuck to her lips, others to her cheek, already caked with grit. She clenched her teeth. "They're everything. When you have them."

"You killed an innocent boy and his mother, among others."

"*I* didn't."

"The men riding with you did."

Her eyes sharpened, and she shrugged. "I can't control what men do. They're animals. They have been since Cain's day. But for the first time in my life, men can't control me either." She looked to Almena. "That's it, isn't it? The reason you ride. Freedom from all those petty rules men make up for an excuse to whip us. People have forgotten that before Eve, there was Lilith. They need to be reminded of what happens when you deny a woman her due."

"Lilith?" I almost laughed. This woman believed she was

some symbolic Second Coming of an apocryphal demon from the Bible?

If there was any humor in the situation, Almena didn't appreciate it. "Get back on the train, Apostle," she said, her voice tense. "You don't want to see this."

"Come on now," I replied tiredly. "If you'd wanted to kill her, you'd have already done it."

Almena shoved the gun forward, threatening, but still didn't fire.

"It's over, Miss Kingery," I said. "Put down the gun, and come peaceably. You've got plenty of reason to be angry, but don't make religion your excuse for evil."

Ruth ignored me. I continued to watch her hand on the Derringer, not taking my eyes off it for even a second. The air pressed heavy around us, weighted with anger.

"We're on the same side," she told Almena. Something about Kingery's expression was strange, almost reverent. It wouldn't have looked out of place on a man crawling toward a cross. "You put the fear of God into men out here. You—a single woman! Imagine what the two of us could do. We could change history." She smiled hopefully, and I confess I felt a little sad for her then. She seemed lonely, at least as lonely as she had when we'd first spoken in Baxter. I knew I'd be revisiting that quiet little conversation for years to come, wondering how much of what she'd told me was true, and what I'd missed that might've allowed me to stop her sooner.

Almena shook her head at Ruth's words, and slowly, ever so slowly, lowered her pistol. "You think you can change history with a bullet. You're not the first." I knew she was thinking of Booth, but I doubt Ruth made that connection.

Her smile fell away. "Men get to achieve glory through violence. What do we get? Martyrdom. Women only mean something when we're suffering or dead. I'm changing that narrative."

"By becoming just as bad as the men you scorn?"

"If that's what it takes."

"That's not progress," Almena said. "That's imitation. But then you'd know a lot about that, wouldn't you?"

"Hypocrite," Ruth spat. "After everything you've done… you dare take the high ground with me? Where do you think I got the idea for all of this in the first place?"

Ruth didn't seem to realize she'd just made Almena's point, but instead of rubbing the other woman's nose in it, Almena replied, "Don't congratulate yourself on following flies to a grave. I don't deny I've made mistakes, but that's in the past now—and I'll be damned before I let you force me into making another. Find your own way to hell."

Right then I knew: Almena wasn't gonna kill Kingery. The Grizzly Queen had gone into hibernation at long last, while Almena Guillory was awakening to a new way of life.

Ruth took a long moment to respond, and when she finally did, her voice shook. "Oh," she said, practically breathless with hate. "You are such a disappointment."

The Derringer lifted out of the shadowy folds of Kingery's dress.

I knew Almena could take a bullet, easy. But I also knew she'd fled before such a close-range delivery once—Lincoln's injury. There were wounds even she couldn't recover from, and I wasn't willing to surrender her life to chance. My gut churned at the thought of losing her, or of Almena losing herself again, forced to kill again to survive.

"Don't go this way, Ruth," I said, but it was too late. She'd already made up her mind.

Well, so had I.

Kingery braced, still unaccustomed to the feel of shooting, betraying her intentions. I raised my own gun smoothly, like it was a weightless extension of my arm. I didn't think about Wade, although I might've done. I didn't think about Dempsey's pulverized face, or the blood spilled in Coffeyville and Baxter Springs. The list probably ran a lot longer. Ruth Kingery had caused so much pain, but this wasn't about me, or my sense of justice. Wasn't about revenge neither. I refused to let myself repeat what I'd done to Casella. If I had to pull the trigger, I promised myself I would do it with my eyes open, and my heart clear. I needed it to feel *necessary.* Unavoidable.

With Almena standing across from her, arms at her side, it did.

I aimed for Kingery's center mass, as I was taught. Nothing fancy, like trying for an arm or a leg. There was too much of a chance I'd miss.

The shot caught her cleanly in the chest, narrowly avoiding the golden teardrop necklace that hung from her throat. She went down so fast, she barely made a sound. After the echo of the shot died away, I walked toward her, stepping carefully through the grass, and leading with my gun. The breeze blew a ripple across Ruth's dark, stained dress. She was still clutching her gun in the rigor of death, but if she felt anything in that last moment—pain or fear or anger—it didn't appear on her face. Her eyes showed an abyss.

Almena stared at me, mouth half-open. "Why'd you do that?"

I knelt down and checked for breath or a pulse, just in case. There was neither. "She was gonna shoot you."

"I could have—"

"I know you could've." I cut her off and helped her readjust her mask, which had slipped down onto her neck. My fingers felt cold and fumbling, but her eyes sank closed when I brushed them against her cheek. "I didn't want you to have to make that choice again."

"Thank you," she said.

I nodded, and we boarded the train.

CHAPTER TWENTY-NINE

Before the train set off again, I had the engineer send a few of his operators to fetch Ruth's corpse. I only had a minute to rest my eyes in a private room in the compartment car before the conductor banged on the door, asking for me.

"We've got her, Marshal. We argued over where to put her. Some suggested the luggage car, but I thought that seemed disrespectful for a lady. Even a dead criminal, so I said…"

I rubbed my eyes. "You have her?"

The conductor's head bobbed up and down. "Yes, sir."

"Good. That's all I need to know. We'll sort out the rest when we hit the next stop."

"Yes, sir." He turned to leave, stopped, and turned back. "Sir?"

I hung onto the doorframe, afraid I'd topple over otherwise. Wasn't just the beating had me wiped, though it certainly didn't help. "Yeah?"

"Is it true what they're saying?"

"What who are saying?"

"The passengers."

He paused, forcing me to ask, "What are they saying?" Felt like the damn near slowest conversation I'd ever had.

"That the woman you shot was Almena Guillory. The Grizzly Queen of the West."

Took only a moment's consideration to come up with the lie. "That's right. She was going under a false name, Ruth Kingery. Lived in Baxter Springs for a time. Wouldn't be surprised if her partners in there try and convince the law otherwise. Men'll say anything to keep in the good graces of a lady, especially one they're afraid'll shoot 'em otherwise."

The conductor issued a low, appreciative whistle. "Well, I'll be. Isn't that something?"

I made a noise of agreement. The conductor continued to stand there thoughtfully.

"Anything else?"

He snapped back into himself. "No, sir."

I went back inside and closed the door.

Almena moved to sit beside me. She hooked a slender finger into her mask, sliding it off her face. I thought she might say something wicked or clever about what I'd just done. Instead, she leaned forward, pressing her lips to my cheek. I inhaled shakily and allowed her to turn my head toward her. Her mouth found mine, and the world retreated into the floor, a soft rumble beneath our feet. Almena's fingers dug into my arm, pulling me closer, and I finally let myself fall completely into her. For a time.

"When we get to the station," I said, "you have to go. You can't let them see you."

"Come with me, Nathan." Her fingertips trickled down my neck.

I removed her hands but continued to hold them. "You know I can't. Someone's got to answer to the law for what's happened today, and better me than you. Just promise me I haven't made a mistake here. Promise me you won't go back to your old ways."

Almena only smiled cryptically and rested her cheek against my shoulder. *Close enough*, I thought. I shut my eyes, relishing these last few moments with her, and fighting the knowledge that when we reached our next stop, she'd be getting off while I stayed on without her.

———

Nearly a month after the Grizzly Queen was declared dead and the remainder of her phony gang was either arrested or disappeared, Kansas finally released its collective breath. By then, the knuckles of my hands had also recovered from the thorough rapping I got for my part in all of it.

Turns out, Judge Foster, who I'd supposed a man of few words from our single previous interaction after Asher, had quite a lot to say on the subject of Coffeyville and Topeka. Say, *and* spray. He pounded his hand as well as any gavel on the desk, rattling his law books, and lectured me about responsibility. Namely, my lack of it. I stood there and took it, not even flinching when a little spittle caught me in the cheek. That conversation went only half as poorly as the one I had with Dempsey, who accepted my apology for Coffeyville but didn't seem to want to sit too close while I gave it.

In the end, the judge didn't take my badge. Killing the Grizzly Queen and capturing the surviving members of her gang was apparently enough to warrant another chance. Feeling I didn't deserve to wear the star, however, I asked that I be relieved of its duties and privileges. I needed to take some time to sort myself out. Judge Foster agreed that was a good idea.

Before I left town, I swung by Song's shop to pick up the mirror I'd bought. I knew by now the mirrors weren't magic none, but part of me still hoped I might find Almena's reflection trapped in the polished surface. No such luck, however, and to complicate the matter, Song had sold my mirror to another paying customer, though they wouldn't say to who. Part of me wanted to believe it had been Almena, though I had no reason to think so. In the end, Song tried to upsell me on buying two more mirrors, but I managed to hold my ground and leave with only one.

Freed from my official duties as a marshal, I went south, venturing as close to Indian Territory as I could get without being shot up by jumpy border folk. I was hoping to find the Osage tribe whom Almena had helped. The sense of injustice I felt regarding the Indians' unfair treatment under the law provoked a response in me I hadn't anticipated. I couldn't shake the desire to act, and I thought the presence of a marshal—even one who'd temporarily shelved his star—might alleviate some of the tension on the frayed edge of civilization and improve trade, or at the very least prevent more bloodshed.

Throughout all this, I told myself I wouldn't go searching for Almena, yet I found myself watching for her, expecting to see her smile on the lips of every passing lady. Disappointment needled me every time a woman turned around wasn't her. I hadn't known how I'd feel about her absence, but it surely wasn't this.

I never ended up finding them Indians neither. Much like Almena did after Topeka, the Osage vanished, loosened into smoke. The message attached to their absence was clear: *We don't want your help. We don't need it.* Maybe that was true, too, if the local grocer's conveniently low stock of John Barleycorn and fresh cornmeal was anything to go by. Man said he'd no clue what happened to it but refused to involve the law whenever anyone suggested it.

Good for them, I thought.

If my time with Almena had taught me anything, it was that a gulf often existed between the law and the people the law was intended to protect. Good could be done for bad reasons, same as the reverse. Once, such ambiguity would have left me drowning in unease, but now?

I could live with it.

EPILOGUE

Three Months Later…

Winter was coming—faster than usual, it seemed—and that meant plenty of job opportunities for those willing. I'd found profitable work helping a local sheriff in Montgomery County with some repairs to his jail, and was just bending down to pluck up another board when a shadow fell over my work.

I turned, expecting the sheriff or his deputy, and instead found myself eye-level with the chest of a tall Osage man. He wore a two-piece suit, though the trousers hugged his ankles, straining to contain his powerful calf muscles. Suppose he was trying to blend in with such fancy attire, but it had the opposite effect. People stopped and stared at us, especially seeing as it was late November and he wasn't wearing gloves.

I lifted the back of my arm to my head, wicking off sweat, while also shading my eyes against the cold winter sun so I could make out his face better.

"I know you, don't I?" I said, only half in question. "You're Footprints-in-the-woods' brother, ain't you? The-traveling-star." Always wondered how that business turned out. When I mentioned his sister, the skin tightened across his face, and his eyes showed a terrible sadness. Guess I had my answer.

The-traveling-star nodded and extended his hand. "Telegram."

"Yeah?" I accepted it. "Who from?"

"The Western Union Telegraph Company thanks you for your business." With that, he turned on his heels and went.

All right then.

I relaxed the board against the side of the jail and dropped my eyes to the small card. At the top, the return address located the sender in Fort Worth, Texas. The telegram itself read:

Could use the help of a friend. Come and find me, Marshal. I'll be wearing blue this time. Deuteronomy 32:35.

It was signed, simply, Mary.

My lips felt the soft curve of a smile for the first time in a long while.

Only one "Mary" I could think of.

Deuteronomy 32:35, I thought, but blanked on the exact verse. Always was more of a New Testament man, never caring much for the begets of the Old Testament. I popped my head into the jail, asking after a Bible, but the sheriff just shrugged, forcing me to cross the street and fetch one from the local church. Sitting in the frosty shadow of the steeple, I rapidly flipped to chapter thirty-two.

To me belongeth vengeance, and recompense; their foot shall slide in due time: for the day of their calamity is at hand, and the things that shall come upon them make haste.

I didn't wonder long who she was referring to. John Wilkes Booth. The woman who couldn't be killed still hunting a man who should be dead. It was almost poetic.

I glanced down at the telegram, rubbing my thumb over the black type.

Come and find me, Marshal.

Maybe I would.

ABOUT THE AUTHOR

 **HAYLEY STONE** is a writer, editor, and poet from California. She is best known for her adult sci-fi novel, *Machinations*, which was chosen as one of Amazon's Best Sci-fi & Fantasy Books for 2016. Her short fiction has appeared in *Fireside Fiction*, *Apex Magazine*, *Flash Fiction Online*, and various anthologies, while her speculative poetry is widely available online.

Hayley loves to hear from readers and writers. Find her at www.hnstoneauthor.com and on Twitter @hayley_stone.

SPECIAL THANKS TO:

ADAWIA E. ASAD	EDDIE HALLAHAN	KYLE OATHOUT
BARDE PRESS	JOSH HAYES	LILY OMIDI
CALUM BEAULIEU	PAT HAYES	TROY OSGOOD
BEN	BILL HENDERSON	GEOFF PARKER
BECKY BEWERSDORF	JEFF HOFFMAN	NICHOLAS (BUZ) PENNEY
BHAM	GODFREY HUEN	JASON PENNOCK
TANNER BLOTTER	JOAN QUERALTÓ IBÁÑEZ	THOMAS PETSCHAUER
ALFRED JOSEPH BOHNE IV	JONATHAN JOHNSON	JENNIFER PRIESTER
CHAD BOWDEN	MARCEL DE JONG	RHEL
ERREL BRAUDE	KABRINA	JODY ROBERTS
DAMIEN BROUSSARD	PETRI KANERVA	JOHN BEAR ROSS
CATHERINE BULLINER	ROBERT KARALASH	DONNA SANDERS
JUSTIN BURGESS	VIKTOR KASPERSSON	FABIAN SARAVIA
MATT BURNS	TESLAN KIERINHAWK	TERRY SCHOTT
BERNIE CINKOSKE	ALEXANDER KIMBALL	SCOTT
MARTIN COOK	JIM KOSMICKI	ALLEN SIMMONS
ALISTAIR DILWORTH	FRANKLIN KUZENSKI	KEVIN MICHAEL STEPHENS
JAN DRAKE	MEENAZ LODHI	MICHAEL J. SULLIVAN
BRET DULEY	DAVID MACFARLANE	PAUL SUMMERHAYES
RAY DUNN	HENRY MARIN	JOHN TREADWELL
ROB EDWARDS	CRAIG MARTELLE	CHRISTOPHER J. VALIN
RICHARD EYRES	THOMAS MARTIN	PHILIP VAN ITALLIE
MARK FERNANDEZ	ALAN D. MCDONALD	JAAP VAN POELGEEST
CHARLES T FINCHER	JAMES MCGLINCHEY	FRANCK VAQUIER
SYLVIA FOIL	MICHAEL MCMURRAY	VORTEX
GAZELLE OF CAERBANNOG	CHRISTIAN MEYER	DAVID WALTERS JR
DAVID GEARY	SEBASTIAN MÜLLER	MIKE A. WEBER
MICHEAL GREEN	MARK NEWMAN	PAMELA WICKERT
BRIAN GRIFFIN	JULIAN NORTH	JON WOODALL
		BRUCE YOUNG